HEIR OF WITCHES

Fictive Kin book three

HEIR of WITCHES

Nico Silver

WHITE RAVEN PRESS

Third Edition, 2024.
ISBN: 978-1-998212-20-0
This book was originally published as *Familiar* by Nic Silver and then as *Heir of Witches* by Nicole Silver.

White Raven Press
North Cowichan, British Columbia, Canada

Cover design and digital alterations by Nik Sylvan
Model stock © Neo-Stock via www.neostock.com
Animal stock © Filin174 via Dreamstime.com
Background stock (misty forest) © Mikel Martinez De Osaba via Dreamstime.com
Background stock (rocks) © Anastasiap83 via Dreamstime.com
Fog brushes © Krist A via brusheezy.com
Title typefaces: Eva Antiqua Heavy by Spiece Graphics, and Snell Roundhand by Linotype

Content warning: This book contains material that is not suitable for all audiences. It is recommended for readers 18+. Some content that may be triggering for readers includes explicit sex, violence, and sexual violence.

*For Bast
who is quite sure I'm her familiar,
rather than the other way around.*

Chapter One

IWAKE SUDDENLY, and I can't breathe. There's something wrapped around my throat, pulling tight, tugging at me, choking off my air.

When I sit up in the darkness behind the bedcurtains, I'm gasping in great sucking lungsfull and even though the feeling of choking is now a lingering memory I still feel like I can't get enough oxygen.

I turn to talk to Evgeny, expecting him to be awake, concerned. But then I remember he's not here. He took a part-time nightshift job at the mall to pay the rent, and his apartment is closer to the job than mine. That's important when you catch fire in sunlight, being able to get home quickly and on time.

It occurs to me that one of us should have asked the other to move in by now, since we spend most of our time together, anyway. Except it's good to be able to have solitude when you need it. I crack the curtain and sunlight floods in. He'll be home now, asleep, safe behind his double-insulated blinds. I wonder why I didn't stay at his place.

I yawn and stretch, feeling fatigue like a throbbing behind my eyes. Oh, right, I stayed home because I haven't been sleeping well and I thought I might sleep better without a beautiful young man sharing my bed.

I put my hand to my throat. I have enough experience with weird dreams to know that they aren't always meaningless picture-shows dredged up by an active imagination, and they aren't always just metaphorical.

I need to talk to Alex.

A couple of months ago, I needed her help … Well, Evgeny needed *our* help to stop a … the witches called it a demon, but it wasn't, exactly. But Ev had to trap it in his own head and for various reasons he wasn't quite strong enough.

And the demon-ghost-thing – an evil presence born from the slaughter of innocents, actually – terrified me. It was something that made even a super-old, super-strong vampire nervous, and he's a guy who so freaked me out the mere touch of his mind is the only thing ever to have made me piss myself. Literally. I was in the shape of a fox at the time, so it wasn't as messy as it could have been, but still. Anyway, the whole story is complicated, but I couldn't help Evgeny on my own. I needed Alex.

The only way for me and Alex to pool our powers (I dislike that word, but I can't think of another that fits) was for her to bind me with a familiar spell. Because Alex is a witch. And you know how witches are supposed to have cats for familiars? Some of them do, but legend says foxes make the best familiars, and *hexenfuchs* are supposed to be especially good. But they're rare. And I'm not explaining very well.

One of my ancestors, as impossible as it may seem, was a *hexenfuchs*, a witch-fox. And I had just learned how to take fox shape, and to keep this short, I'll just say that to help my boyfriend trap the demon, I allowed a witch to bind me to her will, as her familiar.

So, yeah, I'm Su, and I turn into a fox and let one of my closest friends make me her slave.

When Alex did the binding, it was like being leashed with an invisible rope made of her energy. And that's what I've been dreaming about. We haven't been able to find a way to reverse or break the binding, short of one of us dying, so lately we've just sort of ignored it. It's not like Alex would ever order me around.

But now my sex life is suffering, because I know that if she wants to, Alex can feel what I feel, see what I see, hear what I hear. And if *she* chooses, I can listen in on her. If she chooses.

The only thing keeping me from total paranoia about getting naked with Evgeny is that Alex is a lesbian, so she's not going to be interested in what it feels like to sleep with him. But still, knowing she can look in makes it hard to relax, you know? I *think* I would know if she were watching, but I'm not certain.

Also, a year and a bit ago, Alex and I were lovers, on track to having a really great long-term relationship, and now we're still negotiating the current terms of our friendship. So sex is a bit of a touchy topic.

Lately, it's been getting worse. Not the sex. Well, that too, but I mean the feeling of being *leashed*. Of being watched, controlled.

I don't think Alex is doing anything differently. I don't think she's actually watching in on me or trying to make me do things. But I wonder if her developing witch abilities are somehow unconsciously draining me, draining my powers.

So I need to talk to her. Really talk, not the catching up and chatting about life in general that we do every couple of weeks over coffee. The problem is, I can't just call her up, because the last time I saw her, she was all giddy about a road trip she was planning with her new love interest. So I expect her to be out of contact. But if I really need to get in touch with her, I can borrow Evgeny's cellphone, or Magne's, and leave her a message.

When I feel a little more awake, I crawl out of bed and put the kettle on – green tea, because I'm essentially nocturnal these days and I plan to go back to sleep soon. Then I dig around in a drawer and find the bit of paper with Alex's number on it. I have her home phone number memorized – she insists on keeping a landline as well as a cell, says it's a witch thing. Something to do with physical phone lines relaying more non-verbal information, whatever that means.

But her cell number is new. She got the phone just before she left, with the idea that even if roaming charges are ridiculously high, at least she'd have it for emergencies.

Then, number in one hand and tea in the other, I sit on the couch and realize I can't call her anyway, not yet, so I might as well have stayed in bed. I not only don't have a cellphone, I don't have any sort of phone. Or an internet connection. My neighbor and good friend Magne likes to tease me about it, asking if I'd like him to disconnect my electricity, too, or my plumbing. I tell him let me ease into this whole being connected thing. It's only been a few months since I bought a microwave and mere weeks since

I added a secondhand stove so I don't have to cook on a hotplate.

I put Alex's number on the table and glare at it as I sip my tea. My tail starts to twitch in annoyance – I can make it vanish, but since I learned to change shape I find I'm most comfortable, most *myself*, I guess, when I'm in human form with a big bushy fox tail. Fox-tailed girl, that's me. It's weird, but I like it. I have slit-pupiled fox eyes, too, unless I deliberately make them look human.

By the time I get to the bottom of my tea, I'm forced to acknowledge that I'm not going to be able to sleep until I call Alex. So I pad down the hall to the elevator and take it down to Magne's floor. It's only one level and it would actually be faster to take the stairs, but we got into the habit of taking the elevator as a way of letting each other know when we're coming and going. So we can look out for each other. We both have better-than-human hearing – Magne's a werewolf – but our building is a converted warehouse and nearly soundproof. Doors are impossible even for me to hear from one floor up, but we can both hear the hum and feel the vibration of the elevator's ancient motor.

It's still morning and Magne's almost as nocturnal as I am, especially this close to the full moon, so I'm not all that surprised he doesn't answer. Either he's not home, or he's got company and he's ignoring me.

I don't remember hearing him come home, but I was asleep and might have missed it. Anyway, Magne, like Alex, has a new woman friend, and he hasn't been around as much as usual either.

So I'm feeling a bit abandoned when I plod back to my loft, via the stairs this time. Alex is on a road trip with her girlfriend, Magne is probably at *his* girlfriend's place, and my boyfriend is at his own place. It makes me grumpy, and I hate feeling sorry for myself.

So I vanish my tail, make my eyes look properly human, and get dressed in clothes I can actually be seen in public in. Then I go catch the bus to Evgeny's place.

It feels strange to be out during the day. I've gotten so used to being one of those things that goes bump in the night that I forgot how nice it can be to see things in color. Because not only does the darkness reduce the world to shades of grey, but even in daylight my fox eyes don't see the same range of color as my human eyes.

I find myself mesmerized by the movement of light through the leaves of the tired old oak that grows near one side of my building. They're not fully unfurled yet, those leaves, since spring is still new – so new it could snow and not be entirely unseasonal – but they're open enough that I can see the tracery of veins inside their delicate surfaces.

And the sky. It's smudged with the dingy, dusty taint of the city, but it's still glorious. Evgeny's eyes are nearly that color when he's happy. Thinking of Ev happy makes me smile and I laugh out loud.

I realize, too late, that it probably makes me seem like a madwoman, but then I realize that I don't care. As it turns out, there's no one on the street to see me anyway. One of the benefits of living in a largely industrial part of town is that I don't have many neighbors. There are a couple of other warehouses converted to flats and studios, but most of them are rented by vamps and weres and other *others* for the same reasons I live here. It's not a pretty neighborhood, but it's quiet, and it's close enough to the river and several parks that there's room to run.

I sit on the bus stop bench and tilt my face up to the sun, feel it soak into my skin. My fox nature wants to curl up in the heat and take a nap, but my human side is energized by the light.

One of the disadvantages of living where I do is the shitty bus service. They do come here, but only at considerable intervals. So I finally decide to walk, at least to somewhere busier where I can get a bus that goes where I want to go without having to transfer. I stand up, stretch, and head towards downtown via the park.

It was there I killed Ev's papa vamp, which sort of resulted in him gaining his freedom – it definitely ended up with me feeling obligated to help him.

I should point out that I don't go around killing vampires willy-nilly. They're sentient, thinking beings and have as much right to exist as I do. And hell, Ev's a vamp himself. But when they try to make me into a snack, I don't hesitate to fight back.

Killing Papa Vamp also sort of indirectly resulted in Evgeny needing my help with the demon-ghost evil thing he's now got trapped inside his head. It's a long story, and complicated, and I'm not even sure I know how all the connections worked.

But this is where I staked the nasty old prick, when he decided he wanted to feed me to his progeny – after raping me, of course. You can understand, I hope, that I was rather anxious that neither of those things happen. And here, too, is where Ev and I fought off a gang of vamps – who call themselves "Reborn" by the way – who were trying to capture him. Actually, Evgeny did most of the fighting, though I was not exactly a pushover.

I have a lot of memories here, good and bad, but they're all recent, because something over a year ago, a year and a half nearly, I was attacked, violated, and left for dead in a formal Japanese garden outside of town. I woke up in this park, with no memories of my past.

Since then, I've gained a few memories back – a trio of ancient fox women helped with that – but a lot of my life is still a blank. It used to bother me, but since I learned more about my fox nature I've started to care less and less about who I used to be. I am who I am now, and that's what matters, right?

Still, there are times when knowing my past would really come in handy. Like when a good-looking guy, dusky-skinned, late 30s or not much older, with Ben Franklin specs and dressed like an academic in jeans and a sports jacket grabs my arm as I pass by and says, "Panya? My God, where have you been?" And hugs me.

My first instinct is to shove him away and pretend I don't know who the fuck he is. Hell, I wouldn't have to pretend, because I *don't* know who he is. But he knows who I am. Or who I used to be. And he smells – just barely – like magic.

My full name is Panya Su Fuchs, and since I woke up on a park bench – one not far from where I'm being hugged by a stranger – I've called myself Su. Of the two given names on my expired driver's license, it felt the most like me. But I learned when the fox women gave me back a night of my memory, when I remembered loving Alex, that I used to be called Panya. Sometimes Alex still calls me Panya by accident, because that's how she knew me first.

I force myself not to kick this guy in the nuts – I know kung fu, but gonad-crushing is easier from this close up – and I just stand still. After a brief moment he steps back. He looks confused, and I feel kind of bad.

"Um," I say. Yeah, I'm not exactly eloquent. I spend too much time in my own head, I guess.

"Panya?" says the man. He's got a trace of an accent. Indian, maybe. How did I know him? "Are you all right?"

Then this thing happens that sometimes does. It's like déjà vu, only much, much stronger. And it usually brings some fragment of lost memory with it. This man at a podium, giving a lecture. There's a map behind him, showing the Middle East.

I'm dizzy suddenly, and when I put out my hand to catch my balance, he's there, one hand on mine, one at my elbow, leading me to a bench, helping me sit.

"Dr Pradip?" I say. Then I remember another day, an office, he's leading me to a chair just like he lead me to the bench. I've had some devastating news. What was it?

"John," he says. "Have we become strangers?" He touches my hair and I know that touch, intimately. I turn my face against his hand, and remember the heat of his skin, his mouth.

Oh, fuck. This man was my political science professor, and then my lover. I get up and I'm ten steps away before I stop myself, turn back.

"I'm sorry," I say.

"No," he says. "I'm sorry. I shouldn't have… I never explained to you why I… why I broke things off."

"Things are complicated right now," I say. I try to remember more about him, about me, but forcing the déjà vu only makes it recede faster. Another moment, and it's gone. My head is clear and I have a few more facts about my life, but otherwise everything is back to normal.

"Okay," he says. "But I feel I owe you an explanation. Perhaps I could buy you lunch?"

I hesitate. I want to leave, quickly, and not deal with this fragment of my past. I don't want the woman I used to be to intrude any more on my life now. But one thing I've learned in the last year is that you never know when a bit of information is going to be useful. And I've also learned that the past has a habit of catching up to you, whether you want it to or not.

And my past might just hold the answers to how exactly my fox nature fits with my human side. Plus there's that faint whiff of what I think of as the smell of magic, which is more likely the scent of *otherness*, that clings to him like a faded cologne. It's so tenuous I don't think *he's* other, but he's been around someone who is.

So I nod, and take his business card, shake his hand, let him kiss me chastely on the cheek, and walk away.

I make it out of sight around a bend in the path before dizziness hits me again, so hard I fall to my knees on the pathway. This time, it's not déjà vu that does it. It's Alex's familiar binding, and it feels so much like strangling I think I actually black out for a few seconds.

As soon as I fight off panic, as soon as I can breathe again, I walk straight to a bus stop and get on the first bus heading in the general direction of Evgeny's place.

When I get there, I fumble so much with the key that by the time I get the door open Ev's awake, blinking at me from beyond the reach of sunlight through the doorway.

"Su?" he says. "What's wrong?"

I don't cry much. I don't like how helpless it makes me feel. But when I've got the door closed again, I can feel hot tears streaming down my face.

Evgeny puts his arms around me, strokes my hair, and murmurs nice things into my ear until the tears stop. He doesn't ask me to explain, he just waits, holding me until I'm ready to talk. I tell him about the familiar binding and how it's started choking me, about the nightmares of strangling, and even about meeting my professor – my ex-lover – in the park.

He puts his hand on my face, and his touch, unlike John Pradip's, is cool. He's a vampire, so his circulation is slow, so slow he can appear dead, though he's very much alive. But it makes his body temperature cooler than human.

"Is there anything I can do?" he asks.

I scrub my face with both hands. "How are your witch abilities?" I say. Because Ev, though made a vampire, was born a witch, maybe the only male witch currently alive. It shouldn't be possible for him to be both witch and vamp – it should have killed him to be Reborn – but Ev's not exactly a run-of-the-mill guy.

He shrugs. "I've been practicing. I'm not even sure what I'm supposed to be capable of."

"Can you block my mind from… from outside influences?" I'm not even sure I really want to ask him this; I don't like anyone meddling with my mind, but better Ev than anyone else. Usually my fox powers are enough to keep witches and other manipulators-of-thoughts away.

"From Alex?" he says. "Is that what you want?"

Alex, because of the familiar binding, is the one person I can't block. Not anymore. I nod.

"I can try," he says.

"Do it," I say. "Please." And then I kiss him, push my mouth against his, slide my tongue between his teeth, press myself against him until I feel his breath quicken and the heat of his body increase as his metabolism picks up from arousal. I can smell his desire and my own response to it.

And something eases in my head, a tension I was hardly aware of.

He pulls away to say, "I don't think I can keep her out if she really wants to force the issue."

Then I drop to my knees for the second time that day, tug down his pajama bottoms, and render him incapable of saying anything else by applying my mouth to his hardness.

Chapter Two

LATER, WITH THE taste of Evgeny still salty in my mouth, and the dampness still lingering between my legs where he returned the favor, we lie on the bed and talk some more.

"I'm not sure I can deal with this much longer," I say and even I don't know if I mean the weird feeling of our sex life having become stolen moments, or the strangling of being a witch's familiar. Or maybe they're one and the same.

Evgeny kisses the top of my head and shifts his upper body so my chin doesn't jab him in the shoulder. "Is there anything you and Alex haven't tried yet?" he asks.

I shake my head, as much as I can without lifting it from his shoulder. "Just flatlining."

I can almost feel him frown, even though I'm not looking at his face. It's the way his body goes still when he's puzzling something out.

"Death?" he says, concern making his voice strained.

"Alex saw that 90s movie, *Flatliners*. And she had the idea that we could stop her heart long enough to break the binding, like it would if she died. Then start her up again. Or me. I suppose it would work if I was the one who died, too."

He doesn't say anything for a while, and I'm pretty sure he's trying to find a tactful way to say it's a really stupid idea.

"I'm not so sure that would even work," he finally says. "Magic isn't bound by scientific rules."

"You think it would re-bind once she was revived?"

"Assuming she *could* be revived. Things like that are never as easy as they are in the movies."

"I know," I say. "I wouldn't let her do it, even if she could find a doctor to help."

He shifts again, displacing me from his shoulder. He turns onto his side and puts his hand on my face, looks into my eyes. "I want you to be free," he says. "But I won't risk your life."

"Or Alex's?"

I'm not really surprised when he doesn't agree right away. Ev's a sweetheart, but something in the vamp transformation made him liquid-nitrogen-cold in a lot of ways. He once snapped another vamp's neck, killing her instantly, because she threatened to feed on me. He's protective.

"I'd rather she didn't risk her life," he says. "But if it meant saving yours…"

I put my fingers against his mouth so he can't finish the sentence.

"We'll find another way," I say. "I'll call her, and we'll find another way."

"Mathilde?" he says. Mathilde is an older witch, someone we thought a friend, or at least an ally, until she loosed the demon that Ev's got prisoned in his head. Witches are rare and scattered, but Mathilde knows several and can get them together if need be.

"Alex says she doesn't answer her phone or return calls."

"Can't blame her," Ev says.

Mathilde lived through the confrontation with the demon, but several others were not so lucky. But she was forced to admit she'd been wrong, so we probably aren't her favorite people. Plus her intention had been to destroy both Evgeny and the demon at the same time, so she isn't one of our favorites, either.

I stay in bed until my stomach growls, putting off the inevitable, trying to ignore my problems just for a little while, so I can enjoy some time with my boyfriend.

But eventually I'm hungry enough my guts get vocal, and Evgeny stirs next to me. And I feel pressure building in my mind again, like a headache, only not physical. And my throat constricts.

I put my hand to my neck as Ev gets out of bed and pulls on a bathrobe. I'd rather he stay naked, because he's awfully nice to look at, lean with muscle, but not bulky.

"I wonder if familiars feel like this all the time," I say, rubbing my throat.

Evgeny turns and bends and kisses where my hand just was, sending goosebumps across my skin.

"Perhaps it's worse because she's so far away," he says.

Now that's a thought. I did begin having the strangling dreams more frequently after Alex left. Maybe when she comes back, I'll be able to breathe freely again.

That thought is enough to get my lazy ass out of bed. I pull on the nearest garment, which happens to be a t-shirt of Ev's, and while he makes coffee – one of the many things he refuses to give up even though he's primarily a blood-drinker now – I poke the touchscreen of his smartphone and enter Alex's number.

I'm running over the best way to phrase my message, so she'll know it's urgent but not life-or-death. Yet. I'm expecting to get her voicemail, so I'm caught off guard when she actually answers.

"Hello?"

Just the sound of her voice eases something, some trace of the familiar binding. It's not till she says, "Su?" that I realize I haven't said anything.

"Alex," I say. "How's the trip?" I can wait till she's back to hear about it, but it's something to fill the time while I figure out how to bring up the subject I need to talk about.

"It's great," she says. "But I was actually just going to call you."

That, I wasn't expecting. "Where are you?" I say, then before she can answer I decide I might as well just say what the problem is straight off. I don't know why I would feel the need to do anything else, except since she can poke around in my head I guess I've felt a little more guarded.

"We have to do something about the binding," I say. Then I spill out about the nightmares and the choking. I'm about to add my meeting with

Dr Pradip, which isn't even relevant, but then Evgeny distracts me with coffee.

Alex laughs and I realize I was blathering at high speed, as if I had to get everything out at once.

"I'm on my way back," she says. "You can fill in the rest when I get there." Then she pauses, like this time *she's* the one trying to figure out the best way to phrase something. "I told you about Li, right?" Her new girlfriend.

"Sure," I say.

"I think she might be… well, not an *other*, but… gifted somehow."

Others are the things that go bump in the night. Some are born *other* – witches, for example – and some are made – vamps, weres, fox women. But we're all not-quite-human. Some say more than human, some say less, but most just say other than human.

"You think she has some *other* ancestry?" But if she was manifesting *otherly* abilities – it's not magic, exactly – then she'd be considered fully *other*. If not, then human.

"I don't know," says Alex. "It's hard to explain. But the thing is… well, she's a writer. I told you that, I think. A storyteller. But the other day she started making up a story about my ancestor Rose-Perle."

Rose-Perle Holz, a German witch of a few generations back, had taken my *hexenfuchs* ancestor as her familiar. And had then taken the *hexenfuchs'* half-human daughter as her lover.

"Like fiction?" I say. Alex and I had both dreamed about our ancestors, dreams that we believe were more than dreams, glimpses into the actual past.

"It seemed so, at first. Li said she liked the name Rose-Perle, so she started to make up a story about the village Rose-Perle lived in, and her family. I told her what little I know of them, but the parts Li made up… Well, they don't feel made up."

Alex pauses for a breath and I hear her ragged inhale. I can't tell if she's excited or disturbed.

"It felt like a prophecy, except about the past instead of the future."

"Like one of our dreams."

"Exactly. I got her to start writing it down after the first bit, so it would be easier to share with you. She says it feels different from how she usually writes. Like it's written through her, kind of. Not *by* her."

"So what's the story?" I realize I haven't touched my coffee, so I lift the mug and take a big gulp. Ev makes the best coffee I've ever had, anywhere. He's a great cook, too.

"It's weird, and too much to tell over the phone, especially with the rates they're charging me."

I forgot, she's traveling and our local service providers have really crappy cross-country cell plans.

"Shit," I say. "I hope this doesn't cost you too much."

"Never mind," she says. "I'll be back in a couple of days and I'll give you the story to read. And we can talk about a way to break the familiar binding. I have an idea about that."

"Oh yeah?"

"I'll tell you when I get back. But, Su?"

"Yeah?"

"You'll need to get your passport."

"My passport?" Easier said than done when you have no past and only a long-expired driver's license for ID.

"I think we're going to have to go to Germany."

She laughs when I don't answer.

"See you soon," she says, then disconnects.

"Alex wants to go to Germany," I say.

A couple of months ago, if I needed documents, real or fake, I'd have gone to Liam's Market.

Liam was a vampire and a retailer of "sustenance" for Reborn kind, but he knew who to talk to to get just about anything. He'd even get it for you, for the right price.

But Liam had been killed by Mathilde's witches a couple of months ago, walked out into the sun by mind control in a sort of dry-run for what they'd planned to do to Evgeny. He hadn't really been a friend – actually, he was a pretty nasty character – but there are times that I miss him.

The only other person I know who knows a lot of folks, human and *other*, shady and legitimate, is Magne. Magne might know where to get a good fake passport.

He laughs when I ask. "Why not just get a real one?" he says.

When I just stare at him, he shakes his head. "You might not remember your past," he says, "but you do have one. You know your full legal name, and your former employer."

He leans back in his chair, sprawling in a boneless-looking way. I wish I could be so relaxed, sometimes. Or at least *look* that way.

"How do I do that?" I snap at him. I'm irritated because he's making me feel stupid, and I don't like to feel stupid. I think he realizes, because his expression softens and he gets up and goes to his kitchen island, where a laptop displays a random oscillating rainbow of lights on its screen. When he taps the touchpad, the lights vanish, to be replaced by an orderly desktop. His wallpaper is a cheesy airbrushed image of a howling wolf. I hope it's ironic and that he doesn't actually like art that bad.

It seems like mere seconds later he's got a bunch of forms open in his internet browser, and then a wireless printer across the room starts spitting out pages.

Magne seems so much a part of the forest, so wild a creature, that sometimes I forget how technologically savvy he is.

He collects the forms and hands them to me. "Start by applying for a re-issue of your birth certificate, and Social Insurance Number," he says. "You might have to re-take the driving test to get your driver's license back, but it would be good to get that, too. Once you have those, apply for a passport, pay the extra fee to have it expedited, and you'll have all the ID you'll ever need." He grins, a cheeky look in his eye. "Unless you plan to become a spy or an international art thief."

I stare at the sheaf of papers, too bemused to laugh at his gentle teasing. For over a year I haven't had a real job because I thought it would be too hard to get ID again. Or maybe I was just avoiding my past. Then again, I *am* really good at picking pockets.

"How long will it take?" I read the top form, surprised at how simple it is, how little information they ask for.

"A month or two," he says.

I put my hand to my throat. "That long?"

"You've waited this long," he says. "What's a couple of months?"

So I tell him about the choking dreams, and Alex's notion to go to Germany. Magne was there when Alex did the binding. He went through the horror of the demon-thing along with us.

He frowns when I finish talking, then walks back to the kitchen, rummages in a drawer, and returns with a pen. He hands it to me.

"Fill out the forms and give them to me. I know a few people who may be able to see that they get processed more quickly."

When Alex and her new love show up at my door I'm in the middle of kung fu practice, so I meet them sweaty and flushed.

Alex hugs me anyway. A couple of months ago, a hug would have been too much. Too much physical contact, too much weirdness. But I guess she's happy now, not in love with me anymore, and all the awkwardness is gone.

I kind of miss it. Yeah, it's totally selfish, especially since I've got a great thing with Evgeny, but it was flattering to still be loved by Alex, too. To be wanted. And she's a pretty spectacular woman, tall and strong with depthless brown eyes and red hair like a Celtic goddess, kept short but prone to sticking up.

"Su," she says. Not "Panya." I kind of miss that, too, even though I want to set the past aside. Mostly.

"Hey," I say. "How was the trip?"

"It was good," she says. "Li is brilliant at cooking things on sticks over a campfire."

She reaches back and takes the hand of the woman who waits in the hall and draws her forward.

"This is Li," she says.

"Hi," I say, and put out my hand.

Alex's new girlfriend is tiny, barely over five feet and fragile as a bird. Her grip is strong, though, even if the bones of her hand feel like I might accidentally snap them.

I suppose I shouldn't be surprised that she's Asian – I mean, I've known her name since Alex first met her – but I am, a little. It's because

I'm half-Asian myself, and look Chinese, except I'm above average height and fairly pale. I guess I'd have thought Alex would want to find someone less like me.

But that's dumb, isn't it? Alex's new relationship has nothing to do with me. I don't know when I got so self-centered.

"Hi," says Li. Her voice is soft and quiet, but there's a certain compelling quality to it. I bet it sounds great when she's reading a story.

"Come in," I say. "I'll make tea."

While we wait for the kettle, Alex tells me all about their cross-country adventure, camping in national parks all along the highway.

"We didn't see any foxes," she says.

I grin. "A fox is unseen when she wants to be unseen," I say. It's something the fox women told me, or one of them. It's how I learned I could be… not invisible, exactly, but unnoticed. It's almost as cool a superpower as turning into a fox.

When I turn around to carry the tea into the part of the loft I use as a living room, I see Li staring at me.

My tail. I forgot about it. It feels so normal now to have it, that it takes effort to remember to vanish it at appropriate times. And I find it helps my balance quite a lot when I do kung fu. Almost like having an extra limb.

I hand her a cup of tea. "Like it?" I say, and twitch the ridiculous red brush from side to side.

"Alex told me," she says. "But I guess I didn't quite believe her." She drags her gaze away from my backside and looks up at my face. Her eyes are darker than Alex's, almost black. She smiles tentatively. "She says you can turn into a fox, too?"

I nod. "Don't ask me to demonstrate, though," I say. I'm not shy, but changing shape feels sort of private, and Evgeny's the only one I've shifted in front of.

"Oh, no," says Li. "I would never presume."

We sip quietly for a moment, and then I say, a bit hesitantly, "Alex said you see the past."

Li carefully sets her cup on the coffee table. "I never have before," she says. "Or maybe I have and don't know it." She stares into space for a moment, as if gathering her thoughts. Then she picks up her tea, takes a long sip, sets it down again.

"When I started as a storyteller," she says, and her voice takes on more depth, a kind of resonance that makes one want to pay attention. "I told traditional folk tales. Chinese stories. Later, I told tales from many lands, but always folk tales, legends, fairy stories.

"When I tell them, it's like I can see them in my head, playing out like a movie, and I just tell what I see. When I tell the same story twice, I may mention different details, even though the events are the same.

"Then, eventually, I began to make up stories of my own. Fantasy tales, still, but with plots of my own, characters from my imagination. First I just told them out loud, adding them to my performances, and I sometimes made them up as I went along. Once I told them once, I could tell them again and again, but like the folk stories, sometimes I pick out different details. And once I told a story out loud, then later I might write it down and select the details that work best for a written story.

"It takes a different kind of skill to write a story than to tell one out loud, and the details you choose to include are much more important. But I guess I'm not too bad at it."

Alex snorts. "You're pretty close to making a living off it," she says. "Not many writers can say that."

Li smiles softly, looking down at her tea, which she's cradling in her hands now, as if her words are swirling in the depths of the amber liquid.

"Well," she says. "When Alex told me she had an ancestor named Rose-Perle who was a witch I thought I'd make up a story about her to pass the time as we drove. So I spun a tale about a small mountain village where lived a toymaker who first became prosperous, and then got himself cursed by the witch who lived in the nearby woods. I thought I was making up an ancestry for Rose-Perle the witch."

"I almost drove off the road," says Alex. "I hadn't said much more than her name and that she was a witch. I never mentioned that Rose-Perle's family were toymakers, or that they lived in a town on the edge of a forest called the Hexenwald."

I let this information process for a moment. *Hexenwald.* Witch-wood. "Why do you think it's true? Couldn't it be coincidence?"

Alex shrugs. "When she told me, and those details about the village and the Holz family were right… It felt like the time you told me about your dreams, about the *hexenfuchs*. I just knew it was true." She grins at me. "I'm a witch, remember. We're supposed to be able to tell the difference between truth and lies, between story and history."

Li sets her cup on the coffee table again, turns it so the design on the side is lined up perfectly with the edge of the table.

"I thought I was just spinning air into clouds," she says. "Just making up a story like you might invent backgrounds for funny-looking people you see in a coffee shop to pass the time. Except once I started, the words came pouring out and I couldn't stop until they did. And I keep feeling there's more to come, only I can't quite tell it yet."

She reaches for a messenger bag she brought with her and pulls out some pages, handwritten in a precise and tiny script. She looks at them a moment before handing the papers to me.

"It's not in these pages," she says, "but there's a fox in this story somewhere. I don't know how I know that, but I do."

"Read," says Alex. "I'll make more tea."

So I lean back in my chair, and read.

Chapter Three

THERE WAS A VILLAGE in the Oktober Mountains that was cursed. Some people would say that all villages in the Oktober Mountains were cursed, because there was always a chill wind blowing, even in the height of summer. And some would say this particular village – which was named Schönstadt by its founders, one assumes in happier times – was doubly cursed, because it also nestled right on the edge of the Hexenwald.

But Schönstadt had been populated early on by a family of toy makers by the name of Holz, and a witch-wood (for that is what *hexenwald* means, after all) is the best place to find wood for toy-making.

It makes the toys seem more alive, you see.

In fact, the town of Schönstadt had always before been prosperous. The toys made by the Holz family became known far and wide for their life-like-ness. Traders and even tourists braved the frigid breezes of the Oktober Mountains to visit the town and purchase toys in quantity. And while they were there they also purchased the local cheese and ate at the local inn and soon discovered that other local crafts were almost as well-made as the toys. The clocks, especially, were finely wrought and kept time better than any made in the city. So everyone in Schönstadt prospered, but the Holzes most of all.

In fact, the toy making business grew so quickly that Meister Holz did something none of his ancestors before him had done – he took on a journeyman and three apprentices from outside the village. And that was where the trouble started.

The three apprentices were at least born and raised in the Oktober Mountains and had heard stories of the Witch of the Wald since they could understand speech. They were respectful.

But the journeyman had lived in one city or another his whole life and though he came well-recommended and his work would soon enough reach a master's level of skill, he didn't understand the Hexenwald.

Not that anyone could, really, understand that haunted place, but there were *rules*. There were things you did and didn't do and things you must and mustn't do when you went there. Especially if you went collecting wood to make toys.

The journeyman didn't understand, for example, why he should be required to leave a silver coin – in particular a shiny, new-minted silver coin – somewhere nearby when he collected a sled full of wood, stacked and drying not far from the outer edge of the village.

For months, he left the coin because his master told him to, and sure enough, it would be gone the next time he went. But he began to believe it was a scam by some clever local to wring money out of his (or *her*, though *his* seemed likelier) more superstitious neighbors. Witches weren't real, after all.

So one day the journeyman didn't leave the coin. Instead, he tucked it under his pillow. He meant to tell Meister Holz, once he'd held back the coins often enough to prove it was only a silly folk belief and not a custom a prosperous craftsman should keep. But as the coins accumulated enough to make an uncomfortable lump under his pillow, the journeyman, who would soon be a master in need of a place of his own, realized he had nearly enough to buy his own shop somewhere where the wind wasn't so cold. Another year and he would have both mastership and money. So he said nothing.

Then the witch arrived. Of course, no one knew it was the Witch of the Wald, or any witch at all, no one save Meister Holz's young son and daughter, and they were too young for anyone to pay any mind to except to make sure they kept out from underfoot.

To everyone else, she was just an old lady from elsewhere in the Oktober Mountains – for she had a distinctly Oktoberish accent – who had heard of the wonderful toys made by the Holzes of Schönstadt.

"Such lovely toys," she said, in her old, cracked voice.

Meister Holz shivered and reached to shut the window. "Thank you, Frau," he said. He had been working on a particularly fine pair of dolls when the witch walked through the shop's front door and leaned over the counter to watch. They had skillfully carved heads, and arms and legs jointed at elbow and knee, but their bodies were stout canvas instead of wood, stuffed tight with goosedown. Frau Holz had said that this pair of dolls must be warm and pleasant to hug, because they were for their own children. The dolls were twins, as the children were, but Meister Holz had made them too large, his wife said.

And they were too large – they were the size of children twice the age of his twins, which made them nearly twice as large as the children were. They had not seemed so big when Meister Holz began them and he had not noticed their size until his wife had pointed it out. Now he was hastening to finish them for sale, so he could start anew on a pair for his toddlers.

The peculiar incident of the dolls' size should perhaps have given him his first inkling that something was amiss.

"I wonder," said the old lady, "where you found such beautiful wood to carve them from."

"Oh," said the toymaker. "I send my journeyman to collect it from a store we have drying in the Hexenwald. It's witch-wood, all."

"Do you not fear the witch?" she asked.

One of the twins, sucking his finger and staring up at the witch from where he sat at his father's feet with a set of alphabet blocks, began to cry. His sister patted his face and he stopped. Together, the two small children stared at the witch.

She smiled and they simply continued to stare.

"Oh, no," said Holz. "I give my journeyman a silver coin to leave for the witch each time he collects a load of wood from the store, and for each time he cuts new wood and stacks it to dry."

"That's a handsome sum," said the witch.

"It is what we have always paid. One newly-minted silver coin for as much wood as one person can haul on a sled. It's a goodly amount of wood, and our toys sell well. It is a beneficial deal for us," he said. "And for the witch, too, I suppose."

"Do you trust your journeyman with your silver?" she asked.

"He came to me highly recommended," said Meister Holz. "Most highly. He would not risk his place and his mastership."

"It's a shame you trust him so," said the witch.

"Why is that?" said Meister Holz, a slight tremor in his voice.

"He has been stealing from you for more than a year," she said. "I have been patient, but I am patient no longer."

Meister Holz turned quite white. White as the snow that would soon blanket the fields around Schönstadt. White as the cotton dress his wife had made for the girl doll and the shirt she had made for the boy doll. White as old age.

"I will speak to him," he said, stammering in his fear. "I will get the coins you are owed from him, and more, and bring them to you in the wood."

The witch shook her head. She looked sympathetic, but an ancient bargain is still a bargain and bargains must be kept. "It is too late for that," she said. "I'm afraid I must curse you." She looked thoughtfully at the twins, who stared back at her.

Meister Holz went even paler (if that is possible) when he saw what she was looking at. Colorless as ice he turned. Pale as death and bones.

"Please," he said. "Not my children."

"No," she said. "Not your children."

The toy maker became a little less pale. "I will take whatever curse you cast upon me, then."

Now the witch did not look sympathetic, or kind, at all. "I curse you thusly," she said. "Until you or one of your family can bring me a pearl beyond price, this pleasant village will watch its children sicken and die when they reach the age of seven years."

The toy maker opened his mouth to protest but the witch went on before he could speak. "Except your children, who will be hale and healthy their whole, long lives." Then she walked out of the shop and into the

Hexenwald and was never seen again by anyone then alive.

So the families of Schönstadt watched their children grow and thrive until they reached the age of seven years, when they sickened and died. All save the Holz children. And you may think the Holzes escaped the curse, which hardly seems fair. But imagine being the only parents whose children lived and not only lived but grew healthy and happy and beautiful.

In a way, the Holzes were cursed worst of all, and before the twins turned nine, their parents sent them to live with relations in the city.

But the worst part of the witch's curse was that children continued to be born in Schönstadt. And they thrived and filled the village with hope until they turned seven. And then they sickened and died.

So the families of Schönstadt drifted away from their village, where their ancestors had lived for generations. The tourists and the traders drifted away also, and the Holzes never made a toy that looked quite so alive again. But soon the families discovered that they could not have children that lived past the age of seven years, or businesses that prospered, even away from Schönstadt. Even away from the Oktober Mountains entirely. And so they drifted back again, because if they must be cursed, at least they could be cursed in their own homes.

Life went on, only with fewer children, and none older than seven. And when the Holz twins turned twenty-and-one, their parents died within three days of each other. So Jorinde and Joringel Holz returned to Schönstadt for the funeral, and to see what they had inherited.

When I get to the end of the last page I sit looking at the words, letting them blur in my vision.

It's like a fairy tale, and I can easily imagine someone making it up to pass the time. There's not that much specific detail in it – could the name of the village and its nearby forest and mountains just be a coincidence? Maybe Alex had mentioned their names to Li and had forgotten.

Maybe. But did she also mention the Holz twins and then forget that, too? Or maybe Alex didn't even know the names of her ancestors aside from Rose-Perle and they had come entirely from Li's imagination.

But she's right about one thing. It *feels* true. I have goosebumps down my arms and the same feeling in my stomach that I have when I wake from one of my dreams of my own ancestor, the same feeling I get when the déjà vu hits and a small piece of memory of my past surfaces.

"Wow," I say, and look up.

Alex is watching me. I wonder what she can see in my face. "I checked my mom's papers," she says. "She had this old photo album full of snapshots of our relatives and notes on who was born to who. I guess our family noted that stuff down, like some people keep track in the family Bible."

She gets up to fetch the fresh pot of tea she made while I was reading, and pours for everyone.

"I wanted to bring it along, the album, but it's way too big and heavy. But remember how I told you I never knew who my father was?"

I nod and sip my tea. It's hot and strong. Delicious.

"I never really paid that much attention before, but there aren't any men listed in the book unless one of the women has a son. But only his birthday is noted, while all the women and girls' birthdays are listed, and their death days. And not one of the dates has a year."

"So either the men in your family were all sterile and lived forever…"

"Or they weren't important." She sets the tea pot down and sits. "Only one of them is different. A ways back, there's a set of twins. Jorinde and Joringel, girl and boy. They're listed right before Rose-Perle, and you can't really tell which one is her parent. Plus both of their deaths are listed. He died a month after she did, assuming it happened in the same year, which I guess it might not."

"Presumably the girl would be Rose-Perle's mother," I say. "Since only the children of women are listed."

Alex shrugs. "Presumably. But they're listed on the same line. Because they're twins, I guess. But he's the only male who has a death date noted."

"So none of your female ancestors married?"

"Or else husbands were even more irrelevant than sons."

"Or it's not meant to be a complete family tree," says Li, her quiet voice clear for all its softness.

Alex and I look at her and I realize what she's saying.

"It's a lineage of witches," I say. Because witches – Evgeny's unusual family excepted – are female. Always. At least that's so for *hexen*, for German witches.

Li nods. "Alex has told me a little about witches."

It's kind of an unspoken, but strongly-held, rule among *others* that we don't tell non-*others* about our existence. It's safer that way. We don't even tell spouses unless we're pretty damn sure we're going to be with them a very long time. And that we can trust them completely. So that Alex said anything to Li tells me a lot. About both of them. And it's a damn good thing Alex trusts Li that much, since I was stupid enough to meet Li with my tail in full view.

"You might be some kind of *other* yourself," I say. "If you really can tell true stories of the past."

Li shakes her head. "Not that I'm aware of. Is there no magic among humans?"

"We don't really have magic," says Alex. "Witches have the ability to influence perception and probability, and weres and vamps have a symbiotic organism that gives them extra strength and speed and stuff."

"That's one big shift in probability, to make every child in one village get sick and die at the same age," says Li.

Alex frowns, but not at her girlfriend; it's more of a thinking frown. "I don't really know. Mom didn't teach me anything. She didn't even tell me we were descended from witches. I'm not sure she even had any *hexen* abilities herself. Maybe because I didn't show any while she was alive, she assumed I didn't either, and that they had died out in our family."

She pauses for a sip of tea. "What I mean is, I'm telling you what I've been told. And what I've been told is basically nothing."

Li smiles and puts her hand over Alex's. "Maybe what you were told isn't entirely true." She gestures at me. "A woman with a fox tail seems like magic to me."

"*Seems* is the key word there," I say. But I'm not so sure. Everything I've learned about *others* denies magic. Mental abilities have scientific explanations, I've read. Vamps have a symbiont that requires blood and does strange things to their metabolism. Were transformation isn't really shape-shifting, but rather a rearrangement of bones and joints that becomes possible over a long time, where the connections and articulations alter and reconfigure.

I've seen Magne go wolfie, and it's like watching a transformer robot. No magic. And my *hexenfuchs* ancestor supposedly only had the semblance of a human shape. A glamour, if you will.

Except she bore a half-human daughter. And my own shape-changing ability is real enough, and nothing like the way a werewolf takes on their wolf-like form.

Since I became *other* I've been ignoring my own past, but the more it creeps back in, the more the *otherly* explanations for my non-human abilities don't fit. They don't fit the part of my nature that was born *other* – the *hexenfuchs*. And they don't fit the part of me that was made *other* by three old Asian fox women in order to save my life.

And they don't explain the fact that one person isn't supposed to be both born and made *other*. As I was. As Evgeny was. And there's nothing I've learned so far that says humans can have magic without being *other*, like Li seems to have.

"I'm beginning to think," I finally say, after we've all sat pondering our own thoughts for a while, "that there's a lot more in Heaven and Earth than is dreamt of in the *others'* philosophy."

Alex lets a grin tug at the corner of her mouth. "So you think there *is* real magic."

I shrug. "I don't know yet, but I think there's more than the vamps and weres and even the witches know about."

"A deeper magic?" says Li. A smile touches her mouth, too.

"C.S. Lewis," I say, and the smile blossoms.

"I thought, since you quoted Shakespeare…"

Again, we lapse into silence. Then I hand the pages of story back to Li.

"So what happens when the twins return to Schönstadt?" I say, exactly as Alex says, "So now what?"

Li looks from one to the other of us. "I don't know," she says. "Once I said that last line, the story just stopped. I thought it would continue when I wrote it down, but it didn't. I hope perhaps, if we go there, to Schönstadt, I might be able to continue it."

"So that's why we came back early," says Alex.

"Germany," I say. "I wonder if I've ever been there?" I'm pretty good with languages. I must have studied linguistics or something, because I can read several, and even speak some of them, a little. I know German pretty well, but then my dad was German.

"Maybe if you have, you'll remember more of your past," says Alex.

She might be right. I can never tell what will trigger the déjà vu, but afterwards I can see that it's always something familiar, something small and unexpected. Maybe a new setting – new to me as I am now, but perhaps known to the old me – would cause more memories to surface.

I'm still not sure I want to bring up more of the past. I do know I'd rather remain Su than return to being Panya again. But like I said before, the past has a way of finding you, no matter how you try to avoid it. It might be better to just meet it head-on.

"You don't necessarily have to come with us," says Li. "I think I need to go, to get more of the story, and it's Alex's ancestors, so there's no point in going without her. But if you don't want to come..." She trails off, maybe seeing something in my face.

I realize I've got my hand to my throat again. Just the idea of Alex going so far away has made the familiar binding tighten like a choke-chain collar.

Alex touches the hand that rests on my neck. "Su?" The tightness eases.

"I'm okay," I say. "But I think the binding is telling me I have to go with you."

"Okay," she says, and takes her hand away. "I wish I knew more about familiars."

I reach for my tea cup and drain it, then pour another cup from the pot and sip that, too.

"You said you had an idea for how to break it. The binding."

She nods. "Well, sort of. What I need, what *we* need, is more knowledge about how it works. That's the thing about witch abilities, why I can't really think of them as *magic*.

"Magic is like, wave your hand, exert your will, and something happens. Abracadabra. But *hexen* abilities have rules and structure. You have to... you have to pluck and arrange the... I sort of imagine them like strands of time and probability and mind. Like that old Greek myth about the Fates who spin and weave and cut the tapestry of life.

"Know the rules, which threads to pluck and rearrange, and you can do all sorts of things. Nothing that actually violates the laws of physics." Her glance drifts to my tail for a moment. "Not as far as I know, anyway. So if I can learn how a familiar binding really works, I should be able to reverse it. Unweave it, sort of, from the tapestry of our lives intersecting."

"You made the binding in the first place," I say. "So shouldn't you already know how it works?"

"That's the problem," says Alex. "I followed Mathilde's instructions, but I didn't really understand them. I didn't *really* know how they worked or what I was doing. Plus I infused them into that piece of quartz instead of working them directly, and I really didn't know what I was doing there. I'm still surprised it actually worked."

"So you need to know more about *hexen* magic," I say.

She frowns at the word "magic," but nods.

"And none of the witches here can teach you?"

She nods again.

"So how are you going to learn?"

She grins. "I'm going to ask the Witch of the Wald."

Chapter Four

THE WITCH OF THE WALD. I stare at Alex, then look at Li. She's looking at Alex, too, but not in surprise. They must have talked about this already.

"Even if this is a true account of the past," I say, gesturing at the pages of Li's writing on the coffee table, "How do you know she's still alive?"

"I don't," says Alex. "But *hexen* are German witches, so it seems to me that there should be more *hexen* there than there are here. So there's got to be someone we could ask. And maybe they even wrote stuff down there, instead of relying on oral tradition."

"Maybe," I say. "Or maybe all the *hexen* fled Germany years ago."

"Why would they do that?" says Alex.

Li looks at me, understanding in her eyes. "The war," she says.

"It's not like they were Jewish," says Alex. "They wouldn't have been in concentration camps or anything." She looks from me to Li and back. "Would they?"

"It wasn't just Jews who were persecuted," I say. "Anyone different was a target. Romany, gay people, even scientists and journalists and artists who refused to fudge their research or change their work to support the official ideals."

"And witches are powerful women," says Li. "They would try to use them, and if they couldn't use them, they'd kill them."

Alex looks so crestfallen I feel a little bad.

"But *hexen* have always been secretive, right?" I say, trying to sound cheerful. "So maybe they just hid out."

Li smiles thanks at me. "We'll just have to go there and see what we find," she says, squeezing Alex's hand.

"Right," I say. "And I'll have my passport soon, if Magne's contacts are as good as he says they are."

"What about Evgeny?"

I hadn't thought of that. How do vamps orchestrate long distance travel when they have to stay out of direct sunlight, and even indirect sun makes them intensely uncomfortable?

"I don't know," I say. "I mentioned you wanted to go, and he didn't say much, except to ask if you were sure it's what we need to do."

"I'm not sure," says Alex. "I have no idea. But it's the best thing I can think of, besides temporary death."

"Let's make that a last resort," I say.

"Yes," says Li. "A *very* last resort."

I touch my throat, then drop my hand, not wanting to bring attention to it. The strangling feeling has definitely eased with Alex close by, but I can still feel it, like a flexible collar. If I'm distracted, I almost don't notice it, but if I don't have anything else to think about, it just about makes me want to take my nails to my own skin.

It wasn't like this at first. Not at all. It was more like a constant, but very faint awareness of where Alex was at all times, of how she was feeling. Now that awareness has dulled under the sensation of being… I don't want to say "subjugated," but it could easily become that if I didn't know I could trust Alex completely.

It wasn't all that long ago that I didn't trust anyone. Not a single person besides myself. And because of my lack of memory and knowing I wasn't human but not what I actually was, there were a lot of times I didn't even trust myself.

But now I have Alex, and Evgeny, and Magne. I'm even willing to trust Li though I've only just met her, because Alex trusts her. I hope all this trust isn't going to bite me in the ass someday.

Alex is a good organizer, so she volunteers to make the travel arrangements. I just have to come up with my share of the money when the time comes. Thanks to poor, dead Liam, who had a well-stocked safe and the habit of using the same passcode for everything, I've got a good stash of money scattered in several hidey-holes around the loft. I will need to get a job eventually, I suppose, since I seem to be going all official with my ID and all. Hell, maybe I'll even get a bank account. But for now, I'm okay.

Once Alex and Li have left, I head for the shower. It's late and I wonder how Ev's shift at work is going, how many teenagers he's had to evict from the mall's too-easy-to-climb-to roof, if he had time to eat (or drink).

I let my hands drift over my body, thinking to release a bit of tension with a nice, slow orgasm, but my heart's not in it. My hands keep going to my throat involuntarily. The choking isn't any worse – definitely having Alex back in town helps – but it's still irritating. Finally, I shut off the water and dry off, dressing in my most comfortable sweats and a t-shirt with a skeletal dodo bird printed on it.

In polar Inuit and Siberian cultures, myth says shamans could change shape by undressing their flesh right down to the skeleton, shifting the bones around, and then putting the flesh back on. It's not really that far off from what weres do. Well, aside from actually taking the flesh off, I guess. But ever since I read that, I've found I like bones. The idea of them as architectural structure and all that, how we're all pretty much the same when all that's left is a skeleton.

I decide against yet another pot of tea and settle on the couch with a book. And I discover that what I've used as a bookmark is Dr John Pradip's business card. "Professor of Political Science," it says. I wonder if it's usual for profs to have business cards like this one. It seems kind of odd to me, like he's trying too hard to seem legitimate. But if my new memory is right, he really is a poli sci instructor. And also a fairly accomplished lover.

I push that thought firmly aside. Once I mastered my shape-changing abilities, I also hoped I'd gain a better handle on my other foxy attributes. Whether it's the *hexenfuchs* or the fox woman, or just a quirk of my human genetics, I have a really active sex drive. Not quite nympho proportions, but still really distracting. But some of my fox abilities are related to sex, too, and in the last couple of months I've finally been able to get my libido under control, at least a little bit.

Of course, regular sex with Evgeny is probably responsible for most of that.

But I'm thinking that while I wait for my paperwork to come so I can leave the country and look for my roots in Germany, I have some time to kill. So maybe I should let John Pradip tell me whatever it was he believed I needed to know.

I might as well start facing my past right here at home.

We meet at a coffee shop downtown. I picked a busy one, well away from my neighborhood, but one I've never actually been to before. Busy so there will always be something to conveniently draw my attention in case conversation lags or gets awkward, and not close to home or a regular hangout because I want to keep my private life separate from… well, whatever this is.

Back when I was still a loner, when I was pickpocketing regularly to survive, keeping "business" far away from my home base was just common sense. Now, I guess it's a lingering paranoia. Sure, I have friends now, people I trust, but that doesn't mean I trust everyone. I especially don't trust my own past. Maybe because it's been a stranger for so long.

I get there early, of course, and pick a booth that gives me a good view of the whole place, and even a decent look through the windows to the street outside. It's just after lunch, so it's still busy, but the crowds are starting to thin as people head back to work.

When the waitress comes over, I'm looking dubiously at the array of tea tins over the counter, wondering it they're actually an indication of what's on the menu, or if I should play it safe and just order coffee. I'm kind of a tea snob, and bad tea is worse – much worse – than bad coffee. Lousy java you can at least render drinkable with a lot of sugar. And I'm sure coffee snobs would find that statement ignorant as hell.

Just as I'm turning to give the tired-looking young woman my order – I've decided to play it safe – John Pradip's rich voice interrupts.

"They have a very fine selection of teas here," he says, his faint Indian accent somehow giving his words more weight. A stereotype, I know, but you kind of expect someone from India to know about tea. "I recommend the Darjeeling."

There's the briefest flash of déjà vu and I recall him saying once that he spent part of his childhood near a famous tea plantation in Darjeeling. Before I can turn to look at him, the feeling is gone.

I smile. "I'll have Lapsang Souchong if you have it," I say. "Or Russian Caravan if you don't." It's only partly to be contrary that I don't choose his suggestion. It's also because the smoky flavor of Lapsang perfectly suits my mood.

John smiles. "Then *I* will have the Darjeeling," he says, and slides into the bench opposite me.

He looks at me for a long moment, face open and admiring, but something that might be caution in the set of his eyelids.

I took a lot of time getting dressed, trying to get the right balance of professional and casual. I wanted to look like Su, not Panya, but snug-fitting jeans and a motorcycle jacket didn't seem quite right. So I went with pinstripe trousers cut almost like cargo pants and a fitted jacket – not quite a blazer – over a t-shirt, the same dodo shirt I put on yesterday after Alex and Li's visit. I even put on a bit of makeup. I wish I'd been dressing for a date with Evgeny instead.

"You look well," he finally says.

"So do you." And he does. Better than well, he looks damn fine. He's wearing a professorial outfit much like last time I saw him – dark jeans and sports coat with a button-down shirt – but everything fits him so perfectly it looks tailored. He's built a lot like Ev, lean and fit, and I try not to think about what he looks like naked. I have the feeling that if I do think about it, the déjà vu will hit and I'll be treated to a sudden memory of every detail of his body, and I'm pretty sure I can't handle that right now.

The waitress arrives with our tea as we sit there staring at each other, and the next minutes are filled with test-pouring, and fishing baskets of tea leaves out of pots, and inhaling fine vapors. We both ignore the pitcher of cream the waitress left and take careful sips from our cups. Good tea – *really* good tea – should be drunk unadulterated, and anyway I'm lactose intolerant.

And the tea *is* really good. I wonder if I knew about this place before. Because I'm sorry it's taken so long to find it. I could come here every day. In fact, I might just do that.

When the sipping ritual has stretched on a little too long, John breaks the silence.

"Panya," he says, then stops. "What?" he says. "You just scowled."

"Did I?" I say. "Sorry." I stare down into my cup, then make myself look back up at him. "Look Dr Pradip. John. There are some things… A lot has happened since…"

I take several deep, measured breaths. I've dealt pretty well with being violated and left for dead, I think. Or I *thought*. Because sitting here across from this stranger who shouldn't be a stranger, I'm suddenly filled with irrational shame. This is why so many women don't report rapes, I think. Because they're ashamed, even though they have nothing to be ashamed of. I knew that to be true, intellectually, but now I *know* it to be true, from personal experience.

I let anger overwhelm the shame, then use a kung fu breathing exercise to dissipate the anger. "I have almost no memories older than a year and a bit," I finally say. I watch as sympathy and concern play across his face.

"I was…" I still can't quite say, "I was raped." Not to him, though I've said it to other people, though it's been over a year since it happened. "I almost died. And I woke up with no memory."

"Oh, Panya," he says, his voice soft. But there's no pity, only empathy. I didn't expect that. Usually, people pity me. Or get angry on my behalf.

"And that's another thing," I say. "I know I used to be called Panya, but I go by my middle name now. Su."

He's reached out to put his hand over mine and I stare down at his knuckles. His touch is warm, almost hot. I look back into his eyes and see heat in their brown depths, too. He's flushed – not enough for it to show on his cinnamon skin, but enough to make him smell spicy, sort of. He smells good.

I wonder if he'd be getting aroused if he knew the reason I almost died was because I was beaten and violated.

"I'm not really the same woman," I say.

He squeezes my hand and smiles. "How can you know if you're the same woman or not when you don't remember your past?"

When I open my mouth to answer, he puts a finger on my lips, then quickly withdraws it, as if realizing the gesture may be too familiar.

"Do you want to remember?" he says.

That's a good question, and one I've been asking a lot lately.

"Sometimes," I say. "It would make life easier. But going by what I know of her… of me… the old me… I don't want to be that helpless again. And I don't think I can ever be that *nice* again."

He chuckles. His voice is so rich I could drown in it. No wonder I slept with him. Though I'm a little surprised that the woman I used to be would sleep with her teacher. Maybe she… I… wasn't quite the good girl I've been assuming.

"She wasn't so awful. The old you," he says, his voice teasing.

"I hope not," I say. "I mean, I like to think I'm a decent person, with memories, or without."

"You were a lovely person," he says. "As I expect you are still, whatever happened in the meantime." He swirls the tea in his cup and takes a long sip.

"Have you had lunch?" he asks suddenly, and when I admit I haven't, he calls the waitress back to ask for menus. When she brings them, we study the text, both of us, I think, avoiding the reason we actually met. To talk about our past together, and whatever ended it.

I order two vegetarian samosas. I'm not against meat – how could I be when my other shape is a carnivore? – but I prefer those savory morsels full of vegetables. John gets a tuna salad sandwich. With our orders made, we can't avoid the real topic any longer.

"I don't remember being with you," I finally say, opting to be blunt. "Except for a few snippets. So you don't have to explain anything."

"I suppose it wouldn't make a lot of sense to tell you why I broke off our affair if you don't remember having one."

He bites his lip, like he's making a decision he's not sure of. "But I might be able to help with that." He frowns. "If you like."

"Help with what?" I say, a peculiar feeling growing in the pit of my stomach. It's a sort of foreboding, or anticipation. Not entirely bad, but not quite happy excitement, either.

"With remembering," he says. He looks down at his hands, spreads them palm up on the table, fingers wide. Then he makes fists, and nods sharply.

"Close your eyes," he says. I don't. I just look at him. I think I can trust him, a little at least, but I'm not ready to actually do it yet.

He blinks then shrugs and reaches out with his right hand and touches his middle finger gently to my forehead. As before, his touch is warmer than it ought to be, and it tingles. His spicy scent intensifies and I realize it's that odor I always think of as the smell of magic, or whatever it is we call by the word "magic."

Then he withdraws his hand and picks up his tea cup.

I'm not sure what he expected would happen, but I'm more curious about the magic scent. Before, when I met him in the park, it was so faint I assumed it wasn't him, but had rubbed off from someone else he'd had contact with. But now I know it *is* him, and it gets stronger when he does… whatever.

But he doesn't smell *other*. At least not like any I've met before. Which doesn't mean much, really, since I've only met a handful of all the different kinds of *other* there are. Though on the other hand, most *others* I've heard of fit somewhere in the vamp/were category or the witch category, so maybe I don't need to have met them all to know what they probably smell like.

I don't have time to think about it much, though, because I'm suddenly overwhelmed by the déjà vu. Only it's different. Usually it's a nagging feeling of familiarity that stops me in a sort of fugue until I can dredge up whatever fragment of memory that's trying to work its way out, or until something happens to snap me out of it.

This time, the feeling only lasts a fraction of a second before I'm overtaken by a full-on recollection, playing in my mind like a movie, superimposed over the present.

In the memory, like in real life, I'm sitting across a table from John Pradip. But in the memory, I'm in a bathrobe, and he's in a tattered tank top, his skin shining like copper in the early morning sun that slants through the window beside us.

The table doesn't have tea things on it, but a plate of croissants, a pitcher of juice, and a fancy silver coffee pot.

In real life, I stare at John across from me, watching a small concerned frown gather between his eyes. In the memory, I watch him slide under the table, feel his warm hands part my legs, feel him kiss the insides of my thighs.

In real life I sit stock-still, hands planted on the table in front of me. In the memory, I slide my butt forward so his tongue can reach me better and I bury my hands in his hair as his mouth finds all the most sensitive parts of my female anatomy.

In the memory I cry out as he sucks on me, flicks his tongue over me, nibbles gently. In real life I clamp my jaw shut tight, flare my nostrils to suck in more air, and try not to make any sound at all.

Then memory and reality blend together, wave on wave of pleasure building, moisture gathering, my scent intensifying until I'm sure everyone in the coffee shop must be able to smell how turned on I am.

And staring into John Pradip's deep lovely eyes, I manage to say, "Oh fucking hell," very clearly and precisely, before I come so hard I see grey.

Chapter Five

THE MEMORY VANISHES as quickly as it began, and I'm left staring into John's concerned face, trying desperately to catch my breath. I sure as fucking hell hope I didn't yell or moan or something. I'm not really a quiet sex partner, generally.

"Panya… I mean Su," he says. "Are you all right?"

I shake my head. "What the hell did you do to me?"

"I have a… an ability," he says. "To help people remember things. It's inherited, in my family. My mother had it, too."

"You never mentioned it before," I say. But how would I know? So I add, "Did you?"

"It's not something we talk about outside the family," he says. "Except to those with similar gifts."

I wait until the waitress appears with our food and vanishes again, and then I say, "That was one hell of a memory."

"Was it bad?" he says. "You were quite flushed and breathing heavily."

"No," I say. "It wasn't bad." I take a bite out of a samosa, glad of the spices that flood my senses of taste and smell, distracting me from the lingering traces of the memory. I watch his face as he puzzles over that, then his eyebrows go up and his face goes a little pink as he realizes what else might make a person blush and pant.

"Oh," he says, then covers his embarrassment with a bite of his sandwich. I can't help but laugh.

"Was it…" he says, hesitating. "Were you with me?" Then he takes another concealing bite of his lunch.

"You're not the only lover I've ever had," I say, trying to sound unconcerned.

"Oh, of course not," he says. "I mean…" Then he stops, probably unsure of how to proceed without being offensive.

I laugh again. I'm beginning to see why I fell for him, back then. If I weren't happy with Evgeny – more than happy, to tell the truth – I could easily fall for John Pradip again.

"Sorry," I say. "I'm teasing you."

He smiles uncertainly.

"And yes, it was with you, which makes sitting across from you right now feel very, very awkward." Because as good as I've become at feigning unconcern, I'm really wishing I could run the hell out of there, find Ev, and forget all about John Pradip.

"Ah," he says. "I apologize. I only hoped you might remember whatever of your past you've forgotten. I didn't intend to specifically bring back memories of me. Of us."

"I'm sure it was a coincidence," I say. "Or that memory came up because we're in a similar setting."

He looks confused. "A similar…" Then realization hits him and again I watch his eyebrows elevate and his skin flush. He really is adorable.

"That morning, at breakfast," he says, and bites his sandwich. He hasn't got much left and soon he's going to have to go back to sipping tea to cover his embarrassment.

"Tell me more about this memory thing," I say. "Are you *other*?" Like Li, he's not like any other I know of, but he at least smells a little like he might be. Li smelled only human. Of course John smelled more other when working his… should I just give in and call it "magic?" So maybe Li smells other when her abilities are working, too.

A little frown appears between his brows and I resist the urge to reach out and touch it with my fingertip. Evgeny gets a wrinkle like that when he's thinking. When I kiss him there, his whole face relaxes and he gets a happy look – not smiling, but perfectly content.

"I don't know what you mean by *other*," he says, "but my family has had many who chose priesthood over the generations. It's said there were several among them who attained enlightenment, and from them were passed down our skills.

"It's a very simple, specific thing. We can help recover lost memories. Sometimes all it takes is a touch, and sometimes guided meditation is required. Those of us who have it are supposed to dedicate our lives to it, in hopes of becoming enlightened. I'm considered a disappointment, because I wanted to study other things, to teach. I wanted to understand countries and politics and government, when I should have been withdrawing from the world and focusing inwardly."

He smiles, a wry sort of expression that gives him a sweet look. "I thought concentrating inside my own head was useless, and that I could do more for the world by studying and teaching things with real-world applications. But now and then, I use my ability, and sometimes I wonder if Mother was right, and that by concentrating on my own mind and spirit I could gain the strength and wisdom to help people more directly."

He spreads his hands on the table and looks at them. They're large, capable-looking, muscular. I notice callouses on some of his fingers.

"What are those from?"

"I play guitar," he says. "I used to grow my nails long, but my sisters made fun of me."

"Are you any good?" I ask. I'm changing the subject, I know, but I'm buying myself time to think of the best way to explain what an other is, what I am. Or to convince myself to just walk away.

He shrugs. "I enjoy it. A few people like listening. It's not a serious pursuit, just a hobby."

For someone as non-musical as I am, that sort of dismissiveness of talent is kind of annoying, but I let it pass.

Finally, I face the real topic again. "So you've never heard the phrase *other*?"

"I've heard the word, of course," he says. "But not used in the way you seem to mean it. It seems to be something like the anthropological 'other,' as in 'our group vs the other,' but I think you mean something very specific."

I nod. "Maybe I shouldn't even tell you this," I say. "It's supposed to be… well secret, I guess. But what you are… It seems to be pretty close to *other* to me."

He watches my face, carefully attentive.

"*Others* are non-humans, or not-quite-humans. Some of them… of *us*, I should say" – his eyebrows go up again at that, but he doesn't speak, only waits for me to go on. "Some of us think we're better than humans, while most humans would probably think we're less. Bestial, even. I just think we're different. But maybe not as different as we pretend to be."

He nods slightly. "I see why you might call me *other*, I think. Though if these *others* are a separate species, then I have to disagree as many of my ancestors and relatives are entirely normal humans."

It's my turn to nod. "Many *others* have human lovers and spouses. If their children have *otherly* abilities then they call them *other*. If not, they're considered human. Some are born from lineages with *otherly* genetics. Like witches."

"Witches?" A touch of disbelief creeps into his voice, but something about it doesn't ring true.

I just nod. "And some are made, usually by being infected with a symbiotic life form that changes their physiology."

"And those would be?"

"Vampires and werewolves, other shapeshifters." I leave out "fox women," because as soon as I say "vampires," he laughs, and it sounds hollow, affected. It would be very convincing if I wasn't so used to being around vamps, who are mostly incapable of genuine expressions of emotion and have learned to imitate those things that in humans are natural and involuntary.

I don't get any sense of danger from him – though my intuition is far from perfect, so I might not know even if he was something as bad as a serial killer – but I can tell that what I'm saying isn't really a surprise to him. I'm pretty sure he genuinely didn't know the term *other* the way I meant it, but I'm pretty sure he *did* know that witches and vamps and weres exist.

But if he's told me about his own abilities, why not admit he knows about vamps and all? There's something odd about that, but I can't think what it might mean. And now I have to decide if I should flee – leave and not see him again – or attack, metaphorically, of course, and see what I can learn.

I don't know what to do, so I just look at him.

"You must admit," he says, "that it sounds far-fetched. Fairy tale monsters come to life?"

"Hmm," I say. I've never been able to cock a single eyebrow, the way Evgeny can, despite practicing in the mirror, so I make do with raising both and tilting my head slightly. "You bring back a memory from my locked-down brain by touching my forehead and you think those other things are far-fetched?"

He shrugs. "Tell me why I should not."

Now his curiosity sounds genuine. Maybe he knows *others* exist, but doesn't know anything about them. Maybe that's why I'm getting these weird vibes.

"Maybe if they were like in the movies," I say. "But they're much more ordinary once you see them." Also much more scary, but I don't say that.

"Okay," he says. "Suppose I believe you. Which of these non-human beings are you? A witch, maybe? You certainly bewitched me."

"As I recall, you seduced me." And as I say it, I know it to be true. The memory is there as if it had never been missing, and it brings something else with it. My little sister – I have a sister? – abducted from the family home, and my father missing. My breath goes short and choppy. I always assumed my old self had a happy, carefree, *normal* life.

I had continued at school at my mother's insistence, even though it was difficult to concentrate with all that fear and guilt and worry. Then one day in class, a call to tell me my mother had disappeared, too, and I was alone in the world.

But John Pradip was there, strong, kind, comforting. And he *had* made the first move. I was hardly unwilling, but he took advantage of my loneliness and grief. I was nineteen and he was thirty-three.

"I have to go," I say abruptly. I think if I stay, if I continue the conversation, I might learn something useful from him, about why he told me some things and pretended to be ignorant of others.

But I've just remembered my family. The *loss* of my family. I knew, of course, that I must have a mother and father, but they've been absent in my memory so it's kind of hard to miss them. Sure, there's an ache of loss, but it feels like an old loss, even if I've just remembered.

But I have a sister. Or had one, maybe. That's what really hits me. A little sister. And I adored her. And maybe she's dead – after seven years missing one would tend to assume so. But what if she's not? What if she's a *hexenfuchs*, too? What if she's bound as someone's familiar, trapped in fox shape? I have to know.

I manage to escape the café, and Professor Pradip, by promising to meet him again in a few days.

Once I'm out on the street I just wander aimlessly, trying to sort though the flood of emotions. They're both familiar and unfamiliar and I can't quite handle them rationally.

At one point, I find myself across the street from Evgeny's place, and at another, near Alex's. Both times I turn my steps away, wanting to be alone. I wonder if Alex can sense my turmoil through the familiar bond. She must be able to, but maybe she won't notice if she's not actually looking, so to speak.

Though on the one hand, I don't really want to be alone, on the other, I can't stand the thought of having to explain. Not yet.

But if I'm going to Germany with Alex and Li to sort out the familiar binding and discover my ancestral past – half of it, at least – then I have to clear my head and figure out what to do about these unhappy family memories I've just re-acquired.

At last, I find myself in an unfamiliar suburb that doesn't feel as strange as it should. It's late in the afternoon and my feet ache. I must have walked a long way. A little white house complete with picket fence tugs at my memory, and then for an instant I see it not as it is now, but as it was years ago, not white, but slate blue with burgundy trim, paint peeling a little. It has flowers all around it, in pots and garden beds, where in the present the white house has only grass and shrubs. The memory house fades, but leaves behind it more recollections of my family.

My mother was born in this city, to a Chinese-born mother and a half-

Korean, half-Chinese father also born on these shores. My father was born in Germany but moved here as a teenager. My parents met at university when they were only eighteen, but they didn't date until much later. They married in their mid-30s. All this I remember as passed-down lore.

My parents worked together, both staff in the same high school. They didn't realize how well they suited each other until their students decided to set up the shy librarian – my father – with the outgoing, vivacious biology teacher – my mother. Maybe the students thought they were perfect together because they were both brilliant, but they turned out to be a perfect match. The sort of love and devotion you might witness once or twice in your lifetime, if you're lucky. I grew up in a happy house, full of affection.

I was born when my parents were 35. My little sister came even later, when they were on the way past their mid-40s.

My sister was 7 when she disappeared.

I leave the little house and its picket fence behind. There's nothing here for me. My family is long gone – seven years gone if the memories are accurate – and even their possessions will have been removed and sold or thrown away.

I wonder what kind of records the police might have. Maybe Magne has friends who could find out. Magne seems to have friends everywhere. I decide I'll ask him. I'll try what I can to bring back more memories – and maybe I'll even ask John Pradip for help – and I'll put that together with what Magne's contacts can get me.

I can't expect to find out everything that happened to my family in the short time I have before I leave the country, but at least I can try to re-learn what I knew before, and set things in motion to find out more when I get back.

With that decision made, I feel a bit more like facing people again. I think now I can take comfort in their presence and their love.

But first, I want to run, so I aim for the river. There's a long, deep strip of forested parkland along its bank, where city-dwelling weres often run at night, when the pressures of suppressing their nature becomes too much to bear.

Though I actually don't get the same crazy as weres do – especially during the full moon, which shows the old legends do have some truth to them – I do feel better when I take fox shape now and then.

When I reach the trees I stop and breathe in the smell of sun-warmed greenery, and damp shade-cooled soil. The river is a deep moist rumble to my fox senses. Standing and breathing, I shift from listening with my ears to a deeper sort of listening, or sensing the forest with my whole being.

I brush against the consciousness of all manner of living things, squirrels and rabbits, hundreds of birds, a staggering number of insects that feel more like a constant hum or vibration than a group of individual presences.

I don't sense any humans or *others* in the forest. I have the park to myself. So I take off my clothes and fold them up and tuck them in the crotch of a huge old oak tree.

My skin is dappled sun and shadow and the faint breeze feels glorious. Then I slip into fox shape between one heartbeat and the next, and trot into the deeper shadows.

While daylight lasts, I stalk the forest as a fox, exploring, observing, and simply existing. I can't resist snapping up a few grasshoppers – I'm still full from lunch, though, so I don't really hunt. Finally, I end up on the stream bank, watching the sky drain of light and the stars come out. I wonder if my sister can – or could – do this.

My memories tell me she didn't while I knew her, but if she's still alive somewhere… But no, best not to think along those lines. Not yet. Best to assume my family is dead. Murdered, suicided, or something else. It seems pessimistic, but if I assume they're dead and they're not, well that would be a lot more pleasant than assuming they're alive and then finding out they aren't.

When the last light leaves the sky, save the glow of the city behind me, I head for my clothes, take human shape, dress, and head back to the loft.

Evgeny is there when I arrive. He's got an apron on over his jeans and t-shirt, and he's cooking.

His face lights when I open the door, then the tiny thinking frown appears between his eyebrows. He can tell something's wrong.

"Hey there, my heart," he says. He has an endearing tendency to call me by old-fashioned-sounding pet names.

"Hey," I say.

He sets the pan he's holding aside on a cold burner, and hugs me. He kisses my forehead.

"All right?" he says. He inhales the scent of my hair. "You've been in the park."

"Mm," I say. "You can smell that?"

He laughs and steps back, then plucks something from my hair and hands it to me. A leaf.

I laugh, too. "I had a really weird day," I say.

He turns back to the stove, but I know he's still listening. He does that. Evgeny pays attention like no one else I've ever met.

So I perch on the counter and watch him sauté strips of chicken and crisp vegetables and tell him about meeting John.

We're sitting at the table eating when I get to the memory part. Well, I'm eating. Evgeny's sipping a mug of warm blood and picking choice tidbits off my plate. He doesn't need to eat, but he enjoys flavors and textures as much as anyone. And he's a really good cook. Without him, I'd probably live on takeaway.

I finish my food before telling him about the table memory and when I'm done, Ev's gone very, very still. Unlike most vamps, he still mostly moves in unconsciously human ways. But when he's feeling some intense emotion he gets unmoving.

"He didn't mean for me to have that specific memory," I say. "I'm pretty sure." Of course, I didn't tell him every detail.

Ev's not really the jealous type – he trusts me enough not to be, and he certainly has no reason to be. But anything he thinks might be a threat to me makes him very unhappy.

He hisses between his teeth. "He'd better not have," he says.

Hell, he's really angry, and I'm not sure why. Because I had an orgasm with another man would be the obvious reason, but it's not like I cheated on him, and it's not like I could have stopped the memory.

"I don't like to share," he says, and his voice is so vehement I can only stare at him. The last time I heard him speak in a way anything close to that was when he was possessed by the witches and their pet demon-ghost.

Chapter Six

FOR SEVERAL LONG moments we just stare at one another across the table. Then Evgeny buries his face in his hands.

"I'm so sorry."

"It's okay," I say. "I'd be pissed if our places were reversed."

"No," he says. "It's not okay." He looks up at me, and there's too much moisture in his eyes. "You deserve better," he says, taking my hand in both of his, and caressing the backs of my fingers.

He looks down at the table, bites his lip, then looks back up at me. "I've been on edge, I guess," he says.

"The job?" I ask. He hasn't told me much about his actual security work at the mall, just some amusing anecdotes about the people he's had to chase off after hours.

"No, the job is pretty dull. And easy. I spend most of the night sitting on the roof wishing I could see the stars."

The touch of his fingers is giving me goosebumps and I'm starting to think about how nice it would be to fill up my preposterously large bathtub with hot water and climb into it with Ev for a frolic.

"No. The… the witches' ghosts have been restless lately. It's hard to keep my head clear sometimes."

"Is… Are they turning into the demon again?"

The words "ghost" and "demon" don't really fit, but we use them because we don't have better terms. In essence, the thing trapped inside Evgeny's head was an entity created from the slaughter of a village – the agonizing death of innocents that lingered and was captured in the mind of an unstable young man. A rare male witch, and Ev's grandfather. Or great-grandfather; we never did figure that out.

The young man had to die to stop the evil that was unleashed by merging his witch powers with the fear, terror, and pain of all those people. He was burned alive and his bones and ashes became the prison of those terrible memories – what we call "ghosts," even though the people to whom they belonged have long since passed on into oblivion.

Then somehow a group of witches used the bones and ashes to focus their wills together to take over Evgeny's mind. And their will gave the ghosts a singular consciousness. And it escaped their control and became something else, something we called "demon."

We trapped it in Ev's mind, dissolved it back into ghostly memories.

Now he's permanently haunted, and I'm trapped as a witch's familiar. So much for our happily ever after. You'd think that after overcoming two nasty enemies, we'd at least get a break. A couple years, maybe.

Evgeny squeezes my hand. "I can handle it," he says. "It's just sometimes I remember… Well, not remember, but I see the awful things that happened to those people. I dream them as if they were happening to me."

I know what that must be like. I saw them, too, when we were all inside Ev's head – Evgeny and Alex and me and the demon. To subdue them, we had to experience each and every memory, one by one. If we hadn't each had such a strong sense of self, such conviction that these were not *our* memories, if we had not each had the other two to keep us strong, we'd almost certainly have been driven mad.

I really hope that's not happening to Ev now. Especially since I'm leaving soon and won't be able to come to his rescue this time.

"I hope you're right," I say.

And he smiles his sweet, beautiful smile. His perfect lips curve up just enough to show a flash of white tooth and his eyes light up, bright blue behind black lashes. He stands and leans over the table and kisses my forehead lightly, then tugs at the pins and ties that hold my hair up and it cascades around my shoulders like a flood of ink.

He kisses me, slides his tongue into my mouth and I taste the coppery flavor of the blood he's been drinking. I suppose normal people would find it off-putting, to taste blood in their boyfriend's mouth. But I'm not a normal person, and foxes don't mind blood at all.

Then he pulls away, brushes the hair out of my face and looks me full in the eyes. "There's more, isn't there?" he says.

Evgeny can always tell when I have something on my mind.

I want to keep kissing him and not think about anything else, but I also promised myself not too long ago that I wouldn't keep secrets from him. It's too easy for me to keep things to myself, to trust only myself.

I sigh, and nod.

"What else did he do to you?" he says this carefully, calmly, but I can hear an edge in his voice. He's trying to hold back whatever it was that made him so possessive before.

I poke him gently in the chest so he has to sit back down and stop looming over me.

"No," I say. "There's nothing more about John Pradip."

"But you said –"

"There *are* more memories," I say. Then I tell him about my family, my mother and my father. My sister.

When I'm done, he says, "I agree, see what Magne can find out." He's holding my hand again, absently tracing each finger. "They were never found?"

I shrug. "Maybe they were, but that part's not in the memories I got. But…" I hesitate. There's a half-formed idea in my mind, something that may or may not make sense.

"What is it?"

And I can't not tell Evgeny. If anyone would understand, it's him. Hell, he can probably take my uncertain ideas and fill them out for me.

"When I think of my mom and dad, it's painful, but not like I suddenly lost them, you know?"

He tilts his head to one side and the thought-wrinkle appears between his brows, but he doesn't answer. He's waiting for more information.

"It's like I mourned them a long time ago, even though I don't remember, and I miss them, but it's like I've already dealt with their loss."

"Like you would feel if their bodies had been found and you were able to… what's that cliché? Find closure?"

"Right," I say. "There's no uncertainty."

I twine a long strand of hair around my finger, as if giving order to some external thing can help bring order to my thoughts.

"But my sister… I feel astonishment, that I could have forgotten such a thing. And wonder to have rediscovered it. I adored her. But I also feel raw hurt."

"Like you never found out what happened to her."

"Exactly."

"So you think maybe your parents were found dead, eventually, but your sister never was?"

"I don't know," I say. "It would make sense, but I don't really know. I can't know."

He squeezes my hand, but when I look up at him, he's staring out the window. There's nothing there to see, just darkness and lamplight, the wall of a building across the street.

"I suppose you could ask your friend to try his memory trick again," he says. His voice is carefully neutral. It makes me smile. I love that he tries so hard to be fair and trusting and not jealous. But it's also nice to have your boyfriend be a little possessive. Once in a while. As long as it doesn't get excessive.

"Maybe," I say. "But I think I'll talk to Magne first. I need to ask him about my paperwork, too."

Ev looks back from the window, smiles, then stands and pulls me into his arms.

"Yes," he says. "Ask Magne. Later." Then he kisses me again, and again, and pretty soon I've gone well beyond thoughts of bathtime fun and I'm pulling him over to the bed, leaving bits and pieces of clothing – mine and his – behind us as we go.

I wake well into the morning, roll over, and settle against Evgeny's side, intending to go back to sleep. Since Ev's a vamp and can't be out in the sun, we've both taken to a nocturnal life, so daytime is sleep time for me.

Sometimes I think the fox part of my nature would be happier sleeping away the deepest parts of both day and night, and being awake in the twilight times, the in-between times. But foxes are adaptable, and the night shift suits me well enough.

Then I hear a soft footstep on the other side of the door, the rustle of paper. After a moment, the whirr of the elevator motor. That's probably what woke me.

The building I live in – once a small warehouse and now a building half-converted into three large flats, is only three stories, but like I said before, Magne always takes the elevator. He certainly doesn't need to spare himself the effort – he's a big, active werewolf and could probably take each flight of steps in a single bound without exerting himself much.

I consider sleep. It's snug and dark behind the heavy curtains I have hung around the bed. I had them even before I ended up with a vamp lover, because some days I just need to feel like I'm curled up in a den. Some days I can't find a small enough space to crawl into, and other days even the spacious open loft has walls too close together.

But foxes, like cats, are plagued by curiosity, and I have to get up and see what Magne left me. And yeah, even without the fox I'd be too curious for my own good.

So I get up, pull on the first piece of clothing I lay my hands on – which happens to be a t-shirt of Ev's that fits me almost as snugly as it fits him, and barely covers my ass – and pad over to the door. When I open it, there's an envelope there, the big brown kind, leaning against the door jamb.

My name is scrawled on it in Magne's writing, big and sprawling, like he is, but startlingly legible for such careless-looking glyphs.

I take it back inside and sit on the couch, slide the flap open with my index finger, and tip the contents out onto the coffee table.

His friends, I think, are miracle-workers. There in front of me is a plastic card with a hologram and my photo on it. My new – and legal – driver's license. I look startled in the photo, eyes a little too wide, and the image has an odd yellow cast, making me look even more Asian than usual, if that's even possible.

Under that is a deep blue faux leather booklet with the word PASSPORT stamped on it in gold, and the national coat of arms. I pick it up, open it to the first page. Another little picture of me, not so startled, nor so yellow. I look a little lost.

I set that aside and pick up the next item: social insurance card. Then my birth certificate, not laminated, but inside a protective plastic sleeve. Under that is a thin stack of assorted documents – some my copy of submitted forms, and others that I suppose I still need to fill out so the government knows where I am and all that. Income tax forms, changes of address, that sort of thing. I laugh when a card for the local library with my name on it slides out from between two pages. The last sheet is my university transcript. BA in anthropology with a minor in political science. With honors. Fuck. I guess I'm smarter than I feel.

I sit and stare at the cards and documents. They shouldn't matter, not really. I know who I am, and that I exist. Having these things doesn't make me any more real. And yet somehow they do matter. They make me *official*. And hell, I have a degree.

It feels very weird.

After a while, I get up and go back to bed, leaving the cards and papers where I dropped them on the coffee table. Evgeny stirs when I crawl between the curtains, reaches out and pulls me close.

"Mmm…" he says. "Why do you smell like a vampire?" He sounds sleepy, barely awake.

"I'm wearing your shirt."

He nuzzles my shoulder, runs his hand down my back.

"Ah, so you are."

His hand slides off the fabric and onto my bare skin. The shirt rode up when I got into bed, and Ev's hand cups my butt cheek.

"Mmm," he says again. "I especially like how it doesn't cover your behind." His fingers tighten and he pulls me against his body, still naked from our earlier exercise. He's aroused and hard against my thigh.

I wiggle my butt against his hand and he growls in mock ferocity, bites my earlobe gently, and squeezes my butt again.

To my fox senses, the dark cave of the bed is flooded with heavy scent as I twine my free leg over his and tilt my pelvis, trying to bring myself into contact with his hardness.

Vampires have a odd scent, a sort of peppery tang under a basically human odor. On some of them it's sour and repulsive, on others it's metallic. On Ev, vamp scent is spicy and when he's feeling lusty it gets stronger, mingles with the musk of arousal until it fills my nose with a smell so much sexier than any aftershave or cologne. If someone could bottle that, they'd make a fortune.

Of course, I might be the only person who perceives that mix of smells in quite that way. For all I know, other women might find Evgeny's aroma off-putting. Or they might not smell it at all. I do have a really good sense of smell, after all.

I find Evgeny's mouth with my own, nibble his lower lip, and then press my lips to his until he parts his teeth and draws my tongue into his mouth. He rolls onto his back, pulling me over on top of him and suddenly we're pressed together, my moistness sliding over him.

The hand that was trapped beneath him is free now and he tugs the shirt over my head. I don't want to take my mouth away from his, but I don't want that fabric in between us, either.

Once he's tossed the shirt aside, he cups my other butt cheek, lifts and slides me back and forth over himself, and I can't help push against him.

Sometimes we linger and go slow, tease and caress, spend hours just touching. But other times we just want to fuck, to get it on and get off. We've been pretty lucky so far our moods have generally matched.

Today is like that, that urgency. I don't slow down, linger, or try to draw out the orgasm. I want the release, and I want it now, so I slide myself over him, faster and faster, until the tension builds and breaks and my voice is barely muffled by the curtains.

When I feel Ev fumbling for a condom, I know exactly what he wants, so when he's ready I tilt my pelvis just so, take him inside me and keep thrusting until it's his voice filling the darkness and his body that tenses up, then relaxes.

After, lying next to him, I realize that I've got all my paperwork now and it's only going to be a few days, a couple of weeks at most, and I'll be off to another continent for who knows how long. I'm going to need all the sex I can get in that time to tide me over until I get back.

I may have learned how to suppress my sex drive when I need to, or it may just be that I've had access to as much sex as I want. Going without could be really, really hard.

Evgeny is up and making coffee as soon as it's dark enough for his comfort. I lay in bed, watching him move around my kitchen, getting as good a look at him as I can through the gap in the bed curtain.

He's walking around in boxers and nothing else, and the view is fine, indeed. He has the most amazing black raven tattoo, that wraps around the side of his torso so that one wing spreads across his chest and one across his back.

He must sense me watching, because he turns, and even though I've seen it many times, the bright blue of his eyes against his black hair and olive skin is startlingly beautiful.

When our eyes meet, he smiles. His face is lovely enough to look at anyway – all high cheekbones and curvy lips – but when he smiles he looks angelic. If angels have fold-away fangs and a thirst for blood.

"Coffee?" he says as I tug the curtain aside.

"Does it come with sugar?" I say, and waggle my eyebrows suggestively.

He laughs. "I work tonight, but I'll come here after, if you like. Or you can meet me at my place."

"Mmm." I stretch. "I suppose I should call Alex, and let her know I'm all legal and everything."

At his questioning look, I realize I didn't tell him about Magne's delivery, so I point to the pile of cards and papers on the coffee table. "I officially exist," I say.

Evgeny takes two cups of coffee over to the living area and sits down to look at my new ID. I'm forced to get up if I want my hot caffeinated beverage, and once I'm up a shower starts to seem like a really good idea. I still smell like sex, and though I enjoy the musky odor, anyone I run into tonight might not.

First though, I put on a bathrobe and sit with Evgeny to sip my coffee.

"You're cute," he says, holding up my driver's license.

"Ah, but you knew that already," I say.

"True," he says. "But I didn't know you were also photogenic."

After coffee, we shower together – mostly chastely, because Ev really does need to keep his job. There aren't that many places that will schedule an employee's hours around the time between sunset and sunrise, no questions asked.

I send him off to work with a smooch at the door, like a 50s housewife, and then I decide to cook breakfast while I plan what to do next.

I should call Alex first, so she can go ahead with the travel plans. Then I need to talk to Magne. And finally, I promised to meet John one more time. And I have to pack. I'd better borrow Magne's computer to find out what the weather's like in Germany in the spring, so I don't take the wrong sort of clothes.

I didn't think to borrow Ev's phone before he left, so I have to walk down the block to call Alex from a pay phone. I need soy milk and bacon anyway, so I don't mind the trip, even when it turns out Alex isn't home. Or maybe she just isn't picking up, which might be more likely, since she does have a new girlfriend.

So once I polish off the bacon and rinse the dishes and pick up Ev's and my discarded clothes from yesterday, I pad down the hall to the elevator, stab the button, and wait. It's slow, but that gives me time to think.

To ask for Magne's help, I'm going to have to tell him the whole story, everything I know about my family. And I'm probably going to have to tell him why I suddenly remembered. Hell, maybe he has some ideas about John Pradip and whether or not my old prof is some kind of other. Magne's been other his whole life as far as I know. His brothers and father are weres, too, and maybe even his mother. Going by the number of scars he has, he's probably not one of those rare weres who contract the werewolf symbiont in the womb instead of through an infected bite, but he could be. Of course, it takes a lot more than a bite or I'd be a werewolf, too, but you know what I mean.

When the elevator comes I get in and punch the button for floor two, then wait some more. Not surprisingly, Magne's leaning in his open door when I get to his place.

"Thought you might come see me," he says. "Everything look good with the ID?"

"Yeah," I say. "But that's not why I'm here."

"Oh yeah?" He steps back inside to let me in, then hands me a coffee, already fixed the way I like it, sweet and strong.

"Do you have any contacts in the police?"

"A few. Which division?"

"Missing persons," I say, not sure if that's even an actual division. "And homicide."

His eyebrows go up, and his dark eyes shine with curiosity.

"I need you to investigate my family," I say. "My parents were murdered, I think. And my sister was abducted."

Chapter Seven

MAGNE SITS on the couch on the far side of his coffee table. He sprawls, really, but I know him well enough to catch the slight signs of tension that show he's full of curiosity under the facade of complete relaxation.

I nudge a cushion out of the way – Magne's whole living area, both floor and furniture, is littered with cushions of various sizes and textures – and settle onto the opposite side of the sectional.

"Wow," he says.

"Yeah." I can't help but tease him a little, let his curiosity build. There was a time when we might have been lovers – even when I first got together with Ev, Magne kept flirting with me – but recently we've grown into good friends.

Magne was there when the whole deal went down with the witches and their demon, though he wasn't inside Ev's head with me. It was an awful event, and he lost a pack-mate to the demon, but he also gained something good. He met his girlfriend Cara, who was the only one of the witches besides Alex who stood up to their leader Mathilde and told her she might be wrong. I'm a little surprised she's not here now, though I can smell her on Magne, like growing plants and soil and something that makes me hungry. Beetles?

"How's Cara?" I say.

Magne blinks at me. "She's good," he says, slowly, raising one eyebrow at me. I hate that everyone I know can raise one eyebrow when I have to wiggle both at once. "But you didn't come here to ask about my love life. What's this about murder and abduction?"

So I tell him. I include the part about meeting John and the weird sense I got that he knew more than he was letting on, but I leave out the orgasm-inducing memory. No doubt Magne would have something very manly to say about that, which is to say he'd make a crude comment. I tell him pretty much everything else, though.

When I'm done, he leans forward and looks at me closely. "Hunh," he says. "Are you sure you want to dig into this? It could bring up some pretty unpleasant memories."

"I'm sure," I say. "I'm done with avoiding my past, and I need to know what happened." I look down into the remains of my coffee. "Especially to my sister."

"Okay," he says. He reaches across the table to squeeze my hand. "Okay, let me make a few calls."

He gets me a fresh cup of coffee – at the rate I'm consuming caffeine I'm not going to sleep for six days – and then retreats across the room with his cell phone. I stare into space, trying to induce more memories by sheer force of will while his voice murmurs in the background.

I could very easily listen in to his half of the conversation – I might even catch a word or two from the other party – but that would be rude. Magne probably knows, or at least suspects, that that's the case, but I'm pretty sure he trusts me to respect his privacy. Not that he's making any secret calls, but he does like to keep his sources anonymous.

"Okay," I suddenly hear him say, coming closer. "I'll put her on."

I drag my mind out of its reverie and glance up.

"Detective O'Malley is an old friend of my dad's," he tells me, "and one of our pack. He didn't work on your family's case, but he does remember it. He can tell you a few things now, and get you a summary of the case in a day or two." He holds out the phone to me and when I hesitate, he says, "I already told him you lost most of your memories. He knows who you are."

He knows who I am. He's a member of Magne's pack. That means he also knows *how* I lost my memories, and may even have helped punish the were who violated me. I swallow hard and take the phone.

"Hello?" I try to keep my voice from wavering, and I'm almost successful. It comes out only a little squeaky. Suddenly I'm afraid to find out the very things I was just so desperate to know.

Magne retreats into the bathroom and the water comes on.

"Ms Fuchs?" The man on the other end of the call pronounces my last name with a pretty good German accent, and for a moment, I wonder if he's lived there.

"Yes," I say. "Magne said you can tell me about my family."

"Sure," he says, and doesn't sound remotely German anymore. "I didn't work the cases, but I know the guys who did. So do you remember anything at all from that time?"

"Very little," I say. "Bits and pieces have come back, but it's just recently I remembered that my parents and my sister disappeared."

"Well, listen," he says, a note of warning in his voice. "Some of this is pretty unpleasant. So if it's new to you, it could be pretty traumatic."

"It's okay," I say. "I think I mourned for them already, even if I don't remember."

"Okay. Well, what I know is this: your mother called in a missing person's report, what, seven years ago? I don't have the details at hand, but I'll get them for you. I could set up a meeting with the guys who were on the case but… Magne said…"

"No," I say. "I expect I'll remember eventually, and I'd rather not have to explain how I lost my memories and why I want to revisit all this."

"Right. Well, like I said, Mrs Fuchs called in the report, saying your father and sister – just a kid at the time – had gone out for ice cream and never came back. Everyone – here at the station, I mean – figured your old man abducted the girl. The detectives in charge worked your mother pretty hard, trying to get her to admit your dad and her had marital problems. They even accused him of abusing the girl.

"I remember your mom was a pretty tough lady. Real strong and confident that your dad was a great guy. And it wasn't that co-dependent insistence that the husband is perfect that we see all the time in abusive relationships. I remember thinking I'd like to have a woman so confident in me, someday, and that I'd like to be worth that confidence."

I feel a tear slide down my cheek and wipe it away. Okay, maybe I'm not done mourning.

"You sure you're okay hearing this?"

"Yeah," I say. "It beats not knowing."

"Right. You were away at university, as I recall."

"I was."

"So anyway, there were no leads to speak of. Like your dad and sister just disappeared. Until, well, they found your dad. Or some fisherman did, caught in some debris in a bend in the river, about ten clicks upstream from Wonder Island.

Then, a memory that wouldn't come when I tried to force it pops full-formed into my mind.

"That's when I came home," I say. "I went with Mom to the morgue. To…" I have to stop.

"Yeah," says the detective. His voice has gone soft. He must deal with stuff like this every day, yet he sounds like he genuinely cares.

"Sorry," I say. "Please go on."

"The autopsy didn't turn up much. His throat and wrists had been cut. Must've bled out, but the river washed away the blood. Well, you saw what a few days in water can do."

The body hadn't looked like my dad. He'd been tall, muscular, with sandy brown hair and green eyes. He smiled a lot. The thing in the morgue was pale and bloated. But it was, horribly, still recognizable as my father.

"That's when Mom lost it," I say, my voice almost a whisper. "I didn't realize it at the time, but she'd been so strong until then."

"It happens that way sometimes," says O'Malley. "You want to stop now?"

"No," I say. "Tell me the rest."

"The only clue was a business card in your father's wallet, but it didn't give the guys much."

I get a cold feeling in the pit of my stomach. I don't remember this detail, but it makes me afraid.

"Whose was it?"

"Prof of yours. At the time, the boys thought maybe your dad had been checking up on you at school. The guy had an airtight alibi, so he didn't do it."

"Whose business card was it?"

"John… uh… something East Indian, I think."

"Pradip?" My whole body feels cold. I don't think this detail is something I knew at the time. Would I have gone back to his classes, knowing he might be connected with my father's murder, however tenuously?

"Yeah, that's it. Anyway, the investigation didn't go anywhere after that. And your sister was never found."

"So she's presumed dead?"

"Yeah. Sorry."

"And my mother?"

"I guess she made you go back to school. She was reported missing a few months later by the parent of one of her students on the day her high school class graduated, when she didn't turn up at the ceremony."

The memory of being in John's class that summer, of getting a call from the police back home to tell me it didn't look like anyone had been in my parent's house in a week at least, and no one had seen my mom in at least that long. It was only an hour's drive between home and school, and yet I hadn't even known my mother was missing.

And John Pradip used my grief to get me into his bed. He seduced me, made me fall in love with him, and less than a year later, broke off the relationship without a word.

"Was she found? Her body?"

"Not till much later. She washed up on Wonder Island. One of the carnival freaks reported it. Guy by the name of… what was it? Calls himself 'The Illustrated Mannikin'. Short guy, you know. A dwarf. Little person. Whatever."

I went to the Wonder Island carnival once with Alex, when we were trying to distract ourselves from the ghost memories that were still giving us nightmares. I remember a guy – Little Person's the PC term, isn't it? He was covered in tattoos and on display like an old-time circus sideshow. The tattoos were gorgeous, and the man was actually pretty sexy, too, if you like 'em short.

"Wolfram Gottfried," I say. I remember because it was unusual and German, like my surname, like my dad. "His sister's a knife-thrower." I vowed to learn to throw knives after watching her – I once threw Chinese hairpins, but they belonged to a fox woman and pretty much aimed themselves. For some reason, I still haven't taught myself to throw knives.

"That's the one. Anyway, the ME had to ID her from dental records."

That would explain why I had no sudden memory of identifying my mother at the morgue, too.

"Was she murdered, also?" My voice is steady now. I've heard the worst. I can do this. I need to do this.

"Throat and wrists cut," he says. "Like your dad. The guys got all excited about a serial killer. Oh god, sorry," he says, realizing he's talking about my family.

"It's okay," I say.

"Right. Anyway, they figured the same thing happened to your sister, except of course she was never found. They sent unies to keep an eye on you for weeks after, figuring you'd be the next target, but gave up when no one bothered you. And no one seems to have noticed that you dropped out of sight for a year."

I'm startled at that, but of course he knows my story. Magne would have told him the general outline, if he hadn't already learned it when his pack had to punish that werewolf.

"Was anyone else killed the same way?" I ask. "Besides my mom and dad?"

"Not that I ever heard."

"Thank you, Detective."

"Hey, anything for a friend of Magne. So I'll get him some paperwork with more details for you."

"Thanks."

When I snap the phone shut and look up, Magne's leaning on the bathroom door jamb. Leaning is his other usual posture, aside from sprawling.

"All good?" he says, and I nod.

He rubs his shaggy hair with a towel, but it seems to be doing more to fling water droplets around than actually absorb them. He's only wearing jeans, and the muscles in his chest and arms bunch and flex smoothly under the skin. Beneath an ample layer of hair – curse of the werewolf, I guess – his torso is covered with a pale tracery of scars.

I've always wanted to ask about them, but never quite dared. I gather life as a were is brutal and violent, at least to begin with. I have to carefully think of Evgeny earlier today, replace the image of a half-naked Magne – who's really too hirsute and muscley for my taste anyway (or so I keep telling myself) – with a picture of all-naked Evgeny, lean and tattooed, stainless-steel nipple piercings catching the light of the bathroom lamp. Okay, maybe I don't have quite as much control over my libido as I'd like. But I *do* have more than I used to.

"Enjoying the view?" Magne says, and I realize he's caught me staring.

"A little too bestial for me," I say, and he laughs.

"Well, you missed your chance, anyway."

"Mags, have you heard anything about someone – human or *other* – who can influence memories?"

"You're asking about your professor friend?"

"Yeah. I can't figure out if I can trust him."

"Even if he is *other*, that doesn't automatically mean you can trust him."

"I think I have enough experience with nasty *others* – vamp, witch, and were – to know that," I say. I keep my voice flat, but really I'm annoyed. He knows my history. A were almost killed me, several vamps *tried* to kill me, and witches got me in the predicament I'm in now.

And the thought of *that* immediately makes my throat feel tight. I'd almost been able to put the familiar binding out of my mind while I concentrated on remembering my family. I was even starting to think the trip to Germany could wait while I tried to find out what happened to my sister.

"I know, Su. I'm sorry."

"I just meant, is it okay to talk to him about *others* in general? I wonder if I said too much."

"No," he says. "I came across a few mentions of Indian priests with assorted mental powers when we were trying to find out what was possessing Ev."

"I wondered if he might be something like a witch."

"That's the impression I got," he says. "I also got the impression that some kinds of *others*, essentially vamps and weres, are wholly separate from human, while others, like witches, are almost more like humans with extra abilities. Genetically inherited."

"So what you're saying is that witches are like the X-Men, and vamps and weres are a disease?"

I've known a few vamps and weres who'd be really offended at that comment, but Magne just laughs.

"Exactly," he says. "Only I prefer to think of us like Spider-Man. With a disease that makes us stronger instead of weaker, and gives us the abilities of the thing that bit us." Then he adopts a cheesy muscle-man pose, which certainly does show off his assets. "Anyway," he says. "Do you need anything else? I have a date."

"When do you not have a date, these days?"

"You should be happy for me."

"I'm happy you're not hitting on me anymore," I say.

"Liar."

"Am not."

As I head back to the pay phone again, I think I really should get myself a cell phone. If I pick the right one, and the right carrier, I might even be able to use it to talk to Ev while I'm in Germany. I add that to my mental list of things to do before I go.

I should at least have asked Magne if I could use his phone to call Alex before I left. And I forgot about researching German weather. I'll just have to ask Alex about that, too.

This time she's home, and glad to hear I've got my ID all in order.

"I took a gamble and bought the tickets anyway," she says. "We leave Tuesday."

I decide to save all my news for the long flight instead of feeding quarters into the payphone half the night – plus Alex sounds sleepy and I remember she's not a night-dweller like me – so I hang up after getting some idea of what clothes to pack.

Tuesday. It's Thursday today, or actually Friday by now, I suppose. That should just leave me time to meet John one more time, though I have serious misgivings about that now.

Not that I actually think he killed my parents, but his connection to my dad's death, however tenuous, added to his evasiveness at our last meeting, and the realization that he exploited my weakened state to get me into bed all those years ago has left me with a very bad feeling. It's nothing I can even name, but I've learned to listen to my gut.

But that business card in my dead father's wallet also makes me want to interrogate him. I didn't know he'd even met my father. Either of my parents.

I'll just have to use every bit of my foxy cleverness to get information out of him without him realizing that's what I'm doing.

I spend the rest of the night digging through my clothes to decide what to take with me. I realize I didn't even ask Alex how long we would be gone for. But if I take a few changes of clothes, things I can layer depending on the weather, plus all the socks, underwear, and bras I own, I should be okay.

I'm not going to be able to walk around with a fox tail, so I have to sort out the clothes that I added a tail-slit to from the ones I left intact. All my most comfortable things have – unfortunately – been altered for my tail.

Then, as I'm sitting in the middle of the floor, surrounded by piles of clothes, I'm hit by the déjà vu again. It's not overwhelming this time, the way it has been lately. Instead, it sneaks up on me gradually until it's almost like another person comes slowly into focus, facing me across the neatly-folded garments.

The colors in my loft, aside from the industrial white of the walls, are deep greens and blues, russets and browns and rich reds and purples. Forest colors. In the memory that seeps in, the colors are pink and pale blue and gaudy rainbows. Unicorns and sparkles. A little girl's bedroom.

And the person across from me, taking focus in my memory, holding up a pink t-shirt with a cartoon character on it, is just the sort of little girl who'd have a room like that. She's got fair skin and reddish-brown hair and green eyes, but when she tosses back her long, straight locks and grins at me, her eyes and the shape of her ridiculously cute nose show her part-Asian ancestry. She's turning six in a few days in this memory. My little sister.

"See," she's saying. "It's too small already. I've hardly gotten to wear it at all." There's a pout in her voice, but it sounds put on.

"You got it a whole year ago," I tell her. "I bet Mom gets you an even better one this year." Every year for our birthdays, one of our gifts is a t-shirt. Our mom always gets the coolest ones. I don't know where she finds them, but no one else ever has one just the same.

Then my sister's face wavers for a moment, like the memory is uncertain, damaged like an old film strip. It skips ahead and I've got my sister pinned to the bed and I'm tickling her unmercifully, until tears run down her face from laughing.

And then we're both laughing helplessly at some stupid cartoon on TV, while Mom and Dad look on bemused, shaking their heads. My sister points at the TV and a fresh round of laughter begins. This time Mom seems to get whatever we found funny and she starts to laugh. Dad holds out a little longer, but eventually he gives in, too.

The memory fades and it's just me in the loft. I feel moisture on my cheeks, and an ache in my ribs from laughing so hard.

But the moisture doesn't stop and the ache grows, spreads into my chest where it crushes me so I can hardly breathe. The laughter is gone and tears of sorrow have come instead.

I let them. There's no one here to see, not till Ev comes back from work and that's still a couple hours off. I can handle this. Tears are good. Healthy. Healing.

Except then I realize one horrifying fact that somehow seems worse than knowing my parents were murdered and my sister never found.

I cannot remember my little sister's name.

Chapter Eight

I'M STILL ON the floor when Evgeny gets back from work, hunched up in the middle of my piles of clothes. I stopped crying a while ago, but I can tell from the way my eyes feel that I'm all red and puffy still.

Ev says nothing, just drops his jacket next to the door, slips off his shoes, and takes three long steps across the floor where he sinks down next to me and puts his arms around me. I'm suddenly so tired I can hardly get out the words to tell him what's wrong. But once I've told him, he kisses my face and stands up, bringing me with him. He actually lifts me right up, cradling me in his arms, and carries me to the bed where he tucks me under the blankets and crawls in after me.

You might think he kind of sucks at the whole boyfriend thing because he doesn't say anything the whole time. He just strokes my hair and holds me. But you know what? There isn't anything he could say that would make me feel better. And what he does, it's perfect. It's just what I need.

He must be starving, since he can't exactly drink blood on the job, but he stays nestled in bed with me until I fall asleep.

I'm dreaming about John Pradip, about siting in the front row of his political science class, absently taking notes and daydreaming about what it would be like to kiss him.

He's talking about Noam Chomsky and I'm really only half-listening because I've figured out that he seldom strays from the set readings in his undergraduate lectures. Professor Pradip is actually rather disappointing as a teacher, and my nineteen-year-old self is wondering if he'd be less disappointing in bed.

This dream has some of the quality of the dreams I've had of my ancestor Sigrún and the *hexenfuchs*, a certain rightness that makes me believe it's a true dream – a memory rather than a random assemblage of things my mind put together to fill my sleeping hours. And unlike a *dream* dream, in a memory dream I'm fully aware I'm dreaming, the same way you're aware of watching an electronic screen when you're absorbed in a TV show. Except of course it's not just watching the show, but living it.

The dream skips ahead, and that's where things get a little weird. Not what's happening – that's just a series of pleasant scenarios of getting to know John, of flirting, of walking together, of having dinner. Making love. The sex parts of the dream seem more detailed than the others, lingering. But all of it, except for odd moments of clarity – like when I get the news about my mother – seems a little surreal.

There are details about things I don't usually notice much in real life – the brands of people's clothing, the way my hips sway when I walk, the fact that more people on campus are listening to music than are reading – that seem to stand out in the dream. And some of the things I *would* notice in real life, like how people smell and the different regional accents they speak in, or the titles of books in a shop window, are blurry, unclear.

Maybe it's the difference between the woman I used to be and the woman I am now. I don't really know the old me, but I can't imagine I'd be so different.

No, that's not true. I'd like to think I'm the same, but if I really am the same, then why have I been so afraid of facing the old me? It almost feels like I'm watching these memories through the eyes of someone else, or rather filtered through someone else's consciousness. Which doesn't make sense, because they're obviously from my point of view.

Once I shared Evgeny's dream, and this feels even more foreign. Was

I really *that* different a person back then?

It's disorienting, that feeling, and it actually makes me struggle to wake up, especially when I dream about sex. In my dream, as in the memory in the restaurant, John is a fantastic lover. Better than any other lover I've ever had. Better than Alex, and better than Evgeny. Normally I *like* sex dreams, but the weird feeling is keeping me from enjoying this one.

And that's when I get really uncomfortable. Because it suddenly *doesn't* feel true. And then it doesn't matter because something else is intruding through the memory or dream or whatever it is. Something *pushing* at my thoughts, prodding.

And I can't breathe. The memories go on, playing in front of me like a movie, but I'm not experiencing them any more. I walk hand-in-hand with John Pradip, but I might as well be floating. I don't feel my feet touch the ground, or his hand in mine. All I feel is burning in my lungs, tightness in my throat.

I lie in bed with him on top of me, moaning and thrusting and saying, "Oh god, Panya, I'm fucking coming," and I feel nothing but choking. And my vision goes grey as his eyes roll back and he says, "I'm fucking coming, Panya, I'm coming inside you," in a kind of chant, and I'm trying to fight back, to breathe, to escape, to get some air.

"Jesus Christ, Su, wake up," I hear, and I can feel again, see again. Evgeny's shaking me. He must be concerned because he hardly ever swears. He's not religious – especially not after being made a vamp – but he still respects his childhood upbringing and doesn't take the Lord's name in vain and all that. Except when he's scared.

"Sweetheart," he says, pushing back my hair. "Su? Oh fuck, please wake up."

For a terrifying moment I can't move, can't draw a breath. Then the binding on my throat eases, vanishes, and I suck in the biggest lungful of air I can, gasp out, "I'm awake, I'm okay."

I stare up at Ev. It's dark behind the curtains, so dark he probably can't see me very well, but I can see him. His hair is sleep-tousled and there's panic in his eyes that fades when he realizes I'm awake and breathing normally.

"I'm okay," I say. "I'm okay."

"I thought you were…" He trails off. "I don't know. Possessed, or the familiar binding was going bad somehow." He's still crouched over me, arms tense so his muscles stand out through the snug-fitting shirt he's wearing. He's still dressed for work and I realize he must have stayed in bed with me instead of feeding himself.

As if to confirm that idea, his stomach grumbles loudly.

"Get something to eat, pretty boy, and I'll tell you all about it." I try to keep my voice light, but my throat hurts from trying too hard to suck in air.

Evgeny pulls the curtain open a crack and a beam of sunlight penetrates the darkness.

"Oh," I say. I sit up. Every muscle is faintly sore. "I'll get you something to eat."

"I'm fine," he says. His guts gurgle again and he smiles sheepishly. "I can wait," he insists.

I ignore him and get up, careful not to let any sunlight fall on him as I part the curtain to crawl out.

"You were thrashing around," he says. "I couldn't wake you."

While I heat him up a mug of B-positive, I tell him about the dream. I don't quite know how to explain the weirdness, but I try anyway.

"I think I need to ask Dr Pradip some very pointed questions," I say, taking care not to spill Ev's supper as I maneuver myself back into the bed.

He sips and sighs. "I guess I was hungry," he says, gulping down some more. He polishes off the whole mug and I offer to get another.

"Do you think –" he begins as I start another cup heating.

"What, that maybe my memories aren't real after all?"

"Well, it sounds like *some* of them are, at least. But do you think his abilities might extend into giving you false memories?"

It certainly crossed my mind. "If those regression therapy type people can make ordinary humans remember things that never happened, just by asking leading questions, I wouldn't be surprised if a… whatever John is could make me remember untrue stuff." That sounded so much more eloquent in my head.

Back in the bed, curled up so my head rests on Ev's thigh, this whole distinction between real and fake memories seems almost trivial. But if he's

messing with my head… If he made me think we had a past together…
Damn, that just makes me angry.

"Were you even lovers?" Ev says. His voice is aiming for the "I don't
care, I'm just curious" tone, but I can hear just a touch of jealousy in it, too.

"I think we were," I say. "I think he seduced me when I was mourning
my parents, and I was happy for the comfort." I trace a finger along the
inside of Ev's thigh, follow the seam of his trousers to his fly and slowly pull
down the zipper. "But I don't think he was quite the lover he thought he
was, going by that last dream."

I tug layers of cotton out of my way, freeing Evgeny from his clothes.
I feel his hand tighten on my hair, feel how he holds himself perfectly still,
as if a wrong move might scare me away.

I smile, turn my head a little, and stretch out my tongue to trace the
length of him. He jerks under my mouth, as if his hardness has a mind of
its own. Ev's breath hisses as he tries to keep it from going ragged. His skin
temperature rises as his blood quickens and I can feel the pulse of his
heartbeat grow stronger under my cheek.

"John Pradip doesn't make me want to do this to him," I say, and I
push myself up on one elbow so I can slide my mouth over Ev's erection.
His breath comes rushing out as a moan and I don't stop until he comes,
hot and salty.

And then it's my turn.

I meet John Pradip at the same coffee shop, but this time we get our tea to
go and stroll the streets downtown. I'm glad I'm not sitting across the table
from him, because it's a lot easier to avoid staring accusingly when I don't
have to look at him at all.

"Tell me more about your memory ability," I say, trying not to sound
too interested in his answer. "How does it work?"

"Well," he says, "it's rather like removing the blocks people erect for
themselves in their own minds. But with something extra. I don't like to
call it 'magic,' because that makes it sound unreal, but I don't have another
word."

He sounds relaxed, content, and just a little smug. Or maybe I'm imagining it.

"So you're like a therapist?" I say.

"Something like that, I suppose." He looks at me sidelong, a slight smile tugging at the corner of his mouth. From the way his eyes slide up and down, I think he might be checking me out, and it makes me uncomfortable. I hide my discomfort by taking a sip of my tea.

Then I say, "Is it like those counsellors who help people recover suppressed memories?" I wonder if he'll realize I'm just about asking him if he can implant false memories.

He snorts, derisive, but it's not directed at me. "Most of those people are crackpots," he says. "Harmless at best, but causing real damage at worst. You're heard of that book *Michelle Remembers*?"

I have. I don't remember encountering it recently, but I think I may have read it a long time ago. Before. It's about a woman who "remembers" being used in a Satanic cult as a child. She accused a whole bunch of people of terrible acts in a book she co-wrote with her therapist, who she later married, incidentally. People believed it. They were horrified and started trying to root out Satanism in their own communities. Except none of it ever happened.

The woman's therapist used dubious techniques that actually manufactured memories from whole cloth. As far as the woman knew, they were real memories, indistinguishable from other memories, and they traumatized her just as if they were real.

But they didn't happen. Not to her, not to anyone. That's the kind of damage that shit can do. So John knows what I'm asking, but not that I think he might have done something similar to me.

I don't want to accuse him outright, but I also want to know what he did to me.

"But *could* you make someone remember something untrue, like in that book? I mean hypothetically, could you, you know, implant a memory of something that didn't happen?" I look at him, bat my eyelashes – and hope I'm not overdoing it – and say, "That would be so cool." I sip my tea. "Mean, but cool."

His nostrils flare, just slightly, and I think I hit home. "Even supposing I could," he says, "it would be unethical. My gift is about helping people, not hurting them or controlling them."

I can almost feel the flush creeping under his skin. If I was a step closer, I could probably detect the slight change in temperature near him. And I can definitely smell the change in his scent. The tang of magic, of *otherly* ability, intensifies, becomes easily detectable, and I realize he may be about to try something on me.

He lays his hand on my arm, and smiles. "I'm almost insulted you would suggest it." His voice is light, teasing, but with just a bit of sharpness.

And then I feel it, because I'm expecting it this time, a pressure that makes the hair on my arms stand up. Not all the way, but like a mild chill breeze passes over my skin and is gone. It slides up my arm, across my shoulders, and up the back of my neck. I suppress the urge to shiver.

"I wasn't suggesting you'd done it," I say, matching my tone to his, trying to sound carefree. "I just wondered if you could."

The pressure wraps around my skull and I wonder if he's trying to put a memory into my head, or pull one out. Or something else. I think about my fox nature. I can't exactly manifest a fox tail and fox eyes in front of him, but maybe if I concentrate, I can use my abilities to keep him out.

According to the fox women, I should be able to do it automatically, and normally I can, with anyone but Alex. But maybe John used our former connection to give himself a way into my head. Maybe he made himself a back door years ago.

The pressure tightens, then backs off, and I see a little frown hover between John's eyes, then vanish. So he *was* trying something on me, which means he almost certainly *did* do it before. Gave me memories that aren't real, or at least brought out specific things *he* wanted me to remember. But why?

I don't get any sense of malice from him. Really, I can't read him at all, except he seems friendly. A bit possessive, maybe.

"You never did tell me why you broke things off with me," I say, and as he turns to look at a duck splashing in an ornamental fountain in front of a huge office tower – an unlikely sight in this city – I catch just a glimpse of something on his face. Triumph? Does he think I want to get back with him, or is it something else?

"I realized I had taken advantage of you," he says. "When your parents were… Well, when you were vulnerable."

So at least he admits that. "You didn't have to stop speaking to me." At least the dream gave me back memories of the trajectory of my relationship with him, or at least *his* version of events.

"I thought it would be easier. To let you have some distance. I figured you could think things through, and if you did want to be with me, even after that, you'd let me know."

"But you didn't *tell* me that." I let a note of petulance creep into my voice. Let him think I'm the same needy girl I used to be. Maybe I can get him to tell me other things, like why his business card was in my father's wallet when his dead body washed up on the bank of the Wander River.

"No. I didn't handle things well. I'm sorry."

He turns away from the fountain and the duck to look at me and I try to smile without baring my teeth. He's lying. That isn't the reason at all, but I don't think he ever intended to tell me what the real reason was.

"Will you give me another chance?" He smiles, shyly. But he's not very good at it. Maybe it would have fooled me once, but now I've seen the real shy-boy-meets-pretty-girl smile on Evgeny – and it never ceases to astonish me that I'm the pretty girl in the equation.

I can't remember if I told John about Evgeny or not.

I make myself smile back, doing my best shy girl smile in return. "I'm leaving for Germany in a couple of days," I say. "Maybe we can talk again when I get back."

There's not much more to our meeting than that. We talk about trivial things, travelling, airlines. I try once or twice to get him to talk about his abilities again, but he evades my questions, and I don't want it to be obvious I'm pumping him for information.

When we part – he plants a chaste kiss on my cheek, touches my hand, and walks quickly away – I'm left confused and frustrated. I don't even know quite why he wanted to meet again except maybe to ask for another chance.

John Pradip, I learned, is harder to read than a vampire, and vamps are so naturally unreadable they have to practice to seem normal.

The next few days go by far too quickly. I settle on a travel wardrobe, supplemented by a trip to the mall for more underthings and travel-sized toiletries, and I pack it all into a rather handsome wheeled suitcase Evgeny lends me.

I realize we've never talked about places we've travelled to before. I mean, you can't expect to cover every topic in a relationship of, what, a few months? (Is that really all?) Nor would you want to, I guess. But you'd think travel might have come up.

Turns out he's been back to Russia a couple of times with his parents, to visit an assortment of cousins and aunts and uncles. When I ask if he's been in touch with any of them since he was reborn a vamp he just shrugs. "We were never really that close," he says.

"Still," I say, "You have family." I guess I'm a little obsessed with the idea of families lately.

"Not the important ones," he says, and I suddenly remember his parents are dead, too, and he killed them. Not on purpose, of course. His father vampire fed them to him when he was newborn and all instinct, with no memory of his human life.

"Fuck, Ev. I'm sorry."

He shakes his head. "You're my family now," he says.

"You too," I say. Then, of course, I have to stop packing because showing Evgeny how important he is to me is much more important than stuffing another pair of socks into the suitcase. And that takes the rest of the night, so it's a good thing he took my last night in town off from work.

Tonight, it's a slow night of trying to touch, kiss, lick every bit of skin on each other's bodies, to press ourselves close together and memorize every curve and muscle and hair follicle.

We don't speak; there is no need for any more words tonight. So the only sounds are our breathing, the soft brushing of skin on skin, wet sounds of mouths and fucking, moans. I don't want to stop touching him, but eventually even my overclocked sex drive is satisfied and we lie side by side, only our hands in contact.

I can tell from Evgeny's breathing that he's awake, making as much of this last night as I am, I think. Finally, as the sky begins to lighten, he says, "I'll miss you, my heart."

"I'm coming back," I say, and I roll over to pillow my head on his shoulder.

He kisses my forehead. "I know." I can practically hear the grin growing in his voice, even in a mere two words, so I don't have to look up at his face to see he's smiling. "But who will save me from the bad guys while you're away?"

"You're just going to have to stay out of their way. Or learn how to save yourself."

I sit up then, stretch, and get up to close the blinds to shield Ev from the morning sun. I twitch my tail from side to side and he laughs.

"You won't be able to walk around with that showing," he says. "Unless Germany is a very different place from North America."

"I expect it is different," I say, lying back down next to him. I have a few hours before I have to meet Alex and Li in a cab to the airport. "Though probably not *that* different."

Chapter Nine

EVGENY CAN'T SEE me to the airport, or even out to the cab, due to the sun, so I linger in bed until the last possible minute.

Alex and Li are already in the taxi, and the driver helps me wedge my suitcase into the trunk next to theirs. Of course, they're together in the back seat, leaving me to sit next to the driver and make small talk. Luckily, he talks enough for all four of us, so all I really have to do is nod and say, "Oh yeah?" now and then.

It's not till we reach the airport and the cab drives away that I realize I've never flown before. Not that I remember, anyway. I wonder if I should feel nervous.

Alex takes charge and leads us inside to a row of kiosks where we can, apparently, scan the barcodes on our tickets to check in. The airport is bustling and I bump into three people trying to keep up with Alex. I have to suppress the urge to feel my ass to make sure my tail isn't showing. I mean, I know it's not – my balance would be different if it was there, for one thing – but I'm still worried about it. More worried than I am about climbing into a ridiculous metal contraption and letting it hurl me into the sky.

To my surprise, I actually get through my turn at the kiosk without screwing up the process. The printed page Alex gave me scans right away, and my name and flight information pop up on the little screen. Then I wait nervously while the machine scans my passport, irrationally terrified that my perfectly legal new identification will somehow turn out to be fake after all. But it scans without a problem, and a boarding pass pops out of the slot, and I'm done. Now all I have to do is take my suitcase to be checked through, and there's a special line for people who've already checked in. It's over in no time, and I'm left gawking around me like a tourist, or a little kid who's never been in an airport before. And for all I know, I may never *have* been in an airport before. Now Alex, Li, and I are left with an hour to kill before our flight leaves.

So far, this trip has been easy. I mean, we haven't actually *left* yet, but it just feels like something should have gone horribly awry by now. Or at least slightly awry. I don't know why I keep expecting the worst. Maybe I *am* nervous about flying. Or maybe it's because usually the worst is exactly what happens.

But no, it all goes smoothly. We sip coffee, browse the shops, and finally head for security. That's when it does go wrong. Okay, not really *wrong*, but… irritating.

When it's my turn at the x-ray machine, or whatever it is they use these days, I empty my pockets into the bin – only a few coins and my wallet – heft my backpack onto the conveyor belt, and take off my shoes, belt, and jacket as requested. Then I hand over my boarding pass and passport, and the guy behind the x-ray machine chortles.

Really, he *chortles*. Not a laugh, exactly, or a snort, or a chuckle. Something about my passport has him amused. I look at him, trying not to glare, and wait for instructions.

He glances at me, grins, and waves in the general direction of the body scanner. The guard waiting on the other side shrugs and waves me through. The machine doesn't even beep, so I'm allowed to collect my stuff.

X-ray guy asks me if he can go through my backpack while I put my shoes and belt back on. I don't know why they ask. I mean, are you even allowed to say, "No"?

The whole time, he keeps sneaking looks at me and his lips twitch as he tries to hold back a smile. Finally, as he's handing me back my paperwork, he says, "That can't be your real name."

"What?" I say, pausing halfway through reaching for my documents. He pokes them into my hand and I take them automatically. Is there something wrong with my passport after all? I open it up and look. It seems fine to me.

"Panya Su Fuchs?" he says, only he pronounces my last name like "fucks." Usually people say "fooks" or "fyooks" which is close enough to the proper German pronunciation that I don't care.

"Come on," he says. "Fucks? What are you, a porn star? You could totally be a porn star. I'd watch." His grin becomes a leer.

I'm really not a violent person, despite having been forced to live pretty violently in the last year or so. But hell and fuck do I want to kick his teeth in right now. How can he possibly not know how completely gross, how creepy, he sounds?

"It's Fuchs," I say, giving it a crisp German accent. Or at least a decent North American approximation of a German accent. I pronounce it the way my dad did. Then I force myself to grab my backpack and walk away. There are so many things I want to say to that asshat, but I doubt it would make a difference. Guys like that just don't get it.

Though rearranging his face might at least make an impression.

Alex has overheard the whole exchange while going through the next security station over and she's trying so hard not to laugh tears are leaking out of the corners of her eyes. Li, at least, looks pissed, and shoots the x-ray guy an angry look on my behalf.

"Oh, if only he knew," gasps out Alex. Li turns her disgusted look on her girlfriend, and I very pointedly look away and march past the two of them, heading for our gate. As we line up to board, Alex apologizes.

"It's just, you should have seen your face. I bet it never even occurred to you that someone might read your name that way."

I sigh. "It didn't," I say. "But I suppose it should have." Then by way of an apology of my own, I say, "Do you think he actually read the 'h' as a 'k' or do you think he just mispronounced it?"

"Who knows," says Alex.

"Who cares," says Li. "Either way, he was rude, and a pig. Men like that make me very glad I'm a lesbian."

A few people must overhear her, because she gets some not-so-subtle glances – do they think they've never seen a lesbian before and wonder what one looks like? – which she meets so cooly and regally that the people look quickly away.

I wish I had her calm. Oh, I can force it, make myself calm with the mental exercises and breathing my kung fu instructor taught me, but Li seems so naturally calm, even in her anger and disdain.

"Well, at least you won't have to worry about people mis-pronouncing your name once we get to Germany," Alex says.

We didn't manage to get all three of our seats together on the plane, even though we got to the airport in what Alex assumed was plenty of time. She and Li are seated together near the back, while I'm wedged in between a guy who looks like he might once have played football and a thin woman with a lot of makeup who seems to be surrounded in a cloud of perfume. You'd think air travel would be a mandatory scent-free zone, but maybe no one had the guts to tell her. She looks like she's used to getting her way, like maybe she runs a big company or something.

It's going to be a very long flight and the inside of my nose is already starting to burn. I sigh and strap myself in, then turn to peer past football guy and out the window. All I can see is the airplane's wing. Lovely.

Once, I'd have given anything to be a normal, regular human woman, and maybe a human sense of smell would make perfume lady more endurable, but being a fox woman has advantages. Like I can sleep pretty much anywhere.

So I get as comfortable as I can, practice breathing through a thin gap in my lips to avoid inhaling perfume as much as possible, and I've just started to doze when the plane moves. I wake up enough to observe the slow taxi into position on the runway – not that I can see much of what's going on – then wake up all the way when we pick up speed and the engine noise increases in pitch. I can actually feel the wheels leave the runway and it's like we suddenly swoop upwards and we're flying.

Okay, that *is* cool.

But pretty soon, with nothing new to see or feel except the pressure increase and the hiss of recirculated air and the odd bit of turbulence, we almost might as well be on the ground. I stare at the display of the map showing our location on the seat back in front of me for a while, then I sleep again.

I wake up when someone pokes my shoulder. I blink, look up, and Alex is leaning over perfume lady.

"Hey," she says.

"Hey," I say back, blinking some more and wishing I had room to stretch. "Where are we?"

"Middle of the Atlantic-ish," she says. "I thought we could switch seats for a bit."

I wouldn't give up a seat next to Evgeny to sit between football guy and perfume lady, so I assume Alex has a reason for wanting to switch. I climb out of my seat – perfume lady doesn't get up, but just sort of tucks herself smaller in her seat, so I have to climb over her.

Before Alex takes my place, she says quietly, "Li was telling stories to pass the time, and she started telling another one about our ancestors. Well, *my* ancestors. But we agreed you should hear it, too."

I nod.

"She's going to write it down, but it'll make the trip go faster for you both to tell it out loud."

"What are you going to do?" I say. I suppose they must play movies on flights this long. But she grins and holds up a thick paperback novel. There's a bookmark stuck in it, only a fraction of the way through.

"Some light reading," she says. I look at the title, and don't recognize it, but the cover makes me think it's one of those dense historicals.

"Have fun," I say.

Li and Alex's seats are almost in the last row, and Li's sitting by the window. The lady in the aisle gets up to let me in, and Li climbs out, too.

"Take the window," she says. "Alex says you got stuck over a wing."

We all get settled, and aisle lady puts her headphones on and turns her attention to the seat-back screen. The sound is up so loud I can just about make out the dialogue of the movie she's watching with my fox-keen hearing.

Li turns towards me, settles herself in the seat. Out the window, all I can see is sky and clouds. It dazzles my eyes.

"Your ancestor isn't in this part of the story," says Li. "But Alex wanted you to hear it. It's… strange. But I do think it will connect to your story sooner or later."

She takes a sip from a bottle of spring water, tucks it in the seat pocket, and then begins.

Jorinde Holz, who was called Rinde, or just Rin, to distinguish her from her twin Joringel, was the first born of the twins and she had taken the lead in everything since. So it was she who carried the key to the Holz house in her coat pocket, and she who had arranged everything to do with travelling to Schönstadt.

Neither twin remembered very much about the town in which they had been born – delivered at home by the local midwife (said to have regular traffic with the Witch of the Wald, but such things have always been said about midwives), as if it were still the Dark Ages.

But stepping out of the carriage, they both remembered the chill Oktober Mountains breeze. Joringel lifted his chin and seemed to be trying to ignore it, while Rinde pulled her coat tighter. The driver had parked the carriage simply by pulling it over to the side of the cobblestone street in front of the town hall, because there were no designated spaces or even sidewalks, and there weren't even any other carriages in sight, not even a battered old farm cart or saddled horse.

Rin looked around at the old village – not a new-looking house could she see and even the street lamps looked as if they might still be lit by whale oil rather than gas. She had already discovered that the mails were slow to move in and out – daily delivery was not the norm here. That had surprised her, because there were few places mail delivery didn't reach these days, not in a country as populated as theirs.

"What do we say?" said Joringel. He'd been asking variations of the same question the whole trip from the city and into the Oktober Mountains and through them to the edge of the Hexenwald.

Rin shrugged. "We'll just tell them who we are and ask where the house is and when the funeral is to be held." She had said more or less the same thing each time Jor had asked. She loved her brother, but sometimes he seemed so helpless. Not for the first time, she wondered if he had only become helpless because she had always taken charge and done everything for him. She shrugged again and pulled open the ancient wooden door to the town hall and discovered a single large room with shelves and cabinets on one side – a hand-lettered sign reading "Archives" hung from the ceiling – and a large table surrounded by uncomfortable-looking massive wooden chairs on the other.

In the middle, in a space made slightly less dark-wood gloomy by the careful placement of an assortment of dusty old oil lamps, was an enormous desk topped in deep green leather, behind which sat a tiny, thin woman with white hair in a bun. She was knitting a red scarf that already looked far too long for a human neck. There was an even more tiny, even more old, even more white dog on her lap, which opened one bulging pink eye to look at the twins. It blinked once, then closed its eye and began to snore.

"Hello, dears," said the tiny lady. "You're new here. How can I help?" She looked cheerful enough, but there was a deep weariness about her that made Rinde want to sit down.

"Our parents lived here, they just . . . they passed away," she began.

"We've come for the funeral," said Joringel.

The old lady stiffened and whatever warmth there had been in her drained away, leaving only frostiness.

"I'm afraid there was no funeral," she said. "You can visit their graves in the cemetery." She stared at the twins, hostility evident in her posture, but also . . . envy? "We were unaware that the Holzes had any living relations."

Rinde couldn't help but think that the last statement had been a lie, though she couldn't have said how she knew, except why else would the old lady know who their parents were when they hadn't given any name?

Rinde shook her head. "Please, Frau," she said, hoping politeness might soften the elderly woman. "We understood there would be a service. It's why we're here." She didn't add that they had also come to see if their parents had left any clues about why they had been sent away as children to live with relations.

The old lady's look softened a little and – was it pity? – she didn't exactly smile, but the stiff line of her lips relaxed. She reached into a drawer of the desk and drew out a sheet of paper. It was a smudgy document in stiff handwriting of the sort produced by schoolchildren all over the country under the tutelage of strict schoolteachers wielding rulers. Also on the paper was a map. The lady reached into a second drawer and fumbled around for a pen. The ink blotched on the paper, but she didn't seem to notice.

She circled an area on the map. "There's the cemetery," she said. "You can ask the minister in the church there where the graves are. Perhaps he'll even say a few words for you." Then she made a blotchy X. "Here is the town hall, where we are now."

"And our parent's house, Frau? Could you tell us where it is?"

The odd look on the old lady's face intensified – it was definitely pity – and she said, much more kindly, "Don't you remember, then? You were so young when it happened, but not so young maybe, when they sent you away, the two of you."

Rinde wanted to ask, "When what happened?" And she would ask, but just then did not seem the time. She heard Joringel draw breath to speak and stepped gently on his toe. He said nothing, but pulled his foot sharply away.

"Here," said the old lady. "It's in the oldest part of town, right at the edge of the forest. The shop is on the main floor and the house above. There's not likely much there for you, but perhaps you'll find a keepsake or two, to take back with you." She made a smaller x on the map. It was, Rin noticed, exactly as far away from the graveyard and the church as it was possible to get.

"We're a small town here," the old lady said. "There'll be no need for a carriage when you can walk wherever you may need to go." It was not a suggestion, though not exactly an order, and it also seemed to indicate the end of the interview.

The twins thanked the old lady – they had been raised to be grateful and polite – and left.

"Bossy old biddy," said Joringel, once the door had creaked shut behind them.

Rinde didn't answer. Her mind was too full of questions that seemed to echo and intensify as they drove slowly through to town to their parents' house, the house where they'd been born. Nothing in Schönstadt looked new, but a lot of it looked older yet, and quite a few shops and houses – especially those at the outer fringes of town – were boarded up and abandoned. It was as if the town had once rapidly expanded then nearly as rapidly contracted back to its original size.

The only change in this pattern was at the edge of the village closest to the forest, where all the shops and houses looked old, though even then nearly half of them stood unused. The Holz house was alone at the end of the road, marked by painted toys over the door that must once have looked jolly but now only looked tired.

Rinde felt an almost overwhelming sense of familiarity and was glad to be able to sit in the carriage and just stare. She had always assumed she had been too young when they left to have many memories of this place, but she had been nearly nine years old. And here was this place that was home in a way their aunt and uncle's city house had never been, and Rinde discovered she did remember after all. Most of all, she remembered loneliness.

She felt Joringel's hand slip into hers the way it always did when he was emotional, even now that he was supposed to be a grown man. She squeezed gently back, then carefully detached her fingers and got out of the carriage.

The chill wind from the mountains blew past and she shivered but it was almost a welcoming, that wind. Cold, but familiar. It fit. This was home.

She didn't hesitate at all when she went up to the step and unlocked the door, leaving Joringel to follow behind.

The main door opened into a kind of foyer, painted white but dim now with shadows and dust. The shop door – the letters of her father's name were picked out in gold paint that was still as bright as she remembered – was straight ahead, and the house door was to the left. She ignored the shop door for now, as tempting as is was to go in and see if any of the toys she remembered were still there. But of course they wouldn't be, though similar ones might. There would be plenty of time to investigate there later. Instead, she turned to the house door and slipped the key into the lock. It turned with a click that seemed as much to be something opening inside Rinde as it was the house opening, and the door drifted open with only the slightest of creaks. Father, she recalled, had always kept the doors well-oiled. Mother disliked extraneous noise.

She climbed the stairs and emerged through a third door – this one not locked, but left a little ajar – into the kitchen. It was white and black and yellow and blue and now Rinde knew where her favorite colors had come from. White walls and a heavy, ancient black stove made a stark background to cheerful yellow and blue curtains and table linens and crockery. Even the dresser that held the dishes was painted blue, with the shelves backed in yellow.

A memory of gingerbread, fresh from the oven, hit Rin so suddenly she had to brace herself on the dusty table. Why was there so much dust? How long had it really been since their parents had died? How long since someone had thought to inform them?

Joringel clomped up the stairs and dropped their luggage on the floor. Rin hadn't meant for him to carry it all; she would have gone back in a moment. But sometimes he tried to make up for following her every lead by trying to do things without help that he should have help for. When he saw Rin's face – she imagined she must be paler than usual under her honey-brown bangs – he got that look, the one that's all sympathy, that meant he intended to hug her.

Rinde used to take comfort in Joringel's hugs. He was her brother and her best friend, after all. But lately they had begun to grow too ardent. She wished he would find a girlfriend and stop paying so much attention to her. But they were twins, and had only had each other for years, so mostly she put up with him. She accepted the embrace, and only pulled away when his body heat became too noticeable.

Chapter Ten

EVEN IF LI and Alex weren't convinced Li's stories were real, I'd almost have to believe in them anyway. 'Cause that thing they say about truth being stranger than fiction? Well, this story is pretty strange so far.

The twins in the story have got to be the ones recorded in Alex's family album, where only a single male birth and death is included. Though I suppose it's possible there was a second set of twins in her family with the same names. It's already bizarre enough.

I wish there was some way we could figure out *when* this happened. I remember Alex mentioning there were no years noted in her mother's album, and Li's story doesn't have much in it that can be fixed in time. It just has a sort of "ye olden days" kind of feel, and that's not much help.

It happened, this part of the story, sometime before the train went through Schönstadt, because the twins arrived by carriage. Unless there *was* a train, and they just didn't take it.

I spend the rest of the flight staring out the window, and it doesn't even occur to me to sleep, or to give Alex her seat back, because there are too many thoughts running through my head.

On the one hand, I'm excited about this trip. Not just because I might get free of the familiar binding that leashes me to Alex, but also because it might tell me something useful about my past, my ancestry, what I am.

Here, in Germany, I can find my distant past and hopefully that will free me to face my recent past when I get back home again so I won't be so afraid to face the woman I was anymore.

After we touch down and taxi into the airport, we file off the plane. I lug Alex's pack with me, so she won't have to fight her way back to get it. As I get closer to her row – my row, really – I can see football guy is still in his window seat. He seems to be asleep.

Alex grins at me as we stop next to her. She's in the aisle seat, and perfume lady, pointy toe tapping and face pinched, is in the middle.

"Thought I'd wait for you," says Alex. I hand over her pack and drag my own from the overhead bin.

"How'd you manage to get the aisle?" I ask when we're away from the crowd in the relatively open space inside the airport.

"Ask to go to the bathroom often enough and just about anyone will eventually offer to trade seats."

Li snorts.

Alex takes the lead again, ushering us to a taxi, checking us into a hostel, and making sure we eat. I should be gawking around me like a good tourist, but urban Germany doesn't really seem so different from the cities at home. Or maybe it's just that my fox nature isn't interested in cities. Or I'm just so tired nothing matters but a place to sleep. I'm out almost as soon as I lie down and pull the blanket over myself.

When I wake up, it's dark. I can hear the breathing of the other guests at the hostel all around, and for a moment I just lie still and listen.

The bunks are stacked three high, and I'm on the bottom one, but due to the high ceilings in the old building that houses the hostel, each bunk has plenty of space. I've still managed to curl myself into a tiny ball on one corner of my mattress.

I identify Alex's breathing right away, but it takes a moment to catch Li's. She's quiet, even in sleep. Alex is right above me, and Li on the top bunk. There are five others in the room, leaving one of the middle bunks empty.

Once I've determined that everyone is asleep, I open my eyes and slowly uncurl myself. Something nags at me, a faint memory of a dream, but I ignore it for now.

Moonlight fills the room despite the curtain over the big window, and I tilt my head to get a good look around. Not that there's much to see. Three bunk beds of three bunks each, all but one occupied. Suitcases and backpacks. A door out, a door to the bathroom labelled in both German and English. The window.

I wish I dared let my tail manifest, just for a moment, but it would mean taking my jeans off – since I seem to have been so tired I went to bed fully clothed – and that would make me too exposed. Maybe I should buy some long swishy skirts so I can have my tail all the time. I've never really been one for long skirts, though. I prefer short skirts I can hike up out of my way if I need to run. Or kick someone in the teeth.

It doesn't seem like anyone else is going to stir, so I ease my legs over the side of the bunk and stand up. Now that I'm up, I can see that one of the other guests has balanced an alarm clock on the mattress next to their pillow. It's just after three in the morning. I try to work out what time that makes it back home, but I've forgotten how many hours difference it is, and I'm too preoccupied to focus on the simple math anyway. My fox senses are not much help – I can always tell when it's near dawn or dusk, but other times of the day or night feel pretty much the same. And anyway, they're probably attuned now to where I am, not where I was.

I go over to the window and part the curtain and feel almost like I've stepped into a dream. The buildings in this neighborhood are all old, stone and brightly-painted wood. I could be standing in any time period between 1600 and now. But then I notice the glow off a TV screen from the building opposite, a newer car parked in the narrow street below, a candy wrapper glinting from between the cobbles, power lines across the dark wedge of sky, and the illusion is gone.

A thin trickle of air seeps around the edge of the window, and it smells just like any city. Older than those I'm used to, but the car exhaust is still there, the sharp taint of electricity, something sweet and greasy.

I like it. As much as my fox nature craves the forest, the human part of me is still a city girl. And this city has *history*. It has a kind of wildness, too, that's deeper than the feral shiver that runs through North American cities. I try to imagine what it would be like to live here.

And then I catch a wisp of something in the draft from the window – not quite the peppery smell of vampire, or the musky tang of werewolf. Something like the cinnamon whiff of not-exactly-magic. And I can see a figure in the shadow the moon makes on the building opposite. I stare until my eyes ache, but the shape doesn't move. And then it's gone. I didn't see any movement at all. Maybe I imagined that there was even someone there; maybe I imagined the smell of magic.

"What's out there?" says a soft voice from over my head. Li.

"I thought I saw someone," I say, quietly enough that I'm not sure she'll even hear me.

"Mmm," she says, to let me know she's heard, I guess.

"Thought I smelled…"

"Magic?" she says. "Or… you know."

"Not-magic," I say, and I turn to smile at her. She smiles back.

"Tomorrow we'll go see if we can find it," she says.

"It's a long trip?" I realize I didn't even ask how long it would take to get there, or even how we'd be travelling. It's not like me to be so incurious about anything. Especially about something that affects me so directly. If knowledge is a weapon, I like to be well-armed.

"Most of a day," says Li. "Once we get on the train. Not too many tourists go to the Oktober Mountains, I guess."

It sounds like someplace out of a fairytale. But I suppose it kind of *is* someplace out of a fairytale.

I turn back to the window. I want to go outside, to wander this city and see if it's like the city I know. If *others* come out to play in the dark like they do back home. I put my hand on the glass and it's cool, almost cold. Spring is still new, and it's filled me with longing. I want to *run*, on two legs and on four legs.

I wish Evgeny were here.

"I'm not sure I can sleep any more," I say. But I lay back down on my bunk anyway, listen to Li settle herself again. Her breathing evens and softens until it's almost inaudible, even to me, and I know she's fallen back to sleep.

One of the other guests twitches suddenly in the midst of a dream, and another begins to snore – not loudly, fortunately. Right over my head, Alex rolls over, making the springs creak. I listen to her breathing, slow and steady, just like her, and too late I realize I'm falling into *her* dream. I try to pull away, but once I've started to dream with her, the chokehold on my throat tightens and the only way to make it ease is to follow it, in and down to sleep and Alex's mind. Alex's dream.

Her lips are soft, pliant, and she smells faintly of cinnamon, tastes like it, too, as if she has been drinking chai tea. Her small hands are skilled and raise goosebumps as she strokes my bare back.

"Alex," she says, her voice soft and strong and sweet like honey.

"Li," I say, in Alex's voice, because of course I am in Alex's dream, kissing Alex's girlfriend. If I could feel my own body I would probably feel a flush of shame and embarrassment, as if I were a peeping tom, or deliberately imagining my friends making love so I could watch. But though I am aware of dreaming, aware of looking in on Alex's dream, all my senses are hers, not mine. I might as well have left my own body behind entirely.

So I feel instead the heat of desire, the tingle of arousal as Li's hand brushes across Alex's nipple, as her warm, wet mouth traces a line of kisses down Alex's neck and shoulder, as her tongue circles the other nipple, draws it in, sucks.

The rush of moisture I feel between my legs might be all Alex's response, but it might as well be my own. Li is beautiful, I can see what Alex sees in her, and I'd be lying if I said I didn't want to feel how Li's skin feels to Alex's hands.

But it feels wrong, to be here, feeling this. Surely Alex must know I'm in her dream. She must, right? But if she does, I don't feel her trying to keep me out. All I feel is her hand in Li's hair, her nipple throbbing in Li's mouth, her back arching to Li's touch. All I hear is her breathing, Li's breathing, their soft gasps and moans.

Li's hand finds Alex's crotch, slides between the folds, teasing, touching, rubbing, and Alex cries out. I feel her orgasm, feel it double, and realize I must be climaxing, too, in my own body. And I feel ashamed. But it's not like I can close my eyes and block it out.

And hell, it's not like I'm not enjoying it. I do want to explore Li's body in return, taste her skin, bury my face between her legs, lick her until it's her turn to cry out. I think, in my own body, I come again. I sure as fuck hope my dreaming self isn't moaning out loud. Like I've said before, I'm not generally quiet during sex.

They lie together, after, still gently stroking the other's skin, hair, tracing the lines of each other's faces. I feel what Alex feels, and what I feel is an intense love.

It astonishes me, that Alex loves Li so much. As much as I love Evgeny. Maybe more. And I wonder why I'm astonished. Am I so selfish that I thought she'd never get over me so easily? I'm not sure what I think, which means I've been avoiding thinking about it at all.

I decide I'm glad Alex is so in love. She deserves it. Definitely more than I do. Because if I'm going to be honest with myself, I have to admit that Alex is a far better person than I'll ever be. I hope Li returns her love as intensely.

Then Alex falls asleep in her dream, wrapped in Li's arms, and pulls me farther down into the dream with her again. This time, she's not dreaming of herself. She's a honey-haired woman asleep in a child's bed. A life-sized doll watches her from the dresser crammed into the room next to the bed. This time, I'm not in Alex's body – or the body she inhabits – but I hover near the ceiling like a ghost.

The dream has that feeling of realness that my dreams of my own ancestor have, so I think the woman must be one of Alex's ancestors. Rose-Perle, I think at first, but her hair isn't pale enough. It's more a light brown, where Rose-Perle was so fair her hair appeared white. Maybe she's one of the twins. Rinde, I think she was called.

She rolls over in her sleep, throws off the blankets. Her nightgown has ridden up to her waist and she has nothing on underneath. She moans and arches her back, slides a hand between her legs.

Again, I feel shame, and I want to flee, but something holds me in the room.

The door opens, and a young man stands there. His eyes are vacant, like he's sleepwalking, but heat comes into them when he sees the woman splayed out on the bed, pleasuring herself. He looks like a male version of her, only darker of hair and skin. Her twin.

Rinde moans again, and holds out her arms. She stretches them out towards the doll on the dresser, which also looks eerily like her, like the young man, another male version of her, in carved wood and cloth. It doesn't respond, the doll, but the man at the door does. He takes a step forward, then tugs at his long nightshirt, struggles out of it, and steps into the woman's arms. She keeps her face turned towards the doll, even when the man pulls her nightgown over her head, even when he spreads her legs wider and crawls between them.

He stares rapturously at her face as he fucks her, and she stares just as rapturously at the doll. She comes and gasps in ragged breaths, eyes fixed on her doll; he comes, yells wordlessly, eyes fixed on her.

Then silence. A long moment stretches on and the woman's eyes drift closed. The man pulls out of her with a wet sound, stands looking down at her for a long time as his cock goes soft. His eyes are not vacant anymore, not asleep. She rolls over, covers her breasts with her hands as if to keep them warm and his cock slowly rises again. He watches her, takes his erection in his hand, and jerks off with short, rapid motions. His jism splatters her bedclothes and he looks at her a moment longer. Then he pulls the blankets up to cover her, collects his nightshirt from the floor, and leaves the room.

Then Alex wakes up, and pulls me with her again. Except she hasn't woken up, not back to her dream of Li, and not back to actual wakefulness. Instead we are in a forest, the trees so towering there is almost no undergrowth, except a smudge so far ahead it's hard to see what it is.

It's gloomy, but a peaceful sort of gloom that chases away the creepy feeling the last part of the dream left me with. The smudge of undergrowth, or whatever it is, holds a spark of light. A lamp, maybe, or a lighted window.

I'm not inside Alex's head anymore, and I'm not a hovering ghost. I'm me, in my own dream body. I feel my fox tail waving slightly, behind me. And Alex stands next to me, in *her* own body. She looks at me, and I look at her. She nods in the direction of the undergrowth, the light, and I take her hand. We walk, and the smudge gets closer quickly. Despite the size of the trees, it's easy to walk with no brush to trip us up.

Soon we're standing in front of a hedge, looking over it at a house on stilts. The house is overgrown with vines, covered in flower buds. The window next to the door glows with light.

I smell cinnamon, mint, vanilla. I smell tea, and cats, and very faintly, as if it's a very, very old scent, I smell fox.

"Magic," I say. My voice comes out tiny. I tend to speak quietly anyway, but the hush of the forest makes me want to whisper. Like I'm afraid of what may awaken if I disturb it. It's not that it feels threatening here. On the contrary, it feels safe. But it also feels ancient, *eldritch*, steeped in power. And that makes me nervous.

"Yes," says Alex. Her voice is small, too.

We stand, hand in hand, and stare up at the house. It's familiar, but I can't think why. Then I remember Evgeny's book of Russian fairy tales. It has beautiful illustrations, chromolithographs in vibrant color. One picture showed a house on chicken legs. Baba Yaga's house. A witch's house.

But this is not Russia. Though we're in a dream, or something like a dream, I'm certain we're still in Germany. Or very nearby. The Oktober Mountains. The Hexenwald. How I can possibly be so sure, I don't know, but I am. And hell, nothing else about this whole thing makes sense, so why shouldn't I just know something for no reason?

"This is the house we need to find," whispers Alex.

It's my turn to say," Yes."

Then the door opens and a figure is backlit against the flood of light from inside. Tall, slender, female. I blink and my eyes adjust. She has long, pale hair, almost white it's so fair. Or maybe she's old, though she's as straight and strong as a young woman.

She looks a lot like Alex. Not identical, but she could be an aunt. Or maybe a great-grandmother?

"So," she says, and her voice is like Alex's only in its strength. "I hear you're looking for me."

And then I remember the real reason I feel like I remember her house. This is where my *hexenfuchs* ancestor lived, where she was enslaved to a witch. Her familiar.

Chapter Eleven

ODDLY, WHEN I WAKE, it's not the shared dream with Alex that comes immediately to mind. It's the one I had just before I woke at 3 a.m.

It was another one of those memory dreams, where I'm reliving my recent past. It seemed normal enough, a Thanksgiving dinner with my family. Neither of my parents was religious, but they both loved family get-togethers, so any holiday was an excuse to make a big meal and drink nice wine, and watch silly holiday-themed movies together.

Thanksgiving was always the biggest feast, even though it was just Mom and Dad, me and my sister, and mom's Korean grandmother. It's because fall is harvest time so fruits and vegetables are cheap and plentiful. The food was a mix of Chinese, Korean, and German dishes, with North American staples like roast turkey with stuffing, and baked squash drizzled with brown sugar, and apple crisp.

But then John Pradip showed up, and that's where the dream took on that weird feeling of not being quite right, of being altered, imposed.

I lay in bed, staring at the underside of Alex's bunk, and watch in my mind as the memory of the dream plays out. John arrives with a bottle of wine and a lemon meringue pie. We eat, talk, watch a movie. And my sister eats a big piece of pie, gushes over how good it is.

And all at once I remember two things with absolute clarity. My sister's name is Kristine, but we all called her Kit. And she's violently allergic to eggs.

"Fucking . . . Fuck," I say.

Alex's head appears over the side of the bunk, upside down, red hair tousled from sleep. "Fuck what?" she says.

I catch another movement from the corner of my eye, another one of the guests climbing out of bed.

"I just remembered something," I say, and Alex raises an eyebrow.

I pitch my voice low. Not that anyone overhearing would understand what we were talking about, even if their English is good. "I had another memory-dream last night."

Alex blushes and I realize she's probably thinking about a different dream. So she *did* know I was looking in. I hope she knows it was involuntary.

"Thanksgiving with my family, before they…"

"Yeah," says Alex, sparing me the need to give voice to tragedy.

There's a creak and a thump and Li drops to the floor next to me, leans close so she can hear, too.

"And guess who shows up?" I describe the dream, as briefly as I can without leaving out any details that might be important.

"I don't get it," says Alex, when I mention the part about Kit and the pie.

"*Meringue*," I say.

"Made with egg whites," says Li.

"Oh, shit," says Alex. "Either that was a really lousy Thanksgiving, or—"

"Mr John Pradip inserted a fake memory of himself in my head." Oddly, I hear more anger in my own voice than I feel in my gut.

"I wonder how many memories he's made up for you," says Li.

"Maybe you didn't even know him at all," says Alex.

I shake my head. "No, I'm pretty sure I knew him. And I'm pretty sure we were lovers. But now I'm also pretty sure he's not as good a lover as he thinks he is."

Alex laughs.

"And I'm also certain he never met my parents." But then I remember the business card in my dead father's wallet. "At least not while I was around."

Once we get up and get moving, it's not angry thoughts about John Pradip that keep me utterly distracted to the point that I'm hardly aware of where I am and Alex and Li have to keep grabbing my arm or my jacket hem to steer me out of traffic. It's one precious gem that memory-dream gave me back, one thing I know is true however much else John Pradip may have made up.

My sister's name is Kristine. Kit.

When we're on the train, heading out into the German countryside, I finally come out of my reverie enough to pay attention to the passing landscape.

The three of us are in an observation car at the rear of the train, and Alex is reading to us from a guidebook while Li and I peer out the windows.

"The Oktober Mountains are seldom visited by tourists, who find the region's stubborn insistence on tradition to be inconvenient. Cell phone service is spotty at best, and many villages lack amenities like cable television or high-speed internet access. For those looking for a break from modernity, however, the region is a haven, with villages out of fairy tales and pristine old-growth forests to explore. Pack plenty of sweaters, though, because the old folklore that there's always a chill wind blowing in the Oktober Mountains is actually true."

Alex pauses and I glance up at her. She gazes thoughtfully out the window. "I wonder if magic keeps progress moving more slowly," she says.

"Is that even possible?" says Li. Then, "I thought it wasn't really magic."

Alex chuckles. "True, but it *feels* like magic. Anyway, what else should we call it?"

"I suppose."

I look back out the window. The farms here may be old, but they actually bear all the signs of advanced technology. The equipment I see readying the fields for planting looks about as high-tech as farm equipment gets, and there are plenty of power lines and telephone lines, and a whole lot of sleek-looking cars and motorcycles. This part of Germany, at least, is not a place out of a fairytale.

But as the houses pass and the trees close in, and stop after stop more passengers get off and fewer get on, it begins to feel like we're going back in time.

Each train station looks older and more fantastic than the last, though they're all very well-kept and efficient.

Finally, the trees take over completely from the fields, and there are no stops at all. An hour passes and the train zooms along. I know we're gradually zig-zagging higher into the hills, but the trees are so dense they create the illusion of travelling on and on in a straight line and never getting anywhere. Time almost seems to stand still. Then all at once the trees retreat and we're treated to a spectacular view of forested hills and bare stone mountains in the distance and the train stops in the quaintest looking village I've ever seen outside of a book. Hell, I think it may even be quainter than the quaintest ye olde worlde photograph I've ever seen *inside* a book.

The sign on the station wall says *Schönstadt*.

"Nice place," I say, and can't help but chuckle. Li and Alex don't get the joke, so I explain. It's what "Schönstadt" means, basically. "Nice town" would be a reasonable translation. In the US, it might have been called "Pleasantville."

We get off the train, the only passengers to disembark. No one gets on, and there's no one around, though there are lights on in the station. The quiet is almost overwhelming once the train pulls away and rattles into the distance.

"Where the fuck are we?" says Li, softly.

"Nowhere," I say.

"Here," says Alex. "Home." Li takes her hand. There's more emotion in Alex's voice than I would have expected. I don't remember her ever talking much about her family, or her heritage. But then, when I knew her before, she didn't even know she was a witch yet. Maybe that detail changed things for her.

After all, this pretty, deserted little village is where her family originated. And it's right on the edge of the Hexenwald. The witch-wood. This is where the Holz family – and perhaps coincidentally, perhaps not, Holz means "forest" – and the Witch of the Wald met and joined.

"Well, I suppose we should find our hotel," says Alex, breaking the peculiar spell that was creeping over us all.

"And while we eat," says Li, "I want you to read what I was writing." The last while on the train, while we glided on unstopping through the forest, Li had been scribbling madly on a stack of looseleaf paper.

So we check into the hotel, an ancient building with a tiny room for each of us and an immense bathroom to share, all on the third floor. The clerk, who may also be the owner for all I know, is a wizened old man who reminds me of the dried-apple doll my German grandmother sent me for my sixth birthday. Does anyone still make dried-apple dolls, I wonder?

I try not to laugh that the old man's resemblance to shriveled fruit brought me back a small childhood memory.

He doesn't speak English, but he smiles at my North-American-accented German and chatters at me while he shows us the amenities. I wonder if he's lonely. There don't seem to be all that many residents here, let alone visitors.

His accent is a little hard to follow, full of colloquialisms and country pronunciations, but by the time he hands over the keys to our rooms and totters back to his desk, I'm starting to enjoy the sound of it.

The place he recommends we eat might be a restaurant or a café – the sign over the door is unclear and maybe the difference is irrelevant – but it reminds me most of a pub.

We sit at a wooden table scrubbed smooth by countless years of use, and order what the waitress refers to as the "visitor's special" – an assortment of local dishes aimed at introducing tourists to the cuisine of the Oktober Mountains. It's probably also easy to prepare on short notice from whatever the owners happen to have on hand.

Dinner is served with a huge mug of apple cider. Unlike the rest of Germany, which is big on beer, the locals here seem more partial to alcoholic beverages made from local produce. Apparently they also make a turnip liqueur that the waitress assures me is a local favorite, but very much an acquired taste. I'm not much of a drinker, but I decide I'll have to try some before I leave town, just for the experience.

Then, as the plates start arriving bearing more food than even six of us could hope to consume, Li takes out her notepaper and hands the stack to me.

As I read each page, I pass it to Alex, and soon we're both absorbed in the next segment of the story of Alex's twin ancestors.

Joringel let go of Rinde reluctantly. Why could she never let him take the lead? He could be strong, he just needed the chance.

"Do you remember," she said, "when Mother used to make gingerbread?"

He shook his head, but Rin was not looking at him. She bent over the stove and pulled open the oven to look inside. Jor couldn't help but look at her ass. She wanted him to find a woman, but there was no woman as fine as she, no woman who understood him so well. And it was not as if they even looked like brother and sister, not at first glance.

Rinde took after their mother – all honey-brown of hair and creamy of skin. All slender limbs and hourglass curves. Joringel looked more like their father – and like their father's father even more – with black hair and olive skin. Their father's family had Romany blood, some said. Perhaps their faces looked alike, their eyes especially, but most people didn't notice since their coloring was so different.

He had wanted to pretend to be cousins instead of brother and sister, but Rinde had refused. Besides, she had said, people would already know who they were, as they would know which parent each of them took after.

Joringel was not ashamed to admit he loved his sister more than most brothers would. More, perhaps, than any brother should. But he had only just begun to admit that he lusted after her, too. But stubbornly, he thought, was wanting to fuck your twin sister so much different from enjoying masturbating in the mirror? From getting excited at the sight of your own hands on your own skin? From watching yourself stroke your own cock until you spewed semen over your own reflection and then standing and caressing the glass with your slick white fluids until you wanted to do it again?

"Look, the cookie pan is still here," said Rin, and Jor had to focus on reality again.

"Are there cookies on it?" he asked, wanting to make her smile.

She stood up and closed the oven, and she did smile. Joringel felt warm inside.

"Let's go look at our rooms," she said, taking the lead again. "Tomorrow we can go to the cemetery and talk to the minister and all that."

Joringel nodded. He could see it was drawing on to evening and the light through the blue-and-yellow curtains was getting dimmer. They had brought groceries. He would offer to cook – assuming the big gas range still had gas – and they would sleep early, with only a thin wall separating them.

He followed Rin out of the kitchen and into the hall. There ahead was the sitting room, comforting and dark with polished wood and deep-pile rugs. He remembered now the shelves of books – fairy tales, most of them, a photo album, and an improbably large Bible in which all the births and deaths and marriages in the Holz family had been recorded – and the heavy, leather-upholstered chairs.

Upstairs was the washroom, cramped and tucked under a slant of roof, and on the other side, their parents' bedroom with its huge four-poster bed. For a moment Joringel lingered in the doorway, staring at that bed and imagining himself in it. And Rinde. Then she called to him from the attic stair and he followed her up.

And there they were, just as they had left them, their bedrooms. Tiny spaces under the roof, the rooms were mirror images. From the top of the stairs, Joringel could see in the open doors of both. On one side, at the front of the house and overlooking the street, was Joringel's room. It was done all in blues and reds and whites. Soldier colors, he had pretended as a little boy. He had been afraid of the forest, which was why it was Rinde's room, in blues and yellows like the kitchen, but with splashes of purple and green, that looked out at the Hexenwald. Each room had a narrow bed, a dresser, a tiny wardrobe, and a little shelf of books, and that was all.

For a moment, Joringel thought each bed also had an occupant, until he realized they were dolls. Dolls the size of the children Rinde and Joringel had been when they were sent away, and exquisitely made. Jor remembered his father working on them and his mother saying they were too big, but then something had happened and all the joy went out of their father. It had taken him much effort to finish those dolls, and he had not made smaller ones to replace them, though he had intended to, and he had locked them away in his workshop and let his apprentices do most of the toymaking from then on.

"Look," said Rinde. She was always saying *look*. "I've got the boy doll in my room, and you have the girl. I wonder if they forgot which room was whose when we left." Her voice sounded light, but Joringel could tell she wanted to cry. It didn't happen often, but he could always tell when she was going to weep.

"I don't think so," he said. "I don't think they were trying to replace us with dolls." Though that was exactly what he had thought, at first.

"What then?" said Rin. She had heaved the boy doll – his hair was dark and despite the stylization of his features, he looked like a younger version of Joringel, or a darker, male version of Rinde – and looked like she intended to swap it with the girl doll in Joringel's room.

The girl doll had dark blonde hair and looked like a young, stylized Rinde, or a fair, female Joringel.

"I think they're meant to comfort us, when we're apart," he said. "It's why they look like us. And I'd rather have a doll that looks like you than one that looks like me." But both dolls made him uncomfortable. And flushed. He thought about masturbating on a doll of himself instead of on his mirror reflection. Then he thought about masturbating on a doll of Rinde and his pants felt tight.

Rinde frowned and looked at the doll in her arms. She was tall, but the doll was so huge it almost made her look like a child again. Joringel liked seeing her holding a doll version of him. He imagined her masturbating with a doll of him and had to take a long step into his room so she wouldn't see the bulge in his trousers.

He looked out the window at the fading light. It seemed early still, but he remembered that in the mountains, the light went away faster. The street was brown with unswept dirt on the cobbles and the lawns were brown with the fading plants of late summer. How long would he and

Rinde stay in this house? In this town? Might they move here, among familiar strangers, and re-open their parents' business together? Joringel knew nothing about toy-making, but both he and Rinde were good with their hands, and Rinde was also good with people while Joringel was also good with money. Handcrafts, if well made, could be decent money in a world where people were increasingly disillusioned with mass production. It was only too bad that everyone here would know they were brother and sister.

There didn't seem to be anyone around, and it made Shönstadt feel lonely. Jor shook his head and turned to find Rinde watching him. She still held the doll, but seemed to have forgotten it.

"Is this too much?" she asked.

"It's home," he said. "It's strange. Familiar and unfamiliar. But home." She nodded.

"We could stay," he said.

"Let's just deal with Mother and Father's estate first."

He nodded and stood away from the window. "I'll get the food and start supper."

By the time he got back in with the groceries, Rinde had taken their luggage from the kitchen to their rooms and was fiddling with the gas valves just inside the door.

"The stove has gas," she said. "But we don't seem to have any lights."

"They must have shut off the gas when Mother and Father died," Joringel said. "Perhaps the stove is on a different line. There must be candles somewhere, and oil lamps." There were, just where there had always been, so they had a candle-lit supper, which might have been romantic, except Rinde only wanted to talk about everything she had begun to remember from their childhood.

Then they retired to bed early. It had been a long day and full of sudden and strange emotions.

Joringel lay on his tiny bed for a long time, watching the candlelight flicker on the face of the Rinde-doll. He had set her on the dresser, next to the window, and she almost seemed to be watching him. There had always been something oddly lifelike about the toys his father made.

The candle flickered again in a draft and the Rinde-doll appeared to smile and wink. Joringel licked his lips and thought about his sister, sleeping on the other side of the thin wall. He thought he heard her bed creak as she rolled over. He looked down the length of his body and was not surprised to see his erect penis had made a tent of his blankets.

He pushed the quilt aside and looked at his cock. It bobbed, as if in greeting. He looked over at the Rinde-doll and she seemed to smile again.

Joringel took hold of himself and looked at the doll and it seemed mere seconds before he spewed his seed onto the quilt. He didn't quite dare yell out when he came, but he wanted to. He wanted Rinde to hear him, and want him, and touch herself in response. But he was quiet, and fell asleep with his penis going soft in his hand.

His dreams were full of Rinde, or the Rinde-doll – in the dreamworld they seemed to be one and the same.

"Love me," she said, "and I will give you a pearl beyond price."

I don't need a pearl, he thought. I love you anyway.

Then he woke in the chilly night, the blankets still pushed aside and he was erect again in his hand. He began to stroke himself and then he heard her voice. The Rinde-doll.

"Love me," she said, in his head, but clear as if spoken aloud. "Love me, and I will give you a pearl beyond price." He turned his head and the doll seemed to be watching him. The room was so small he had only to sit up to reach the doll down from the dresser. He held her in his lap and she was warm. His cock poked up between her legs and tangled in the folds of her dress.

"Love me," her voice said in his thoughts.

Maybe he was going mad. Maybe he was still dreaming.

Joringel leaned down and kissed the doll's wooden mouth and it seemed to open for him, to let his tongue into its wooden depths. He must still be dreaming, then.

It was not much like kissing a real human woman, but it was still good. Joringel ran his hands over the doll's body, as excited by wood and stuffed canvas as he was when he touched his own skin in the mirror. The doll was warm, as warm as the living Rinde. And she smelled like his sister.

Joringel sat in bed with the Rinde-doll in his lap and stroked himself. He looked at her perfectly carved face and imagined spurting his jism onto it.

"Love me," she whispered. "Love me."

His hand left his cock to fumble under her skirt. Maybe he could wrap her wooden legs around himself somehow, and pretend to fuck her. His fingers found a hole in the canvas between her legs. It was warm and soft with goosedown.

"Oh, love me," her voice moaned in his thoughts. "Let me give you the pearl beyond price my brother, my lover, my all."

And Joringel hiked up the doll's skirt, rolled over her on the bed and thrust himself into the hole between her legs.

He cried out as the tiny goosefeather quills stabbed into him, but it felt good, too. He looked down at the Rinde-doll's face and saw his living sister and he fucked her as hard as he could until he yelled out, loud but wordlessly, and seemed to come forever into the down-filled doll's body.

He fell asleep on top of her, slowly going soft inside her.

He was cold and stiff-jointed when he woke and the Rinde-doll was perched on top of the dresser where she had been when Joringel fell asleep.

A dream, then. But when he pushed back the blankets to get up, he found himself gouged with tiny, bloody scratches, and suddenly he felt their sting. One fluffy goosefeather was stuck in his urethra like a flag and he almost screamed when he pulled it out.

He got out of bed and grabbed the Rinde-doll and peered into her face. For a dizzying moment, her wooden lips appeared to part and an enormous pearl rolled off her tongue and dropped into her lap. After that, she was just a doll again, no matter how Joringel shook her or caressed her or whispered to her.

He picked up the pearl and sat on the edge of the bed. A pearl beyond price. Where had he heard that phrase? It had something to do with the Hexenwald, he was sure. He looked at the doll and remembered a part of his dream — a part that was not filled with fucking and cock-sucking and Rinde who was and was not a doll.

"Take the pearl," the not-quite-Rinde voice had said. "Give it to your other self as a med'cine, and he will give your sister a pearl beyond price. That pearl will save Shönstadt."

Joringel heard clattering from downstairs and smelled coffee. Rinde was already up. He looked at the doll again and at his abused cock. He didn't care about saving Shönstadt. Did he?

"She will love you," the doll-Rinde had said in the dream. Or had it been a dream after all?

Joringel got dressed and went next door to Rinde's room. He discovered, as he went, that he remembered where each board creaked and which spots stayed silent when stepped on. He had memorized them as a boy.

The Joringel-doll sat on Rinde's dresser, its back to the window and the view of the Hexenwald, as if the sight made the doll as nervous as it did the living Joringel. It seemed to be watching him. He stepped over to it and held out the pearl in his fingers and was almost not surprised when the wooden lips parted and the pearl rolled onto the doll's wooden tongue. Then the carved face was still again and the carved mouth closed and Joringel muttered to himself, "It was a dream."

Then he went downstairs to breakfast and the sister he loved, and a day of visiting graves and talking to ministers and going through their parent's things.

Chapter Twelve

ALEX'S CHEEKS ARE pink by the time she hands the last page back to Li.

"You could have warned us," she says.

Li laughs. "I wanted to see your face."

Then they both look at me. I'm thinking about the dream I shared with Alex. Not the part with Li or the part with the witch that seemed to be as much communication as imagination, but about the part where I hovered near the ceiling, watching her twin ancestors.

So I say, "It's the same story as your dream, almost." But it's not really. Maybe the dream was the literal version of the fairytale events in Li's story.

Alex looks confused. "I don't think I dreamed *that*."

"Last night in the hostel," I say. "We shared a dream."

"Yeah," she says. "We were in the Hexenwald, and met a witch."

"And you have to find her house, now that we're here," says Li. I must look surprised, because she adds, "Alex told me on the train."

"Before that," I say.

"Before that, I dreamed –" She flushes deep red. "I dreamed about Li." She looks at her hands.

So maybe she *didn't* know I shared that particular dream.

"No," I say. "We dreamed … or I dreamed about a young woman who looked like you, but she had brown hair. Almost blonde, I think. And a young man." I tell them the dream, or the outline of it anyway. I'm not prudish, but dinnertime doesn't seem like a good time for graphic depictions.

"Are you saying … he raped her in her sleep?" Alex looks not a little horrified. These are her ancestors we're talking about, after all. It's got to be creepy to think you are, even indirectly, the product of incest.

"He didn't force himself on her," I say. "But yeah, I suppose he did. She didn't really seem to be awake. But then neither did he." *Sleepfucking*, I think, but I don't say it out loud.

"But this story" – Li holds up the pages – "is about dolls, not incest. Well, not exactly."

I shrug. "I don't know. Maybe I'm losing the ability to tell what's a true dream and what isn't." I pause and poke at the food on my plate. I'm hungry and not hungry at the same time, like my human side is too weirded out to eat, but my fox side *always* wants food. It's a bizarre feeling.

"I suppose the next part of the story I write will answer that question."

"Do you think this stuff with the dolls is *real*? Like, literal?" Alex says.

"Maybe it's metaphorical. Like … a brother and sister … it's too messed up, so the story comes out as …" I trail off. Not only do I not know quite what I was trying to say, but I just called Alex's family "messed up."

"Who knows?" says Li.

"Let's just concentrate on finding the Witch of the Wald," says Alex.

Thankfully, the rest of the evening is spent with maps of the town and its surroundings, trying to decide where to look first. The Hexenwald looks immense on the maps, and I bet local superstition about witches keeps people away, so there aren't a lot of paths. Even if most of the forest is free of undergrowth, as it was in my dream, it'll still be way too easy to get lost.

Luckily, I have a fox's sense of direction and one of my more inexplicable abilities lets me sense everything around me in the forest, like I can feel everything alive as if it's an extension of myself. No, actually, not like that at all. It's not just inexplicable in the sense of *how the hell can I do this?* but also it's impossible to explain what it feels like.

The next morning we all sleep in, like jet lag hits all three of us at once. When we finally get up, the hotel is deserted, and even the little old man who showed us our rooms is nowhere to be seen.

The first order of business, of course, is coffee. We find a tiny café on a corner between two old houses that lean out over the street like you read about medieval houses doing. And these buildings certainly look like they could have been around that long. Hell, they look like they haven't been *painted* in that long.

No one's in the café when we go in, but I can smell coffee and pastries, and not too far away is a human male who could use to shower a little more often. I sneeze.

When Alex taps on the bell on the counter a few times, the man of the smell appears from a back room. Okay, he doesn't really smell any worse than most men, but I have a sensitive nose. I guess I'm just really lucky that Evgeny bathes a lot.

Before any of us can say anything, the man – middle aged, lean, and dirty blond – says, "You are English, yes?"

"*Nein*," I say, ready to explain were from North America, not England, but he doesn't give me the chance.

"But you speak English? This is good. I can practice. We have so few visitors, it is difficult for me to practice."

"We speak English," says Alex. "But you don't sound like you need practice."

"You are kind," he says. He shows us to a table and apologetically explains that breakfast is over and lunch not yet available, but he can bring us a selection of pastries.

"How am I supposed to practice my German when everyone insists on speaking English to us?" I mutter as he leaves to fetch our coffee, which is unfair, because the hotel clerk was quite happy to speak German with me.

When the man comes back, Alex says, "Do you know anything about a family named Holz?"

He frowns, and places each cup precisely in front of us, fusses to get the large plate of pastries in the exact middle of the table. The "selection" he promised looks like enough to feed us twice over. For several days.

"I think I have heard this name," he says. "But no Holzes live in

Schönstadt now." He looks up at the ceiling as if he might find enlightenment there.

"Holz. Hmm. Oh –" and now he looks right at Alex. "I *have* heard this name. Of course. The museum."

"Museum," says Alex.

"Yes, on the other side of town, right near the forest." I swear his voice drops in volume when he says "forest." "There is a small museum. A ... you would call it a local history museum, maybe? It is in a building that once was a toy shop. Many years ago, before my father's time, this shop was famous. People came from all over Europe to buy toys there. It was owned by a master toymaker, and they say he used witchcraft in his toys."

His voice *definitely* grows quiet when he says "witchcraft" and he glances to each side, like someone in a cheesy spy movie, checking to see if anyone is listening in.

"The *meister*, the master toy-maker, his name was Holz."

He leaves us then to enjoy our food and coffee in the otherwise empty room. As we're getting up to leave, though, he comes back and gives Alex a dusty, faded brochure.

"This is the museum," he says. Then, "What is your interest in this name, Holz? Are you a scholar, perhaps?"

"Sort of," says Alex. "But Holz was my ancestor."

"You are a Holz," he says. He's gone quiet again, almost whispering. "But surely ... that means ..." He clamps his mouth shut. Then he suddenly bows, a gesture that seems anachronistic even in this great big anachronism of a town. "No charge for your coffee," he says. "Can I get you any pastries to take along with you?" He grabs a paper bag out of the pocket in the front of his apron and starts filling it from the food we left on the table.

"Really, that's not necessary," says Alex. "How much –"

"No, I insist," he says, and makes as if to hand the now full bag to Alex. Midway through the gesture, he seems to change his mind and hands it to Li instead. "Please, with my compliments. It is good to see you back here again." He smiles at Li, tentatively. She looks confused, but smiles back.

"Thank you," says Alex. She sounds bewildered and I almost laugh, but I have to take pity on the café owner. He obviously knew all about the Holz family all along, despite pretending to have forgotten, and he can't get us out of there fast enough, but he's also desperate not to give offense.

Out in the street, I finally do laugh, Alex and Li look at me, puzzled, "He thinks you're a witch," I say. "Alex, he's afraid you'll curse him."

"I *am* a witch," she says.

"Yes," says Li, "but most people don't know that. They don't know about hexen. That man has heard legends of the Hexenwald all his life, I bet. He thinks you're a *fairytale* witch."

"I bet he was relieved you didn't sprout a big warty nose and glowing eyes."

"Oh ha, ha," says Alex. "If people are afraid of the name Holz, and the witch, why wasn't Herr Oberst at our hotel afraid of us?"

"He was awfully nice to us," I say.

"Maybe he's from out of town originally," says Li. "But I wonder why that man thought I'd been in the café before."

"All Asians look alike?" I say. "He must have had a Chinese visitor recently."

"He didn't seem to think he'd seen *you* before," she says.

"I don't look as Asian as you do," I say, and flash my cheesiest grin.

We stroll along the street, gawking at the postcard-perfect old buildings, as tourists are supposed to do. Li even snaps a few pictures on her cellphone. Finally, Alex hands me a piece of paper. It's the museum brochure.

"Can you read this?" she asks.

The front has a photograph of a ye-olde-looking shop. "Schönstadt Historical Museum," I say. "There's an address." Inside is a potted history of the town and area – pretty much what we had already read in Alex's guide book.

"Though most of the original toys are long gone, the master toy-maker's tools and workbench are still as they were when the last member of the family left Germany for America."

"Does it say when that was?" asks Li.

I shake my head. "Don't you know, Alex?'

"Mom never said. She didn't talk a lot about her family. Every now and then, when she was in a good mood, she'd tell me an old family story, but that was about it. When she got sick, she didn't say much at all."

"Sorry," I say.

She shrugs. "Old news," she says, but she seems grateful when Li takes her hand and twines their fingers together. "So what's that address?" she says.

I read it out and she checks her guide book. "Should be that way," she says, pointing. "Then left to the end of the road." We head the way she indicated, and it's not long before we're turning left onto a shady street with houses even older-looking than the ones nearer our hotel. I wouldn't have thought that possible.

"It's right on the edge of the Hexenwald," she says, and sure enough, a dark barricade of trees looms beyond the houses.

As we get close to the last house on the street, I can see that it's even more run-down looking than it is in the picture on the brochure. It was once brightly-painted, but the colors have faded and peeled. The sign over the door has come loose and hangs crooked, and the windows are dim and grimy.

"In Li's story," says Alex, "the toy shop was downstairs, and the house above. That looks right."

"I wonder if the whole place is a museum, or just the shop," says Li.

We stop and look at it from across the street. It looks forlorn. The sign in the window says "open" but no lights are on, like someone forgot to take the sign away when they closed up. Months ago. Years, even.

There's a bus stop here at the end of the street, though I can't imagine buses even coming here. The sign doesn't have numbers on it like a city bus stop; instead it has the names of neighboring towns. A faded sticker at the bottom of the sign says, "This stop no longer in service." The bench next to it is covered in fallen leaves and since it's now spring, they've been there since last year, at least.

Alex brushes some of them aside and sits down.

"Don't you want to see if anyone's there?" I say.

Li sits next to her. "It's worth asking, before we head into the woods," she says.

"I don't know," says Alex. "I'm nervous all of a sudden."

"Well," I say. "I'm curious. I'm going to go look in the window."

I leave them sitting on the bench and cross the street. Just as I'm about to step onto the cobbled sidewalk, a gust of wind blows up a little swirl of dust and I shiver.

Wasn't there something about cold winds always blowing in the Oktober Mountains in Alex's guide book? I guess that really wasn't just a folk legend.

Most of the front of the former toy shop is a big window. There are various things displayed there, like old agricultural instruments, a cider press, some hunting gear that makes my fox self nervous just to look at. Exactly the sort of thing you'd expect from a small local history museum.

There's also a large doll with a carved wooden face and a cloth body, dressed in what I guess must be the local traditional peasant costume. Not *lederhosen*, thankfully, but something that looks more like a dressed up version of a farmer's overalls and workshirt.

The sign next to it says "replica" and explains how the local toymaker – I notice he's not mentioned by name – was famous for the quality of his lifelike carved faces. I'm ridiculously relieved that the doll has ordinary brown hair and looks nothing like Alex or the creepy twins in my dream.

I turn to the door. It's all glass and beyond it there's an inner door, half wood with a big window. I can just see where there were once gilt letters that specify that it's a toy shop. And there, so faint most people probably wouldn't even notice it, the name Holz.

I'm turning to beckon to Alex when a movement on the other side of the glass startles me. I turn back to the door. A tiny old man is just closing another interior door, one to the left that presumably leads up to the house above. He straightens up and notices me. His eyebrows – huge and white – shoot up his forehead, and his mouth opens in an "O" of surprise.

He stares at me for the length of a few heartbeats, and then breaks out in a beaming great smile of proportions to match his eyebrows.

He says something and I hear a muffled, "*Guten tag.*" He opens the door and I have to step back out of the way.

"*Guten tag*," I say.

"Have you come to see my museum? How marvelous!"

I glance back to Alex and Li. They're watching from the bench, so I motion to them.

"We did," I say. "My friends and I are visiting and heard this was once a toy shop."

"Indeed it was," says the old man. He straightens himself up in pride, and he still doesn't reach my nose in height.

"Are you a relative?" I say. "Of the toymaker?"

"Heavens, no," he says. "It is terrible enough for the people of this town that I live in this house and use the toy shop for a museum." He leans forward and says, in a joke-conspiratorial fashion, "They thought the family were witches, you see." His eyes twinkle merrily. "They even made me take away all mentions of the family's name, is case it might summon them to return. How infantile is that?"

I can't help but smile back at him, and as Alex joins us, I take a chance and say, "This is my friend Alexandra Holz." I put my hand on Alex's shoulder.

She scowls and shakes her head sharply, but the old man smiles again and claps his hands together. "But how wonderful! Come inside and I will give you a tour. I only wish I had more of Meister Holz's own toys here." As we follow him in, he looks over to where Li is still sitting on the bench. She's got some paper spread out on her lap and is writing on it. More of her story, I hope.

"Will your friend not join us?"

"She's not a fan of museums," says Alex.

"Ah, that is too bad," says the old man. "But we cannot appeal to everyone."

"When you say Meister Holz," I say, "Is there one master toy maker in particular you refer to, or the whole family?"

"Ah, well, that is a good question," he says. "And to be truthful, I do not know the answer to it. There was supposed to be a family of toy makers named Holz, and I suppose many of them could have been masters of toymaking."

"There's a story in my family," says Alex. "One of the few stories my mother passed on, that one of my ancestors – a woman – defied the tradition of the time and became a toymaker herself. Not just soft dolls, but carving and all that."

"Yes, I have heard this," says the old man. "The last two Holzes who lived here were women, many decades ago. I think maybe this is why the townspeople believe the Holzes were witches."

"Because of course a woman who does a man's job must be a witch," I say.

He laughs. "Back then, that is exactly what people would think, yes. And this was only a few generations ago. Things are different now, and yet they still think a witch."

The old man shakes his head and leads us on a tour of the shop. First, we have to listen to stories about all the various farm implements and other items, but he's mercifully quick with that part of the tour. I think he's eager to show us the things that actually belonged to the Holz family, but he wants to save the best for last.

And then we're standing in front of a long, battered wooden workbench. More recent cuts in the wood show where it was once much longer – maybe even the whole length of the shop – but now it's about ten feet, and of a height that would be comfortable to work at standing up, or seated on a tall stool. On the wall behind the bench is hanging an assortment of tools, and scattered on its surface is a variety of doll parts in various stages of manufacture.

"Most of these are new," the old man says. "Replicas, you would say, yes?"

I nod.

"But I have one piece." He lifts a box down from a shelf and stands holding it. "I have not told you why I chose this place for my museum." His hands trace the angles of the box and he looks at it, not at us.

"It is a … a penance, I suppose," he says. He looks up and his watery old eyes are bright blue and sharp. "Not that I believe the old tales are literally true, but it still seems fitting." He pauses, looks from me to Alex and back.

"They say," he says, one gnarled finger tracing a design on the lid of the box. "Which is to say, the old tale goes, that one of the Meisters Holz made a bargain with the Witch of the Wald, to collect wood in the Hexenwald. It was supposed to be magic, that wood, and it made the best toys."

"But the toymaker was betrayed," says Alex. "And the family cursed."

"It is so, as the old story goes."

"But they were redeemed. By a girl, Rose-Perle."

"Yes," says the old man. "But my great-grandfather, many generations ago, he was the journeyman toymaker who took the witch's payment for himself. So you could say, if the old stories were true, then my family owes your family – owes all of Schönstadt – a debt."

Then he hands Alex the box. "This is a doll head carved by one of the Meister Holzes. I believe it was Rose-Perle who made it, before she disappeared into the Hexenwald for good."

I want to ask about Rose-Perle disappearing, but Alex has opened the box. Inside, resting on a bed of deep green linen, is a doll head. But it's not a human doll head. It's a fox. A flame-red, beautifully carved fox head. And suddenly, I can't breathe.

Chapter Thirteen

I STAGGER WHEN the familiar binding clamps down on my throat and catch myself on the edge of the work bench.

"Su?" says Alex. I feel her hand on my shoulder. At her touch, the binding lets go and I can breathe again.

"Is everything all right?" says the old man. "Are you ill?"

"I'm fine," I say, pushing myself away from the counter. "I'll be okay in a minute."

I look up and there is real concern in the old man's eyes. I force out a smile and hope it doesn't look too fake. "Just asthma," I say. "It hits me like that now and then."

The old man is holding the box again and the lid is closed, shutting away the sight of the doll head. The fox head. Why would the sight of it have such a sudden and terrible affect on me, on the bond that keeps me leashed to Alex?

I catch her eye and she quirks an eyebrow. She doesn't know, either.

"You should get some rest, maybe," says the old man. "I would make you some tea, but I was about to go buy some when you arrived. Perhaps coffee? Or juice? I have local apple juice. Very good."

"Thank you," says Alex. "But that's all right. We should go back to our hotel so Su can rest."

He nods uncertainly.

"We've already taken up too much of your time," I say.

"Can we make a donation to the museum? An admission fee?" says Alex.

"Oh, no," says the old man. "No, you are my guests." He looks thoughtfully at the box in his hands. "I would like to give to you this doll's head. It belonged to your ancestors, to your family. Your great-grandmother, perhaps. You should have it." He holds out the box to Alex.

"Oh, I can't," she says. "It should stay here. This was her house, her workshop."

He shakes his head, and keeps holding out the box. "My child, I would give you this house, too, but then where would I live? At least I can give you this one thing. Maybe I will put you in my will for the house." He laughs at Alex's shocked expression.

"I am a very old man, yes? I won't live for many more years. Even now, few visitors come here. But you, you are a *Holz*. This is the place of your ancestors, and I want you to have this small token. Please."

Reluctantly, Alex takes the box, and I'm glad when she doesn't open it again.

"But you never told me *your* name, child," he says, turning to me.

"Su," I say. "Su Fuchs." I almost cringe, thinking about the guy in the airport and his comments about my name.

For a moment, he looks taken aback, and I think he's thinking the same things as that obnoxious airport security monkey. Then he looks worried. Finally, he smiles. "Maybe I will become superstitious in my old age. You know what this name means? Fuchs?"

"Fox," I say.

"A descendant of a witch, and a fox," he says. "I wonder who is your friend who waits for you outside, so intent on her papers?"

Alex smiles. "No one, and everyone." Her voice is soft and the old man looks at her knowingly.

"Ah, I see," he says. "Well, daughter of witches, and daughter of foxes, if you decide to walk in the Hexenwald, the best path is the one that leaves from my back door."

"Do you walk there often?" says Alex.

"Not as often as I once did," he says. "When I was younger, I imagined 'what if I met the witch?' What would I say so she would forgive my ancestor and restore the good name of Meister Holz, restore the fortunes of Schönstadt?"

"Did you ever meet her?" says Alex.

He laughs. "I think that in order to meet a witch, one must first believe in witches."

"Have any of the townspeople met her?" I ask. "They seem to believe."

His laughter becomes even more merry. "You know, I do not think any have. Not for a few generations."

We thank him, then, and he still refuses our offer to donate money to the museum. He follows us out the door, then slowly makes his way down the street towards the center of town as we cross back to where Li waits.

"What happened in there?" Alex says, hefting the box a little in her hands, as if to test its weight.

I shake my head. "I just saw that thing and couldn't breathe. Like the familiar binding suddenly tightened up."

We try to explain it to Li, who says, "One more thing to ask your witch." Then she hands me a stack of papers, so hastily written on it takes me a minute to get used to her writing.

"It's a continuation of the past part," she says. "Same weirdness."

"Doll sex?" I say. Alex glares at me. I *am* talking about her ancestors, after all.

Rinde could hardly look at Joringel all that day. She had woken sometime in the very early morning and had at first thought the moans were a continuation of her dreams. Then she had thought Jor was in pain and even jumped out of bed to rush to him.

She had her hand on the doorknob before she recognized the creaking bedsprings and realized he was masturbating – violently, it sounded like – and the moans were not of pain, but of intense pleasure.

Her skin had flushed hot in the cool air, and she had opened the window, easing the pane upward so as not to make a sound. She leaned out and tried to let the night sounds of the nearby forest drown out Jor's pleasure, but the Wald was too distant.

Eventually he stopped. Rin considered going for a walk in the wood anyway, to banish the echo of his moans from her thoughts, but she remembered all the cautions her mother and father had schooled into her. It was quiet in the house now – Rinde hoped Joringel was asleep, and what man wouldn't fall immediately to slumber after a release such as that one had sounded?

She slid the window shut except for a crack and got back into bed, careful not to make it creak. The doll seemed to be watching her from atop the dresser and she wanted to turn its face away, but instead she had put her head under her pillow and ignored it until she fell asleep.

In the morning she bustled and chattered and hardly let Joringel say a word. She was silent only when they reached the graveyard and the minister – a much kinder person than the stern old lady at the town hall – had lead them to the far corner of the graveyard and said some words of prayer with them.

Both the church and the cemetery were ancient, as old as anything in Shönstadt, and older than most of it. Many of the gravestones were worn smooth by time and weather, but even those upon which the names and dates could no longer be read were neat and tidy and the grave plots well cared for. The grass was nowhere mown, but it was full of late-blooming wildflowers and three contented sheep wandered about, grazing it to a pleasing height. It was the loveliest place in Shönstadt that Rinde had yet encountered.

She let Joringel take her hand as they listened to the minister's words and when the ordained man left them there by the grave, she let Jor keep holding her hand. For a long time they stood and looked at the two graves, side-by-side in a cluster of other gravestones bearing the name Holz.

"Our family's been here a long time," said Rinde, just as Joringel said, "Why didn't they want us?" His grip on her hand tightened, and Rinde stepped closer and leaned her head on his shoulder.

"Something happened, when we were children," she said.

"But they didn't send us away just then," said Jor. "I remember."

Rinde turned her face into Jor's jacket. He smelled like soap, she noticed, and of the cold Oktober Mountains wind. She had never noticed before what he smelled like, or had never allowed herself to. "I remember . . ." she began, her voice muffled in Jor's shoulder. She paused as Joringel let go of her hand to put his arm around her and draw her close. Here, now, it was all right. Grieving over their parents' grave, a brother and sister could hold each another closely in consolation. She put her arms around his waist and felt his leanness.

She tried again to put memories into words. "One of the earliest things I remember was an old lady in black and green looking at us. She had something to do with . . . with whatever took away father's joy in toymaking."

"I thought she was a witch," said Jor.

"The Witch of the Wald," said Rinde, and Joringel shuddered. She shifted her feet to press more of herself against him, to warm him from the fear she knew he felt. He had always been afraid of the Hexenwald, and of the witch, as a child.

He wrapped his arms tightly around her. "She frightened me," he said. And then, as if he was just remembering, he added, "I dreamed of her last night."

Rinde stiffened. She had also dreamed of the witch. There was something she must give the witch, in her dream. Something that would save the village of Shönstadt from a terrible fate. Something very dear, that would wound her to give, but it was the only thing that would begin to make up for the tragedies their father's misplaced trust had caused.

"A pearl beyond price," she and Joringel whispered together.

"But what is it?" she wondered.

"A huge big pearl," Jor said. "Though every gem can be priced, so it would have to be spectacular." His voice had a peculiar note that Rinde couldn't identify, but she suspected there was more to his dream than he would tell her, even if she asked for details. Maybe even . . . maybe something to do with his moans that had awakened her. Her skin flushed at the thought and she wanted to pull away, to run from Joringel and hide in the woods. She felt him warm against her and there was a faint stirring at his crotch and she wanted to shriek in shame and flee. And she also wanted to feel him grow hard against her.

The idea of making love to her own brother filled her with disgust, yet she couldn't deny he was a handsome young man, and he knew her as no one else could. How easy it would be to give in, to let him love her, fuck her, pleasure her. And she had no doubt there would be pleasure. No one else ever need know. He would surely tell no one. She felt his lips on her neck and shuddered. She was nauseated and aroused at once. She wanted to raise her mouth to his, and she wanted to hit him, to knock some sense into him. It would not, must not, be.

Finally, she disentangled herself. There was still paperwork to track down and legal matters to settle before they could explore their old home fully. Joringel clung for a moment, and as her hip slid away she felt how hard his erection had grown.

But then he let her go, and he followed when she headed back into the village to look for the solicitor's office, where their parents had left their will on file. The man had been, it seemed, a family friend. It was a simple will – everything had been left to the twins, to hold jointly or divide between them equally – and the paperwork was relatively easy. After the signing was done, Rinde sat back in her chair and regarded Herr Ehrlichmann solemnly.

"Our parents never told us why they sent us away," she said. "Perhaps, Herr, you might give us some clue."

The solicitor looked uncomfortable. "They did not inform me of any specific reason," he said. "But around that time an affliction came on the children of Shönstadt, and I believe they wanted to spare you its effects."

Rinde was able to get little more out of the man, save that the sickness seemed only to affect children of this one village, and though more children were born, they always died young. No doctor had been able to determine a cause. The people – and here the solicitor spoke hesitatingly, as if unsure how much he should tell them – the people said it was the curse of the Hexenwald. He could not, or would not, thought Rinde, say what the cause of the curse was supposed to have been. It fit too neatly with her dreams and her childhood memories to be comfortable.

"That explains why the people here are so hostile," said Joringel. "We lived when their children didn't."

"Hostile?" said Rinde. "Only that old frau at the town hall was hostile. We've hardly spoken to anyone else."

Jor got that triumphant look he always had when he did something better than she did, which happened seldom enough that Rinde allowed him his victory without comment. "Haven't you noticed?" he said. "Every street we walk down, people look at us from behind their curtains, and glare."

Rinde hadn't noticed, but she did after that, and she began to think she didn't want to stay here after all, no matter how much like home it felt.

The mountains cast their early shadow over Shönstadt as the twins walked back to the Holz house. The gas to the lamps was back on, so they didn't have to eat by candle-light, but Rinde still decided to go to bed early. There was much to think about, and she was confused, and having to make conversation with Joringel was making her uneasy for the first time in her life. So when they had eaten, Rinde selected a book of fairytales – Oktober Mountains fairytales – from the sitting room shelf, and left Jor looking through old photo albums, and went up to bed.

She looked through the book for anything about the Hexenwald or its witch and found nothing until more than halfway through. It was just a short passage, and said little, only that the Hexenwald was named for a witch who, from ancient times, had aided those who kept to her rules and treated her with respect, and cursed any who crossed her or violated a bargain. She was not evil, the book said, she merely had her own code, like a fairy, and could be baneful or beneficial depending on how she was treated.

Rinde set the book aside. There were other folklore books in the family library; surely one of them would have more information. Rinde was a modern woman and would have said she was not superstitious. Yet she had been born a child of the Oktober Mountains and raised to respect the Wald and its witch. Being back here, on the very edge of the forest, filled her with odd feelings and fears, and her dream last night would have her believe that her father's journeyman had betrayed his trust and brought down a curse on Shönstadt and its children. A curse that had only spared Rinde and Joringel, and that only their family – the twins were the only two left of the Holzes of Shönstadt – could break.

And who even used silver coins these days?

She closed her eyes and put such thoughts away, and instead her mind was filled with Joringel. How nice he had smelled, how warm he had been, the gentle touch of his lips on her neck. She opened her eyes and met the carved gaze of the Joringel-doll. She could just reach out and touch one carved bare foot. It was warm. Even as a child she had never needed the comfort of dolls, but now she felt that holding something soft would be nice, especially if it was something that didn't want anything back from her.

She sat up and pulled the doll into bed with her, curled around it like spooning with a child, and she immediately felt better. The doll smelled just like Joringel – soap and the Oktober Mountains wind – but it was not shameful now. It was nice. Rinde fell quickly to sleep.

She woke to Joringel's voice, yet it was not quite his voice. Somehow, in the night, the doll had got turned around and now it faced her in the bed.

"My love," she was sure she heard it say, though not aloud.

She smiled. Of course, she had only seemed to wake. She had been dreaming of the witch again, and this was a part of it. The Joringel-doll was witch-wood, after all.

"Mmm?" she replied, sleepy and warm. She closed her eyes.

"Let me love you," he said. "And I will give you a pearl beyond price."

"So I can save the village?" Her lips brushed wood and she opened her eyes again. The doll's head was level with hers, and he had grown to man-size. His carved wooden lips were warm and dry against her mouth.

"Yes," he said, though she didn't feel his lips move.

"How?"

"The pearl will save Shönstadt," he said, and now his lips did move, but only to press against hers, to slide his wooden tongue in and kiss her until she burned. "You only need possess it."

"Then give it me," she said, reaching out to embrace the Joringel-doll. "And I will help save Shönstadt, even if it means giving the pearl to the witch."

"You may not like it when it comes to that," he said.

Rinde pressed her mouth to his wooden lips hungrily, pressed her body to his canvas-and-goosedown and discovered he had been equipped with a carved wooden cock, erect and ready for her. How had she not noticed it before now?

She lifted her mouth from his only to say, "It would save the children?"

"Yes," he said.

"Then I will do it," she said.

"Then you must love me," he said.

"Gladly."

Rinde tugged her nightdress off and undressed the doll. His arms and legs had been carved with beautiful smooth muscle and were sanded silky-soft. She laid him on his back and looked wonderingly at the erect penis of dark smooth wood, gleaming faintly in the moonlight, that stood proud from the doll's crotch.

She pushed aside the thought that her father must have carved it and took it in her hand. It was so warm it was almost hot. She looked at the Joringel-doll's face and he seemed to smile. She smiled back, then bent and put her mouth on the wooden cock. It was smooth against her tongue and she sucked on it, played with it as if it belonged to a living man. This was her dream, after all, and she could do as she liked. It was only too bad the doll had such limited ability to move.

"Oh, my love, yes," she heard his voice say. "Suck me, love me, fuck me," he said.

She let the cock slide out of her mouth, then touched its tip to one nipple, then the other, using it to tease and arouse herself. She pinned it between her breasts for a moment, held them around it with both hands, and tweaked her own nipples.

"My love," the doll said. "Make me yours."

"Oh, I will," Rinde said. She released her breasts, watched the wooden cock bob against the doll's canvas belly, then crawled up the bed to lie atop him.

"Now love," he said. "Love me."

She kissed his wooden mouth, felt it open to her, and straddled the doll to slide herself against his hardness. Her fluids made it slippery, made it glorious, and for long moments, she slid over him and over him until she was about to come. She trembled on the edge of orgasm, and he said, "Fuck me, my sister, my lover. Fuck me and take this pearl." She looked at his beautiful glistening member and saw that, indeed, a pearl did seem to shine in the moonlight, trembling at its tip, and she twitched her hips in just such a way that the wooden cock slid inside her. She sat up, throwing off the blankets, and thrust again and again, letting the smooth wood fill her over and over.

With one hand she caressed a nipple, and with the other she sought her center of pleasure and rubbed while she fucked the Joringel-doll.

She couldn't help but cry out as orgasms washed over her like trembling waves. She thought she felt a hot spurt inside her, but that could just be her own wetness – could you even feel a man come? – and how could a doll ejaculate, anyway?

For while, Rinde sat braced over the doll, feeling her muscles clenching and unclenching around the wooden penis. Then she slid off the doll and curled up next to it in bed, and fell asleep.

She woke again – for real this time, she thought – a little later, and the Joringel-doll watched her from the dresser-top, fully clothed. She heard Joringel – the living Joringel – on the other side of the wall, bed creaking.

"Oh god," she heard him say. She thought she should feel embarrassed, awkward, to hear him masturbating again, but she was not. Her hand strayed briefly to her crotch, but she was still satisfied from fucking the doll – but that had been a dream – that she felt no need to rub herself off.

She curled up and listened until Jor's moans stopped and he was still, then she began to drift off again. Just before she fell asleep, she peered at the Joringel-doll through half-closed eyelids.

"So where's my pearl beyond price?" she said.

She might already have been asleep when he answered. "Don't worry, my beloved. You shall have her in nine months' time."

Chapter Fourteen

EVEN THOUGH I'M expecting the story to be much the same as the last part, only from the sister's point of view, it's still weird enough to creep me out. Alex has one fucked up ancestral family, but I can't exactly tell her that.

"Fuck," she says, when she hands the last page back to Li. "I really wish I didn't know that about my family. I think I'm starting to regret this whole trip." She looks down at the box she's holding on her lap, that the old man in the museum gave her. The one that holds the fox head. Fox *doll* head, sure, but *that* gives me the creeps, too, beautiful as I could see it is, even from the brief glimpse I had.

Alex looks up at me. "Sorry," she says. "I only regret this part. Not the part where we figure out how to free you."

"Unfortunately," says Li, putting her hand over Alex's, "It seems like there's no way to learn that without also learning about the people you come from."

Alex nods.

"Now what?" I say. I'm eager to get into the forest, to drop into my four-legged shape and run in the shadows. It's not an overwhelming urge, I just *like* being a fox. Not that I would want to be one all the time, though. Besides messy human sex with my sweet and delicious boyfriend, my two-legged form does have its own advantages. Thinking, for one thing. I *like* thinking, and that's way easier with a human brain than with a fox brain, even if a *hexenfuchs* is considerably more sentient than a regular fox.

Alex taps the top of the box. "Fancy an experiment?"

"You want me to look at that thing again?" My hand goes to my throat before I even think about what I'm doing.

"If we can figure out why it affects you the way it did, it might help us figure out how the familiar binding works. And if I'm expecting something to happen, I can be paying attention."

"Let me sit down first," I say. I step closer to the bench, but instead Alex gets up.

"I thought we could walk into the forest a little," she says. "For privacy." She glances around. The windows in the nearest houses look empty, but she's right. Anyone could be watching.

I take a deep breath. I don't like the idea. I want to stay very far away from that decapitated fox, or whatever you call the bit that's decapitated *from* the fox. Yeah, okay, fox head. There should be a better word. Fox decapitation, as a noun instead of a verb, maybe.

Honestly, though, I'm also intrigued by it. I think back to the dreams of Alex's ancestors and to Li's stories and try to remember if there are any foxes in them. I know they're connected, Alex's family and *hexenfuchs*, but I know that from dreams about my own ancestors, not from dreams about hers.

"Okay," I finally say. "Just don't let me stop breathing for good."

"I know CPR," says Li, then blushes, as if realizing how silly that sounds when we're talking about witch magic. But I find it comforting just the same.

We cross the street again, back to the museum, the former Holz toy shop, and then go around to the back. There's a small square of lawn, neatly trimmed and surrounded by a hedge of something prickly. Holly. A path of random-looking flagstones leads from the back door of the shop to an ironwork gate in the hedge. Beyond the gate is the gloom of the forest.

A cold breeze wafts through and brings me the scent of the forest, and it's the most intoxicating thing I've ever smelled. I could drop my human shape and run away in red fur and never look back.

It's then, I think, that I realize this trip is dangerous. That it's more than just a genealogical investigation. We're looking for a sort of … dammit, I don't want to say "magic," but there is no other word. We're looking for a kind of magic that none of us really knows anything about. I don't know if Alex is ready for what she may find. I know I'm not ready.

But the only way through is forward. Further up and further in. For an instant I remember reading that to my sister Kristine. Kit. She was old enough to read to herself, but since she was little we've taken turns reading to each other. Not everything. Just the special books. *The Wind in the Willows. The Secret Garden.* The entire chronicles of Narnia. Neither of us noticed the Christian allegory – to us it was just a beautiful series with magic and courage. *Further up and further in.* I just hope this witch we're heading for is more Aslan and less White Witch.

I realize abruptly that we're all three clustered by the gate, staring through the hedge, and none of us is moving to go through.

"Okay," I say, and it's like a spell has broken. I step forward, taking the lead for once, and open the gate.

I supposed I was expecting some sudden change to happen after taking that step, but the forest side of the gate is merely shadier than the yard side. I can do this.

There's a narrow path ahead, which is good, because even though the trees are huge, there's enough light here at the edge of the forest that the undergrowth is thick. I turn back to make sure that Li and Alex are following. They're right behind me, looking so solemn I want to laugh, but that seems inappropriate somehow. And I realize I was wrong; it is different on the forest side of the gate. It's *hushed.* There are birds, and they sing, but it doesn't sound to me like the raucous din I'm used to from the park back home. It's as if every bird is careful to sing perfectly, like a trained choir and not like a schoolyard full of enthusiastic children.

If nothing else, that should tell us something about this Witch of the Wald we're going to look for. I feel the first stirrings of fear in my gut. I wish I had someone's hand to hold, but Alex has Li now, and Evgeny is far away.

We walk into the muffled wood, following the path. It doesn't branch or wander, it just heads right into the forest, until we're deep enough in that the light is dim and very little undergrowth crowds between the tree trunks. Then the path is less obvious, just a somewhat more tamped-down ribbon across the forest floor. Here's where we could start to get lost.

I breathe deep and let my fox nature out a little. I wish I thought to bring one pair of jeans with a hole in the back, so I could let my tail out, too. But at least I can let my fox abilities make a scent map as we walk along, so even if I lose track of direction I'll still be able to bring us back the way we came.

"Why's it so quiet?" Li's voice is a whisper.

"It's a witch wood," says Alex. "Maybe that's why."

A little farther on and we come to a clearing. Or what was once a clearing. The trees are much smaller than in the rest of the forest, but it's been a long time since this place was fully open to the sky. Still, a little sunlight filters down, and there are smaller plants and grasses. And a few tree stumps.

There are other signs of human interference. The stumps are cut, partly by axe, partly by saw, and there are cut boards, warped and rotted by time, but still neatly stacked for drying under a blanket of ivy. I trip over a rusted saw blade.

We stop. "I wonder if this is where Meister Holz cut wood," Alex says softly. None of us wants to speak loudly here, I think.

"It could be," says Li.

"Who else would dare come here?" I say. "If the townspeople back then were as afraid of … you know … as they are now." For some reason, I can't bring myself to say "the witch" here in the forest. As if it might call her. I've suddenly gone all superstitious and anyway, we want to find the witch. It's why we're here.

"Let's stop here," says Alex. "It feels … safer."

We sit together on the patch of grass at the center of the former clearing, our backs to the small trees, and Alex puts the box between us.

I stare at it. The fear gnaws my belly again but I push it away. The only way out is through. Further up and further in.

"Li," says Alex. "Can you open the box so I can focus on Su?"

Out of the corner of my eye, I catch the small movement of Li's nod. I keep staring at the lid of the box. I make myself breathe. Kung fu breathing exercises. I barely hear when Alex asks if I'm ready.

"Yes," I say, and Li opens the box.

I can't breathe, but I'm not afraid. Here, now, breathing is not important. I feel the collar of the familiar binding tight on my throat. It should be choking me – I feel the pressure, but it doesn't bother me. I seem to be *paused*, floating in limbo.

Alex's presence is close, not quite *in* my head, but nearby. She's watching me through the binding and I know she can feel what I'm feeling. I feel safe, protected.

In that moment, the binding feels so perfectly right I'm ready to give in to it completely, to become Alex's possession entirely. It would be so easy.

But there's something else that holds my attention. The box. No, what's *inside* the box. A fox head looks at me, amber glass eyes meeting mine. It is perfectly carved, the wood so cunningly worked it looks like fur, soft and warm. And even though it's just a head alone, it looks alive.

I reach out and touch it, and it *is* warm. It *is* soft. It is *alive*. I jerk my hand back. It looks at me, and blinks its sad eyes. It has eyes like mine, rich orange-brown with vertical-slit pupils, like a cat's, but in the shadows of the forest the pupils have expanded so they're almost round. Then a breeze rustles the branches overhead and the shadows shift, the pupils in the glass eyes contract to pointed narrow ellipses.

I reach out again, touch the fox head. It feels like fur and carved wood at the same time. *This* is not the *hexen* abilities I know. Every bit of *other* lore I've ever found, or heard, or ferreted out of an old book says magic isn't real. What *hexen* can do is use a little psychic power, some mental tricks, some tweaking of the threads of probability, and nothing more. Not that that is a minor thing; you can do a lot by changing people's perceptions, or by making one outcome more likely than another. You can cause revolutions, plagues, even.

But this fox head, this is something else. Something real. Magic.

I lift it out of the box, hold it close to my face, and breathe in. It smells like wood, not one that I'm familiar with. Not oak, or ash, or pine. It smells like the old man's hedge. Holly. And it smells like fox. A female fox.

Suddenly I want to cry.

She blinks at me, that fox, but if she can speak, she doesn't. She just looks at me, eyes full of sorrow. Then her eyes shift, towards Li. She blinks, then turns her eyes the other way, towards Alex. I turn her head a little, so she doesn't have to strain. Then I see something else in her look besides sadness.

There is fear, and wonder, and finally, there is *hope*.

Then the fox head is just a beautifully-carved chunk of wood in my hands and the fact that I'm not breathing becomes a problem.

I drop the fox doll head as my hands go to my neck and I try to breathe. Can't … breathe …

Then Alex is there, her hands on my shoulders, and there is cool air flooding my lungs and everything is okay. For the moment.

"Holy crap," I say, when I am capable of speech again.

"Yeah," says Alex. "You okay?"

I nod. I look at the fox head. Just dead wood now. Carved and painted and lovely, but not alive. Or at least dormant. I reach out, run my fingers over it. Who was this fox? Was she ever alive, or only animated by magic? Is she related to me, or just something one of Alex's ancestors created? I lift it, put it back in the box, and shut the lid.

"What happened?" says Li. "You both went completely still, not even breathing. It seemed like forever."

Neither Alex or I say anything. I don't even know how to *begin* to explain what happened.

"I was ready to start giving you both artificial respiration," Li says.

"It was weird," says Alex. I let her try to fill Li in on what just happened, glad that she was experiencing it along with me. I suppose I should stay and listen, because she might have seen something I didn't, but suddenly I'm restless.

I get up and walk around the clearing, looking into the woods. From here, the faint path splits, but it's impossible to tell, no matter how I peer into the gloom, where each fork might lead.

I make myself stand still then, where the path leaves the clearing, and

I slowly open my senses to the forest. I'm cautious, because who knows how a witch might react to someone surveilling her woods, even if said witch is probably expecting that someone.

I can feel the age of the trees. The ones here in the clearing count their years as a century, two centuries, a little more, or very much less. But farther out in the Hexenwald are ancient giants, living slow tree lives, and ignoring the brief, bright flickers of faster-paced life.

This place is so *old*. I know from reading that a lot of Europe has been populated by humans for so long my mind can hardly fathom it, and for just as long, humans have been altering the landscape. But *this* forest is untouched. Any alterations beyond a few clearings and a slow, creeping contraction of its borders have been by natural processes.

The Hexenwald feels like a place that has been inhabited by – guarded by – witches since humans and *others* first adventured out of Africa and onto other continents.

All around, I feel life. The insects, bacteria, fungi, plants, are so innumerable I can't hold them all in my mind. They're like bright sparks flickering in my peripheral vision.

Birds are in the hundreds, thousands, more. They're quiet, for birds, but they go about their lives just the same. In my senses, they are like crackles of tiny lightning – static charges in the blanket of trees.

I find badgers, hedgehogs, feral cats, mice, weasels, deer. Too many animals to name. I do not find foxes, and I do not find a witch.

But just before Alex and Li join me on the path, I *do* find a blank spot in the heart of the woods.

It's a glimpse so brief I wonder if I've imagined it. But what other direction do we have?

"We take the path to the left," I say.

"We should have prepared better," says Li. All we have are a bottle of water each and the bag of pastries left from breakfast.

"Maybe we should come back tomorrow, with proper supplies," says Alex.

I push back the urge to take fox shape and run, to leave them behind. Or at least to leave Li behind. I don't think I *can* leave Alex behind, no matter how fast I run.

"It's still early," I say. I look up, but of course I can't see the sky, just branches and way, way overhead, leaves. I can sense the time, though. We have hours of daylight left. If you can call the gloom of the forest "daylight."

"Why don't we follow the path a little ways?" I say. "We can turn back if it gets too late and we still haven't found anything, then come back tomorrow."

Alex looks at me oddly, but she nods. "Are you sure you're okay, after that?" She nods back towards the clearing. The box is still in the dappled shade at the center.

"Yeah," I say. "I actually feel better."

"Okay," she says, and turns back to fetch the box, while Li grabs the bag of pastries.

As I turn back to face the forest, a glint near my feet catches my eye. I bend over and look, and directly between the toes of my boots, almost buried in the dirt and leaves, is something silver. I pick it up. It's a coin, dull black where it was exposed to the elements. Where it was protected by the earth, the coin is shiny silver, and I can make out words. I'm not familiar with the currency, though I can tell the language is German, and there's a big, fancy number one on it. The other side has a raised design of oak leaves and a blackletter H, so old-fashioned it takes me a while to figure out which letter it is.

For some reason I can't explain, instead of showing it to Alex and Li, I slip it into my pocket. *Silver coins for the witch*, I think. You never know when that might come in handy, especially when you're looking for one. I wonder if the "H" is for *hexen* or *Hexenwald* or something else altogether. Maybe it's for *Holz*.

We set off under the trees, and I find myself leading the way again. Even Alex is deferring to me, though she's the one who planned this whole trip, and I'm supposed to be *her* familiar, *her* servant.

It's hard to keep from breaking into a run. I can feel the cold breeze on my face and the backs of my hands. I swear I can feel it creep under my clothes until I'm all goosepimples.

It's glorious, that breeze. It smells like autumn, even though it's early spring by the calendar and the forest is full of sprouting, growing things. I wonder if the Oktober Mountains got their name from that autumnal wind.

Also, it smells like freedom.

"Hey, wait up," Alex calls, and I realize I've started walking faster without realizing it. I slow down, shake my head. *No.* It would be too easy to lose myself here.

That thought brings back the fear I felt earlier, and this time I don't push it aside. I let it build into an uncomfortable lump in my belly to remind me that I am not just a fox that can take a two-legged shape. I am much more than a fox. I have a human life, too, and friends. A lover. A *beloved.*

And tears spring to my eyes suddenly when I realize that I have let myself forget that I have – or at least had – a younger sister. A sister who, slim though the chance may be, could still be alive.

I'm repeating that to myself in my head – *remember Kit* – when I hear Alex call out again, and I stop. But she's not asking me to wait, she's looking around in bewilderment. She looks at her own hand, then at me.

"Where's Li?" she says.

Chapter Fifteen

ALEX AND I face each other in the shade of ancient trees, bewildered. We're so deep in, now, that the undergrowth is limited to fungi and a few thin strands of ivy and creeper. Back the way we came, a brighter, greener patch marks where the old clearing is, where there is a little sun, and more growing things beneath the canopy far overhead.

In every other direction, there is undulating forest floor, carpeted in years of shed dried leaves. Unless she stepped behind one of the massive grey-brown tree trunks, there is nowhere Li could have hidden.

"We were holding hands," says Alex. "And then suddenly she wasn't there."

She turns in place, takes a few steps away, then tries another direction.

"Alex," I say. I extend my *hexenfuchs* senses into the forest, searching for Li, for a human presence. There is Alex, and … nothing. No, there is something, faint and moving away from us more quickly than a walking human would.

"I think," I say, then stop. It's Li. I *think* it's Li, but somehow her presence doesn't feel right. I try to remember what she felt like before. Quiet, soft, gentle, strong. With the faintest cinnamon scent of magic. The presence I feel is that, but it doesn't seem quite human. It reeks of vanilla and anise and other spices I can't name, so strongly that the parts that feel like Li are almost overwhelmed.

There's a similar presence much closer by, flickering into being. Not sort-of human, though. Sort-of fox. I look at the box in Alex's hand. I shake my head. Whatever presence is masking Li, it's not hiding her completely, and whatever it is, it has also touched the fox doll. I can follow Li. *We* can follow Li.

"She's still heading the same direction," I say, finally. I want to tell Alex how strange Li feels in my wider senses, but the words don't come out. I want to tell her to feel what I feel through the familiar binding, but my tongue won't shape the sounds.

The ball of fear in my belly blossoms, making my limbs feel shaky.

"Are you okay?" says Alex.

I try to smile. Li has just vanished and she asks if *I'm* okay.

"Let's go find Li," I say. "And meet this witch."

We walk quickly, side by side, following the faint path. There's something pale on the ground ahead, like a misshapen mushroom, so we stop and look. It smells sweet.

Alex bends over, then straightens with a frown creasing her forehead.

"Pastry?" she says. There's another one farther up the trail, then another.

I laugh. I can't help it. Overwhelmed by something – the witch, maybe, or some other thing that lurks in this wood – and Li still has the presence of mind to try to leave a trail.

Alex looks hurt, so I say, "Hansel and Gretel," and her look changes to confusion. She stares at the torn-off hunk of breakfast sweet in her hand.

Then she laughs, too. "Good thing you can follow her without this, though," she says, pointing ahead. There are several drab brown birds pecking at the pastry bits. One flies up as we approach, lands on Alex's hand when she holds it out, and pecks at the pastry she still holds. Then it opens its beak and sings the loveliest song I've ever heard.

Except I *have* heard that song before, in a dream of my *hexenfuchs* ancestor. She was running an errand for her witch mistress, to fetch back a little brown songbird. It was then, under a tree full of cheerful birds, that she met the young man who would capture her heart, and who would father her half-human child.

I can't breathe, but this time it isn't the familiar bond. It's an overwhelming sense of wonder. I guess maybe I never fully accepted those dreams as real. They were too fantastic, and I was still trying to fit my own magic into the framework of the others – weres, vamps, and witches.

But seeing those little birds, hearing their song, I know those dreams were real. I come from a pairing that should have been impossible by every law I know of how the world works, human and other.

"Are you okay?" says Alex, again, and realize I stopped moving to listen to the bird.

"Yeah," I say. "Let's hurry."

The birds fly away as we stride along the path, and I don't look behind to see if they settle back down to their pastry feast when we've passed.

Darkness sneaks up on us. I couldn't see the appearance of dusk due to the already dim light under the trees, and for the first time since I woke on a cold park bench with my memory gone, I don't even *feel* the twilight.

They may call midnight the witching hour, but twilight, the hours between night and sunrise and between sunset and night again, is the true magic time. And that's when even ordinary foxes are most active.

I should have felt dusk coming, but I didn't. We've been walking for hours, and it feels like minutes, and suddenly it's dark.

"How did it get so late?" says Alex, her voice hushed.

"It's a witch wood, I guess," I say. I try to keep my voice light, like it doesn't matter, but it *does* matter. It bothers me more than I can say that I didn't notice the time passing.

Alex walks closer and closer to me, finally putting her hand on my arm. At first I think she's scared, but I realize I've started to be able to sense her emotions through the familiar bond, and that's not it. Well, she *is* scared, but the kind of scared that makes a person braver, not the kind that makes them crave comfort.

But of course it's dark, and witches have only human eyesight. I can see perfectly well, but she must be completely blind. I walk a little slower so she won't feel like she could walk into a tree at any moment, but I really want to break into a run. I want to get wherever it is we're going, because night in the countryside under the forest canopy will soon bring a darkness so deep even my fox vision will be seriously impaired. Sure, I've got other senses, but humans are visual creatures and I'm still mostly human.

I open my wider senses again to the forest. I wish I could just keep them open all the time, but it's too much information to take in constantly, and I'm not practiced enough at it to keep it up while still paying attention to my immediate surroundings. We're moving slowly enough now that I should be able to do this without braining myself on a branch or something.

Li's presence isn't moving any more, and she isn't too far ahead. For a brief moment, I think I sense that emptiness I felt before, but it's gone before I'm sure. That's close by, too. I shiver involuntarily and my senses contract back to normal again.

"We're close," I say.

"To Li, or to the witch?" says Alex.

"Both, I think."

We almost trip over her. Li is sitting with her back to a tree, legs splayed out in front of her, empty paper bag crumpled up in one hand. It's her leg Alex catches a toe on, but we aren't walking fast enough for her to even stumble.

"Li!" Alex says. She drops to her knees next to her girlfriend.

Li doesn't respond. Her eyes are open, but she stares into the darkness, head turned to look in the direction we were headed.

"Su, can you tell if she's hurt? I can barely see her." Alex sounds like she's holding in worry, forcing calm on herself.

I step over Li's legs and kneel on her other side. She looks okay. I'm in her line of vision now, but she seems to stare right through me.

Last time Alex and I had dealings with witches in the woods, people died, and Evgeny ended up with a demon trapped inside his head.

I inhale. The heady scent of exotic spices that cloaked Li's presence in my wider senses is gone. I don't smell blood or fear, so she's not physically harmed.

I inhale again, deeper, then deeper still. I smell the human warmth of her skin, the faint jasmine of her shampoo, the sugar of the pastries. Not only is the stronger magic smell gone, but so is the faint cinnamon hint I smelled on Li before. If she has any magic, like we thought she might, it's not active now.

"She's not hurt," I say. I touch her neck, gently. I don't need to feel her pulse to know her heart is beating, I can feel it before I touch her. It's slow, but strong. Her breathing is even and quiet.

I try my *hexenfuchs* senses again, and she's there, human and alive, but faint even though she's right next to me. Compared to Li, Alex is a blazing beacon. Even the fox doll head in the box still gives off a faint crackle of almost-life, and good whiff of magic. Vanilla and nutmeg, and a whole host of others.

"What's wrong with her?" says Alex. "What do we do?"

I know Alex doesn't really expect me to respond, and I don't have an answer anyway. I get up, take a few steps in the direction Li's eyes are focused, then stop.

"We can't leave her here," I say.

"We could bring her," says Alex. "Between us."

"If we head back," I say.

"Yes," says Alex. I can hear the fear creeping into her voice now.

I turn back, sit next to her on the leaves. I'm suddenly exhausted and I just want to curl into a ball in the soft mulch at the base of this tree and sleep.

"Do you think it would help her," I say. "To go back?"

"Maybe if we get her out of the forest," Alex says. "She might recover. Then you and I can come back alone. To meet the witch."

"I think the witch did this to her," I say.

Alex says nothing. She's staring at her hands, but I know she can't see them in the dark.

"So we take her with us to find the witch," she says, her voice just above a whisper.

I put my hand on her shoulder. The tightness grows in my throat and I have to fight off the urge to just help Li to her feet and start walking towards where I think the witch will be. I understand, now, that if Alex ordered me to do something, I would have to do it. I would be unable to disobey.

"No," I say. "I think you should stay here with Li, while I scout ahead, find the witch, and bring her to you."

She stares at me, eyes wide and straining to see. She reaches for my face and almost jabs me in the eye before she finds my cheek with her fingers.

"Shouldn't we stay together?"

"Maybe," I say. "If you judge by all the cheesy horror movies ever made, we shouldn't split up."

She laughs, a clipped and hollow sound.

"But this will be faster," I say. I put my hand over hers and my cheek grows warm from our combined body heat. "I'll go as a fox. I should be able to find the witch quickly, and at least find out if she *will* help us. You and Li should be safe together."

She takes a deep breath. I hope she doesn't say, "No," doesn't argue. If she argues, I'll have to do what she wants. I wonder if she knows that.

"Okay," she says. "I don't like it, but you're right."

"You're strong," I say. "You're a witch. And I'll be able to sense if you're in trouble."

"You will?"

"Yes."

She's quiet. Thinking, maybe. Then I … sort of *feel* her thoughts turn towards me.

"Oh," she says. For a moment, I can feel her clearly, like her thoughts are my own. Then it fades, but the connection doesn't close.

"It's stronger," she says.

"Yes."

"It's … kind of nice. Comforting."

"For you, maybe," I say.

She doesn't say anything and I think I must have hurt her. I didn't mean for it to come out quite like that.

Then she reaches out with her other hand and touches my other cheek, puts her lips lightly against mine. It's not a lover's kiss, not anymore, but something more sisterly.

"I'm so sorry," she says.

I shake my head. "It *is* nice," I say. "And that's what terrifies me. It would be so easy to give in."

"Don't give in," she says, her voice suddenly strong and sure. "We will fix this."

I nod and stand. *That* is the Alex I know. Strong as a Celtic goddess, fierce and protective. She will be safe, and Li will be safe with her.

Then I take off my clothes and put on my fox shape, and vanish into the shadows to seek the witch.

The farther behind I leave Alex and Li, the more I wonder if I've made a terrible mistake. I love being a fox, but I also love being human, and this forest makes me want to stay a fox.

It's so hard to keep my thoughts focused on the witch, on my friends, on my human self.

The cool breeze wafts by, tickling my fur. It's not a constant trickle of wind, like the guide book led me to expect, but rather sudden random gusts, like living things flitting between the trees. I want to chase the wind that whips at the fur on my tail. It would make a fine plaything, appearing and disappearing between the trees, romping for hours.

I'm not sure how long I've been frolicking before I realize this was supposed to be quicker, not more distracting.

I have to re-orient myself, let my senses widen. When I find Alex and Li, I realize I've been heading away from where I think the witch is hiding, in her elusive nothingness.

I shake my head, think about taking human shape again, but decide that I just have to pay attention. *Think*, I tell myself. Hang onto conscious thought.

I pick up speed, trot purposefully towards the nothingness. I make good progress until a bat swoops out of the darkness, so close I feel its wings stir the air next to my ear, and I just *have* to chase it.

I think I catch myself more quickly, remember more readily what I'm here for. At least I don't seem to have gone as far astray when I sense Alex again to figure out where I am. I'm closer. I keep going, repeating the word "concentrate" over and over in my head to keep focused.

But you know how when you say a word over and over so many times that you realize it's just an arbitrary string of nonsense syllables? Turns out that happens when you're only repeating the word in your head, too. Con-cen-trate. Con-cen-trate. Con-cen-trate. It becomes a game of sounds and when I realize my mind has drifted I also discover that I'm chasing my own tail.

But again, I'm closer than I was before. Much closer.

I stop now, and expand my senses again. Li and Alex are behind me, and safe. The nothingness is just ahead and it's, well, not tangible, but *obvious*. It doesn't become undetectable so rapidly that I wonder if I imagined it this time. It stays, just beyond a huge old oak tree, obviously not there, if that makes any sense.

It's too dark now for even my *hexenfuchs* eyes to see much beyond tree shapes and shadows, but there is something hidden in that nothingness.

And all around me, suddenly, as if they emerged from the nothing, are other living beings.

Nine cats. I don't know how I know, but I am certain there are nine without having to count them. Nine is an important number to witches, so I wouldn't be surprised if it was a deliberate choice. Three are toms, and six are female. One is pregnant with four kittens. So much for the witch's perfect number. I wonder if she will keep them, the witch. If it's the same witch, she let my ancestor keep her litter of ordinary fox cubs once, as long as they didn't interfere with her duties as a familiar.

There are also two owls, one very large, and one smaller. A crow, edgy at being out and awake in the dark. Several mice that move too quickly for me to count. A very large spider. The bat.

I wonder if the number of familiars a witch has is an indication of her power, or if it's a way of compensating, the way some men feel the need to buy shiny, expensive cars, or juggle multiple girlfriends. I really hope this witch is friendly, either way.

I think about continuing, approaching the place where the emptiness waits, stepping into it. But that's where the witch's house will be, if it's anywhere in these woods, and in the dream – a dream I'm beginning to think was sent by the witch herself – Alex and I arrive together. Without Li.

So I wait.

The cats circle me, prowling in the darkness, nearly silent. Nearly, but

I can hear the faint crackle of dry leaves under their careful paws. All nine make one complete circuit, then another, and stop all around me, perfectly evenly spaced like they're performing a synchronized swimming routine. Synchronized stalking.

The crow stays where he is, just this side of the nothingness, huffed up and watching me from a branch. I wonder if he can even see me. The owls come closer. The big one lands high in a tree over my head, and the little one keeps to the air, wings so silent I only know she's there because I keep my senses wide open.

The mice are all around, and I've lost track of the spider and the bat. No, the spider keeps her distance, stays near the crow, but lower down on the tree. And there's the bat now, swooping past my ear again, to land just off to my right, clinging upside down to the bark of an oak.

It's hard to keep my attention on so many at once. I've never done kung fu breathing exercises in fox shape – I've never needed to – but I try it now and it helps. I relax into full watchfulness, relax into my wider senses, and all at once I *can* keep track of all the witches familiars, even the mice, and Alex and Li, and a variety of other animal life nearby. I don't need to think about it any more, I just do it.

There are thirteen mice, another magic number. Two male, eleven female, and miraculously only one is pregnant. The witch must have good control over her familiars if only one out of eleven mature female mice is pregnant.

The mice begin to move even faster, scurrying around me like mad and I suspect that they are there to distract me, to take up all my attention and shake my ability to keep them all in my focus at once.

One gets too close and I pin it to the ground with my paw without thinking. My fox self wants to eat it, but consuming a witch's familiar is probably a really bad idea.

It wriggles away and escapes, and all at once the nothingness vanishes – if that even makes sense – and a new presence enters my awareness like a nuclear explosion.

She's old and she reeks of spices. Cinnamon, vanilla, anise, and mint, plus others I can't name.

"Impressive," she says and I know without having to be told that I've just met the Witch of the Wald. She looks like Alex.

Chapter Sixteen

I STARE AT HER for a long time, the Witch of the Wald. She really does look like Alex, or close enough to be related, but with long white hair instead of short red hair. And older. Much older, but more ageless than ancient, if you know what I mean.

For a moment, I can't remember why I'm here. Then I feel pressure in my head and shake it, like I would shake off a fly.

"I see," said the witch. "A pity someone has claimed you already. Though she'll have to complete the binding if she wants to keep you." She laughs and it's like Alex's laugh, but without the warmth.

The binding. I shake my head again and change into human shape. Or I try to. There's something in the way.

The witch laughs again. "You are not quite what you seem, are you?"

I try to take human shape again, and fail.

Alex. I reach out with my mind, along the familiar binding, and feel her like she's right next to me.

Her presence seems to block the witch out and I snap into human shape with a shock like a rubber band breaking. It *hurts*. It has never hurt to change shape before.

"Interesting," says the witch. I struggle to stand up as she steps closer to me. "Bring your friend and we'll have tea," she says. "I think there's a story you'd like to hear the end of."

"There are three of us," I say, amazed at how difficult it is to make words.

"Of course," she says. "There are always three." She steps closer again. "It seems your friend is rather attached to the human girl. A pity. Humans make good tools, but they break so easily." Another step closer. "Still, if it's the only way to get her here."

I don't understand what the witch means, but I can sense Alex moving closer, and faintly, I sense Li with her.

"Now," says the witch, taking one final step. "You're exhausted. Rest until your friends arrive." She puts her finger in the middle of my forehead, and I feel sleep wash over me.

No. Maybe we need her help, but I will not be put to sleep like a mechanical toy. I fight the drowsiness.

"Stubborn," the witch says. "And strong. Very well, they'll be here soon anyway." Then she vanishes back into the shadow, into the nothingness, and her familiars trail after her.

It seems an eternity before Alex and Li arrive. Li walks steadily forward, seemingly unaware of anything, including Alex's hand on her shoulder. She avoids trees – and me – mechanically, though I don't think she can even see them. She keeps walking right past me.

"Su," says Alex. She has my clothes, and she stops to hand them to me. "Li, wait," she says, but Li keeps going.

"She's going to the witch," I say. "And so are we."

Alex turns and looks at me, but I don't know how much she can see in the darkness. But then I realize it's not so dark anymore. Dawn has arrived as suddenly as dusk did. I don't think I like this forest so much.

Alex looks after Li, who has already disappeared into the gloom. "Should I…?"

"I think she'll be okay," I say. "But I'm pretty sure the witch is controlling her somehow." I dress as quickly as I can, and then Alex and I together follow after Li, and the witch.

The nothingness becomes something as we reach its edge. A hidden bubble in the forest. There is a house just like the one in our dream. It's on stilts, with a ladder to the door, and long ago someone cleared branches away, high in the canopy, to let sunlight in, so there is a garden. It's not cheerful, despite the increasing sunlight. Too much foliage has grown back for it to be bright, but at least it's not quite gloomy.

Li is nowhere to be seen, so I reach out with my senses, and find her. She's already in the house. So is the witch and a small assortment of familiars.

"She said the binding was incomplete," I say, as we stand looking up the ladder at the door of the house. "She said she would tell us the end of a story."

"My ancestors' story?" says Alex.

"She looks like you."

Then the door opens and the witch invites us in, and I feel like a girl in a fairytale, about to do the stupid thing that gets her in trouble. But we go in and stand next to a table, where Li is already sitting, sipping tea, vacant-eyed.

"You've come for your story," says the witch, after looking at Alex for a long time.

"No," says Alex, to my surprise. I mean, she's right, we came about the familiar binding, but I thought she'd want to hear the story since we're here anyway.

The witch looks taken aback, but it passes quickly. If I wasn't used to observing the tiniest of reactions in vamps, I'd have missed it.

"We came," says Alex, "to learn how to break a familiar binding."

Again, brief surprise in the way the witch breathes, in how her pupils dilate slightly.

"Perhaps you have," says the witch. "But this is my house, so first you will hear this story, because I have been waiting for you to come and hear it. It may also change your mind about what happens after."

She seats us at the table, serves tea and gingerbread. Yes, gingerbread. I wonder if it's a deliberate Hansel and Gretel reference, or if she's unaware. I wonder if I should be more scared than I am, though I'm already terrified.

Then she sits, too, and begins to tell her story.

That the child who was to rescue the people of Schönstadt from the curse was a product of incest was a fact not lost upon the villagers. But Rose-Perle was a sweet and lovely child, and it was hardly her fault that her father had fucked his own sister and got her pregnant.

From the moment she could understand speech, she knew that one day the Witch of the Wald would come for her. She was not afraid. It would have been like being afraid of growing up. It was simply something that would happen, will she or no, and that was that.

And from the moment she could read, Rose-Perle devoured the books in the library of the Holz home. She had the old master bedroom as her own, while her parents kept their separate tiny bedrooms in the attic and hardly spoke to each other, let alone touched. They had been like that for as long as Rose could remember. Gradually, the best books from the sitting room found a new home in Rose's room, and the twin dolls stayed there, too, on opposite ends of a small sofa under the window that looked out on the Hexenwald.

Rose-Perle would often curl up on that sofa, a doll on either side, and read. In time, she began to think of those dolls as her real Mama and Papa, and of Rinde and Joringel as sort of a dotty aunt and uncle – always present, but never really there.

They lived on the scant remains of the Holz wealth – it had never been quite enough to call a fortune – which covered their needs, but left little extra.

In her reading, Rose-Perle discovered that, in every tale about the witch, the hero or heroine (or the unfortunate victim, depending) approached the witch, or accidentally stumbled across her, in the Hexenwald. Then a bargain might be made or a curse laid, depending on the respect or lack thereof of the seeker (or stumbler). The witch, it seemed, didn't like to leave the Wald, and would generally only do so to avenge a bargain broken.

And so Rose-Perle began to wonder, round about the time she turned seven, why her parents – the living ones in their attic rooms – didn't just take her to the witch. She also began to notice that the two children she played with came out to play less and less often. Eventually, she was made to attend their funerals, while her parents stood on the edge of the crowd apart from the rest of the village, and everyone else avoided looking at them.

But they looked at Rose-Perle. They looked at her as if they expected something of her, and they clutched their other, younger, children close, as if they were afraid to let them play with her.

When she asked what sickness her playmates had that made them die, the villagers would only say, "It was the curse. The curse of Schönstadt. The curse of the Hexenwald." And then they would look at her, waiting.

So she asked her vague, unhappy parents why this was and what the curse was, and Rinde began to cry and said, "She is only a child," and Joringel tried to put his arms around his sister and she fled to her bedroom and locked the door, and he also went to his room and also locked the door.

So Rose-Perle asked her doll-parents, but they were silent. As much as she wished that they would, they did not speak to her, if ever they had spoken. Still, their wooden limbs and stuffed bodies were warmer and more comforting than her living parents, and their carved gazes more kind.

Then when Rose-Perle was nine, and had attended more funerals of more children and endured more expectant looks, she suddenly wondered why no one ever went in the toy shop anymore.

She had returned from a funeral, distressed that they were now too poor to buy a small toy to place on the child's grave, as Rose had always done for the dead children, and she had watched her parents weep and retreat up the attic stairs. And she thought about the toy shop below and wondered if there might be something there she could put on the boy's grave. The key to the house didn't fit the toy shop door, so she put the thought aside for the time being and set about making herself some supper. And looking for a misplaced can opener, she opened a drawer she had never opened before.

It was full of boring things like paperwork and old advertisements, but at the very back she found a key. It was a large key, and where most keys had a flat spot to help turn them in the lock, this key had a face. It was a smiling face, a plump-cheeked old-man face. When Rose turned the key over, she saw a smiling, equally plump old woman face.

"Grandpapa," she said. "Grandmama." Though she knew the key was too old to really bear the likenesses of her grandparents, it comforted her to think of them that way.

She put the key in her pocket, and eventually found the can-opener in a pail of greasy water under the sink and by the time she had eaten her soup, she had forgotten all about it. Later, when she was changing for bed, it fell out of her pocket and onto the floor with a clatter.

"Tomorrow," she said to the parent-dolls, because speaking to them aloud made her feel less alone. "I will find out what this key unlocks." They seemed to smile at Rose-Perle and after she put the key on a ribbon and slid it over her head to hang around her neck, she fell asleep and dreamed the most wonderful dreams about toys. In her dream, the grandpapa-and-grandmama key unlocked the door to the toy shop.

In the morning, Rose-Perle breakfasted alone. He parents would be up late, if they ever got up at all. Then she washed her plate and wiped the table and put on her favorite shoes and wrapped her favorite scarf around her neck. I was red and so long that she had to wind it around many times. But it was soft and cheerful. She wasn't going to go outside, but it would be cold in the toy shop, and probably very dusty. She remembered the oil lantern that sat high up on a shelf in the kitchen, and took that, too, because the lights would most likely not work. The house had only had electricity for a very few years, and Rose-Perle was sure her parents would not have spent the extra money to put lights in the shop.

When she reached the foyer and turned left to face the old oaken door with its grimy glass window, Rose-Perle felt the first inkling of fear she had ever felt in her life. It was not so much fear of what she might find in the toy shop as fear of what she wouldn't find. What she hoped for was a small toy to take to the cemetery to put on the most recently dead child's grave, and some answers.

If Rose-Perle was to someday be taken by the Witch of the Wald, then there must be a curse or a bargain, and if there was a curse, there must be a way to break it, and if a bargain, there must be a way to keep it. If there were any answers at all, Rose-Perle reasoned, they would be in the toy shop. They must be, because they weren't in the house.

Rose-Perle set the oil lantern on the floor and took the key out from around her neck. She looked solemnly at the door with its dusty window and letters painted in gold, still oddly bright after all this time. She wasn't tall enough to reach them all, but she traced over the letters of her family's name with a finger. H-O-L-Z. And where she traced, the removal of dust made the letters blaze brighter in the dim foyer light.

Then she took a deep breath, slid the key into the lock, and tried to turn it. At first, she couldn't, and she was afraid that the marvelous key didn't open the toy shop door after all. She tried again, twisting one way, then the other, and there was a grating noise. Once more she tried and there was a sudden twist and "snap!"

Rose-Perle didn't move. She was sure the key had broken in the lock. But eventually she got tired of holding her arms out to the lock and she pulled the key away. It stuck. She turned it and tried again and it came free, unbroken. With a soft "creak" the door eased open a few inches and a draft trickled out.

The smell of dust and wood and tool oil trickled out, too, and tickled Rose-Perle's nose and made her sneeze. She picked up the lantern and pushed the door open farther with her toe. Just inside the door was a long counter of wood – when it was not dusty, it would probably gleam – with a huge old brass cash register that had enormous keys and a window at the top to see the metal numbers in.

Rose-Perle stared at it. Then she put the lantern on the counter and noticed a light switch near the door. Her parents must have had lights put in here after all, despite the cost, because when Rose-Perle tried the switch, several bulbs lit up. Then, one by one, the lights went "pop" and darkened until only one was left, midway through the shop. It flickered and cast a dim light.

Rose-Perle said a bad word she'd heard her father-uncle use once, that had made her mother-aunt slap him. Then she fumbled the safety matches out of her pocket – she'd have been in trouble to be caught with them, but that would be better than being sighed over, or wept over, or ignored. She lit the lantern and adjusted the wick and the big room filled with warm light. It was not enough to see everything clearly, but it would do, and Rose could move it where she needed it.

She looked around. It was a very old-fashioned sort of shop, lined with wooden shelves on three sides, with a big table in the middle, and a big window in the front. The long counter where the cash register was blocked easy access to that side of the shop, which had a big workbench under its shelves. An array of dusty carving tools hung behind the bench and it had drawers of all sizes below. There was a stool in front of the bench with rungs worn from somebody's feet. Grandpapa's feet, Rose thought.

The shelves and the window-display and the big table were all empty. The floor was empty of everything but the footprints and droppings of mice. Only the counter and the workbench showed any promise.

Rose-Perle walked around the long counter and into the space behind. There was a wooden block on the floor, almost hidden under the edge of the bench. It was painted red and had a "T" on it, and pictures of a truck and tractor. The boy who had just died had been the son of farmers and had liked tractors, though he was a little old for alphabet blocks. Rose-Perle picked up the block, wiped the dust off on her skirt, and put it on the counter next to her lantern. It would have to do.

Now where, she thought, might answers be?

The drawers of the cash counter held only ledger books and coin wrappers, and the register itself was empty. The drawers of the workbench were more promising. In them, Rose-Perle found screws and wooden pegs of various sizes, sharpening stones, and linen thread. One was full of carved left arms and another of carved right legs. Some were skillfully made, and some less so. Another drawer held heads, and another right arms and left legs jumbled together. One held canvas bodies, but the one Rose held up to the light fell to pieces in her fingers. Another drawer had carved wooden bodies in two pieces – some fronts and some backsides.

Rose-Perle was tempted to lay the doll parts out on the workbench and see if she could assemble a whole doll, but she didn't know how they were held together.

In another drawer, Rose found a plush fox, a little moth-eaten, made from real fox fur and with clever amber glass eyes.

"Hello, fox," she said, and fancied the toy winked at her. She put him on the counter next to the lantern, turned towards the door to keep watch for her.

In the next-to-last drawer, Rose found a book. It was a journal, but in two different kinds of writing, alternating. One was blocky and masculine, and one looked like calligraphy. On the front page were two names, the same names that were painted in gold (one large, and the other much smaller) on the toy shop window. Grandmama and Grandpapa.

The last drawer was locked, and Rose-Perle did not have a key to fit. The door key, which looked about the right shape, was too big. She looked at the rows of tools above the bench and thought about trying to pry the drawer open. But it seemed a poor way to treat good tools, and she thought Grandpapa would disapprove.

The journal was bound to have answers of some kind – maybe it would include an answer about where to find the key for that last drawer.

Rose-Perle thought she heard the floor creak above – one of her parents, at least, was out of bed. She quickly put the truck block in her pocket and tucked the journal and the fox under her arm and put out the lamp. Then she left the toy shop and quietly closed the door and locked it and hid the key under her blouse.

Chapter Seventeen

THE WITCH PAUSES finally, and gets up to get the kettle off the big black stove in the corner. I feel even more like I'm in a fairy tale than I did before, and a day ago, I'd have sworn that wasn't possible.

Alex, who's holding Li's hand while Li sits unresponsive, like an automaton or a doll – and *that* thought makes me shudder – sits up straighter.

"Are you Rose-Perle?" she asks.

The witch doesn't react at all. "I am the Witch of the Wald," she says.

"But –"

"No questions," says the witch. "Let me tell you this story, then you may ask questions." Her voice slips into a heavy German accent, just for a word or two, and I realize that the whole time she's been speaking English in a perfect generic North American accent. In the middle of an ancient German forest with no other people around for miles.

I don't have much time to think about it, though, as she launches back into her story. At least there's no weird sex, unlike Li's story. Not yet, anyway.

Upstairs, her father-uncle looked at her through dull eyes. "Are we out of milk?" he said.

"It's in the icebox," she answered, and he nodded and turned away.

Rose-Perle went into her room and shut the door. She took off her favorite shoes, and unwound her favorite scarf, and then climbed onto the couch between the parent-dolls with the fox and the journal in her lap.

She patted the fox's head and said, "When I go to the witch, I will take you with me." She had decided it was about time she went looking for the witch, instead of waiting for the witch to come and get her. But first, she would read the journal and find some answers.

Grandpapa seemed to try to say as much as possible in as few words as possible, while Grandmama used a lot of words and said much less, but in more detail. Grandpapa also used a lot of abbreviations, which Grandmama had later gone through and spelled out, which was good, because most of them would have been impossible for Rose-Perle to figure out otherwise.

Between the two of them, Grandmama and Grandpapa told the story of the Holz family bargain with the Witch of the Wald. In it, the first Holz ever to live in Schönstadt had gone into the forest to find suitable wood to cut and dry for his toy business. He was newly a master, and eager for his own shop. He had found a fine walnut and begun to cut it down, when an old woman appeared as if from nowhere and demanded to know what he was doing.

He apologized, and offered to pay for the wood, as he had not known the forest had an owner and the witch, impressed by his good manners, had agreed. All the money he had was the new-minted silver coin he had been given by his old master when his own masterwork was approved by the Guild (because back then, Grandmama explained in a note in the margin, there were still craft guilds, and that was how craftspeople were trained). And there began the Holz bargain with the Witch of the Wald.

That early Holz was so pleased with his success with the witch-wood that he went into the forest the next year with a beautifully-carved marionette as a gift for the witch. When he found her at last, she was not the old lady he had expected to see, but a younger woman, strong and beautiful. And he fell in love.

Alas, the witch would not marry him, and after a week sent him home.

A year later he visited again, with more gifts, and she sent him away again, with a baby boy in his arms.

"Give me a girl child," she said, "and that would be a pearl beyond price." But there were no more children, and still the witch would not leave her wood. The Holz's half-witch son became a toymaker like his father, and kept up the bargain, and so on through the generations, though no other Holz met the witch face to face until…

There was a break in the writing. And Rose sat and looked out the window. Her family had witch-blood, she thought. She had witch-blood. She ran a strand of hair through her fingers. It was long and fine and so blonde it was nearly white. Her eyes were dark green like both her parents. She wondered what hair and what eyes the witch had had. None of the stories ever said.

A pearl beyond price, she thought. There was something about that phrase. She pondered. The people at the cemetery, the other villagers, sometimes they would say those words when they looked at her. The words made her father-uncle grim and her mother-aunt sorrowful. My name is Pearl, she thought, because Rose-Perle means "rose-pearl." A flower and a gem.

Rose looked at the journal again. Grandmama's writing took over and told about her generation. Always, the Holzes had boy children. Each boy would learn the toymaker's craft from his father, and marry a local woman, and they would have a son. Each generation, one boy child only.

But then Grandmama and Grandpapa had twins, a boy and a girl. Maybe they should have known right then that something had changed, or would change. Or was changing. The family was healthy and the business so prosperous that when Grandpapa's own father died peacefully in his bed, they had to take on more help. And the journeyman, though highly recommended, had been swayed by silver, by gain, to dishonesty. In those days, Grandmama said, few used silver coins anymore, and theirs had to be specially-minted to keep the witch's bargain. The journeyman had probably never seen such wealth before. And so he kept their silver and doomed not only the Holzes, but all of Schönstadt.

And the witch came. It was the first time she was seen by any Holz since the one who'd made the bargain. And she laid down her curse and the children of Schönstadt began to die, all save the Holz twins.

"Bring me a pearl beyond price," the witch had said. Either one of the living Holzes or a child of theirs must deliver such a pearl to break the curse. Rose-Perle smiled. She had been right. She *was* the answer. She was the pearl that would save Schönstadt. And she had to be taken to the witch.

Well, she thought. As soon as I have solved the last mystery, the locked drawer, I will take *myself* to the witch.

After that, the journal was full of speculation about where they might find a pearl beyond price. Rose shook her head. How had Grandmama and Grandpapa not seen that the answer was right in the very story they had just set down? How did the other villagers not realize the child was not to find and deliver the pearl, but *was* the pearl.

And Rose-Perle thought, *I* am the pearl. *I* am the answer. And I am doubly a Holz, and part witch myself. She turned pages, seeing nothing more of interest. There were passages of notes about famous pearls and pearl folklore – something to read later, maybe, but there were no more answers for now – and sections where Grandmama wrote sad descriptions of Grandpapa who was no longer happy making toys and spent more and more time staring out the window with its view of the dark and gloomy Hexenwald.

Then there was nothing but a wad of pages stuck together. It was done so neatly it seemed deliberate, and Rose wondered if there might be more answers – answers her grandparents had felt the need to keep secret – on those pages. She flexed the pages back and forth, and slid her thumbnail against the edges, seeking a hold from which to peel the leaves apart. The glue was brittle with age, it seemed, for eventually several sheets came free and revealed a hollow in the book, out of which fell a key. It was little, and old, and looked just the size to fit the locked drawer in the toy shop.

When Rose left her room she found both parents in the kitchen, looking at each other across the table. They both had tears in their eyes. She thought about sneaking past, but they turned to look at her, and Mama-Auntie tried to smile, so Rose got a plate of cookies and made tea and they sat together, almost like a real family. Then Rose-Perle pretended to read picture books in the living room until her parents drifted back to their rooms and locked their doors.

She left the books where they lay scattered on the floor and slipped down the stairs to the toy shop and unlocked the door. The dim light in the middle of the shop was still on – she must have forgotten to turn it off when she left – and it flickered and faintly buzzed. It was enough light to see her way to the workbench and fit the little key into the lock. It turned smoothly, like it was new-oiled, and the drawer slid open easily.

Inside was a drawstring bag made of the same canvas as the mama-doll and papa-doll's bodies. It felt weak and old in Rose's hand – perhaps the temperature of the toy shop had been harder on it than that of the house had been on the dolls – but it didn't fall apart the way the unused, unstuffed doll body had the last time Rose looked in the drawers. It was heavy, and it clinked.

Rose opened the bag and saw it was full of silver coins. The journeyman's stolen silver, she thought. The witch's silver.

Rose-Perle would return the coins to the witch when she presented herself. Maybe the witch still wouldn't want it, but it seemed the proper gesture to make.

She decided she would go to the cemetery first thing in the morning to place the truck block on the dead boy's grave, and then she would pack a lunch and go into the forest. Surely if she went, the witch would find her, even if she didn't know where she was going.

Rose-Perle went back upstairs – this time she shut off the light in the toy shop – hid the coins under her pillow, and sat looking out at the Hexenwald until it got too dark to see anything but vague shadows. Then she went to bed and dreamed of old ladies who became young, and dolls that talked, and little stuffed foxes that grew teeth to bite.

"Little stuffed foxes that grew teeth to bite," says the witch again. She smiles and her teeth bear more than a passing resemblance to a predator's.

"Foxes," says Alex, but she seems distracted, like she's only half paying attention.

The witch's smile had been turned on me, but now she looks at Alex. "You are quite attached to that China doll, aren't you?"

That snaps Alex out of her distraction. "Don't call her that," she says, anger giving her voice an edge.

The witch smiles wider. "Ah, good, you do have some fight in you." She picks up the tea things and takes them across the room.

"She is a doll, though," says the witch when she returns. She lifts one of Li's arms by the wrist, then drops it. It smacks limply onto the table, and Li doesn't even blink.

"Stop that!" says Alex. She stands up, pushes herself between Li and the witch as much as she can with the table in the way. I reach out and take Alex's hand, hoping to calm her. We still need this witch's help, after all. At least *I* do. And I suppose Li does, too.

"What did you do to her?" I say.

The witch looks at me like she might look at a talking animal. It's much the same look she gave Li. Like we're less than human.

"I gave her life," she says. "Or gave her *back* life. Temporarily, so she could serve me."

I stare at her. Then I look at Alex. She's staring at the witch, too, but the look on her face is not one of confusion, it's one of horror.

"You —" She feels behind herself for her chair, sits as if all the energy has suddenly drained from her limbs. "That isn't possible."

"Neither is making a fox into a toy, or a toy into a fox," says the witch, tapping the lid of the box we carried from the museum, the box holding the carved wooden fox doll head. "And yet it is." Her voice actually sounds kind.

Alex shakes her head. "No." She stares at her limp hands.

"Child," says the witch, and Alex's head snaps up.

"You weren't meant to love her," the witch says, and for a moment I think she's talking about me. But no. Li. "You were only meant to fuck her, to desire her, to follow her here so I could give you the education our lineage deserves."

"But I do," says Alex. "I love her more than anything." More than she loved me, but that doesn't even sting now. Not much, anyway.

"This is an interesting conundrum," says the witch. "It should be fun finding the answer."

Fun. Not really a word I'd associate with this dour woman. Yet she does seem to have softened since we've been here, from the severe, terrifying woman I first met to … someone sympathetic. Sympathetic to Alex, at least. I doubt those feelings extend to me. Or Li.

"What do you mean, you gave her life back?" I say.

The witch glances at me, then away, like I've just behaved inappropriately, instead of asking a perfectly reasonable question.

"You really must keep your familiar on a shorter leash," she says.

"She's not my familiar," says Alex. "She's my friend."

"And yet you have bound her. Incompletely, perhaps, but a familiar all the same."

"Only out of necessity," Alex insists. "Only to … save another friend."

"You really must tell me that story," says the witch. "But first you must let me finish mine."

This time, I'm the one who jumps up in anger. "What did you mean, you gave Li back her life?" I growl.

The witch raises an eyebrow, but doesn't look away from Alex. "Will you tell her, or shall I?"

"I'm not sure I really understand myself," says Alex.

"Disappointing," says the witch. She tucks a long strand of white hair behind her ear and tilts her head slightly. In that instant she looks so much like Alex it feels like a punch in the gut. I sit down.

"A pretty young student from America came hiking in my woods," says the witch. "I discourage visitors, but don't murder them outright." She looks sidelong at me, and I know she's said that to head off any accusations I might make. My gut clenches, the fear I felt earlier returning in full force.

"But my forest is dangerous, even without its *hexen*. She hiked alone, as those who know the wilderness say never to do. She met an unfortunate end when she became lost and discovered how cold the Oktober Mountains get in the autumn night."

"She died," I say. "You let her die of hypothermia."

"I did not let her die," says the witch. "I simply ignored her presence. One of my birds brought me the news in the morning." She gestures at a crow perched on the windowsill and it bows its head like it knows what she's saying.

"She was not otherwise damaged, so I sought out her spirit and offered her a bargain. I would return her to life in exchange for her service."

"She works for you? All along?" I almost get up again, as angry now at Li as at the witch.

The witch smiles. "She was unaware. I gave her back her life and her memories, but erased any knowledge of me. Then I sent her to you." She looks at Alex. "Implanted with the desire to know you, and to convince you to come here. To convince you it was all your idea, naturally."

Alex stares back, saying nothing. She's holding tightly to Li's hand again.

"We could trade, you and I," says the witch. "I've wanted another fox familiar for a very long time."

"No," says Alex, flatly, but I can see the strain in her face. I may be her friend, but Li is her beloved. I could hardly blame her if she did trade. But what catches my attention in the witch's words is "another fox familiar."

"You had a fox," I say. I don't ask it as a question.

"Yes," says the witch. "He … was passed down through my family," she says.

"You *are* Rose-Perle," I say. "Even if you don't look old enough."

"Patience," she says. "Not all is as you assume it to be. Patience."

"Please give me Li back," says Alex.

The witch sighs. "You, too, are impatient. I have a story to finish, and it is not a short one."

"Can't you just lay out the facts?" I say.

"Youth these days have no appreciation for the art of storytelling," says the witch. She gets up again, crosses the room, and rummages in the kitchen. I'm about to get up and start breaking things when she comes back in with bread and cheese and sausage. Pickles in dusty old jars. Butter in a crock. Fresh tomatoes, from who knows where this early in the year. My stomach grumbles and I realize it's been hours … days? … Since we ate a proper meal.

She arranges the food, snaps her fingers, and Li begins to feed herself mechanically.

Alex glares.

"Really, child," the witch says. "It's easier on her this way. For now."

I assemble a sandwich, but hesitate to take a bite. I'm ravenous, but who knows what a witch's food will do?

"If I intended to drug you," she says, like she can read my thoughts – and hell, maybe she can – "I would already have done so."

Because we each drank several cups of tea. *Fuck.* I take a bite of my food and it's so good I have a hard time refraining from stuffing as much in my face at once as I can.

After I swallow, I say, "Can you just hurry up and finish the story already?"

The witch draws herself up and seems suddenly to tower over us, though she hasn't even left her chair. He features grow sharp and shadowed and cruel, and I don't feel so hungry anymore.

"This is my place, my home, my forest. I am the Witch of the Wald, and I will tell you my story in my own way, and in my own time. And you will listen."

Alex and I stare at her, and even Li pauses in her robot-like movements. The crow on the windowsill ruffles its feathers.

Then the witch smiles and it's the first real, genuine expression I think I've seen her make.

"I still have it in me," she says, as Alex and I continue to gape at her. "Now eat, while I tell you about Rose-Perle."

"You," I say.

"Perhaps me," she says. Then she tilts her head, like she's thinking. "Or maybe she was one of my ancestors. I was never really clear on that point."

Alex and I exchange glances as the witch takes a deep breath and goes back to her story.

Chapter Eighteen

T HE WITCH SITS with her hands folded on the table in front of her, and speaks like she's reading a story from a book, only there's no text. She just stares ahead, past Alex's shoulder, and talks like the blank wooden wall opposite is a teleprompter.

She doesn't *tell* the story, like a real storyteller would, with gestures and inflection and voices. She recites it like a literary verse she's memorized. It's creepier than you might think. But after a while, I'm absorbed in Rose-Perle's story, and it doesn't matter how the tale is told, only that I find out what happens next.

And maybe that's a bit of witch-magic, too. That I don't care how lousy a storyteller the witch is, only that I hear the story. Or maybe it's not witch-magic at all, but only the spell of a good plot.

It was easy to get permission to go to the cemetery in the morning, even though both parents were at the table when Rose-Perle got up for breakfast. She simply told them that she meant to visit the boy's grave and they nodded absently. Her father-uncle was examining a letter with a frown and barely glanced up when she explained. Her mother-aunt was more responsive, but barely.

At the cemetery, Rose-Perle put the block on the newly-filled earth of the grave. She'd have liked to have put it in the grave on top of the coffin, but she could hardly ask to have the grave re-dug just for her. So she pressed it into the soil and stood for a while, looking at the headstone. There were far too many new headstones in the old graveyard, and many of them showed lifespans of just seven years.

"I'm sorry," said Rose-Perle. "I'm sorry it took so long to know what to do. I'm sorry my parents didn't take me to the witch as soon as I was born." She walked along the rows, sorrow and responsibility heavy in her heart. "But no one else will have to die so young."

When she got home, her parents had vanished into their rooms again, and only the letter remained on the table to show they had been there at all.

So Rose-Perle made a pack lunch and filled her school bag with it, and her grandparents' journal, and the bag of silver coins, and the little plush fox. She strapped him in so his pointy face stuck out the flap, so he could watch her back. Rose-Perle might have been a rational, practical child, but she was still a child, and a neighbor of the Hexenwald, and a toy fox as guardian seemed perfectly reasonable. She wished she could take the parent-dolls along, too, but each one was nearly as large as she was, so they would have to stay behind. She would miss them. She kissed each of them on its smooth wooden cheek, then put on her favorite red shoes, and wound her favorite red scarf around her neck and left the house.

The Hexenwald was quieter than Rose-Perle had expected. There were birds, of course, but they sounded far off, and once under the trees a dense cushion of fallen leaves muffled Rose's footsteps. Most of the trees were so tall that even the rustling of branches in the Oktober Mountain wind was high overhead.

In the Hexenwald, the chill wind was baffled by thousands of tree trunks and the air felt almost warm.

At first, Rose simply headed straight into the forest. She supposed the witch must live deep within somewhere. Then she wondered if she should be looking for Grandpapa's wood store, where he put the cut witch-wood to dry. She didn't know where that was except that it was far enough in that no one but the Holzes had gone there, but not so far that hauling a sled loaded with wood was a long task.

Just when she began to get tired, and was thinking she would like to find somewhere to sit and eat one of her sandwiches, a bright streak of sunlit green came into view ahead, and gradually there was undergrowth where there had been only tree trunks and fallen leaves. Rose pressed through and saw the canopy overhead was split, allowing light to hit the forest floor, which was why there were shrubs and grasses and flowers. And then – Rose-Perle discovered by almost falling into it – there was a river. Or a stream, anyway. Too wide and deep to cross without a bridge, but not so far across you couldn't throw a stone and hit the far bank, if you had a good arm.

Rose found a boulder in the sun to sit on, and she perched there and opened her bag. She put the plush fox on another stone, facing the forest to keep watch, and she dug out a sandwich. Before taking a bite, she took out a bit of ham, and put it on the stone in front of the fox. She knew it was silly to feed a toy fox – Rose-Perle had never been one for imaginary tea parties, either – but it seemed right to do, here.

She was about to take a big bite when she heard a voice like the wind in dry leaves, or sandpaper against wood – rattling, raspy, old.

"If you can spare a morsel for a plush dog," it said, "can you spare a bite for an old woman?"

Rose-Perle's heart jumped, and she lowered the sandwich. There, at the edge of the forest, standing on a path Rose hadn't noticed, was a woman in a cloak, leaning on a staff. She was tall and straight, with long shining white hair, and she didn't look so old, really.

"I didn't see you there, Frau," said Rose. "But I have another sandwich you're welcome to, if you like." This must be the witch, though she didn't look like any of the illustrations in Rose's folklore books, except perhaps for the old-fashioned cloak and staff. "And he's a fox, my toy," she added.

"Of course he is," said the witch. She came closer and seated herself gracefully on a stump not far from Rose's boulder. The witch reached out with her staff and tapped the plush fox on the head. "But he can hardly eat without teeth."

And then, between one blink and the next, the plush fox was a live fox and he gobbled up the bit of ham and lolled his long, pink tongue at Rose.

He sat primly on his stone and watched her. For a moment, Rose-Perle just stared, but then she remembered her manners and took out the second sandwich and hopped off her boulder to give it to the witch.

"Thank you, child," the witch said, and took the sandwich, unwrapped it, and began to eat. Rose tried very hard not to gape at the witch and concentrate instead on her own sandwich. When they had both finished, the old woman — for now that she was closer, Rose could see the lines and creases in her fair skin — leaned forward to look closely at Rose.

"Where are you headed this fine day?" she asked.

"Well," said Rose, wondering how direct she should be. "I'm seeking a certain inhabitant of this forest, to repay a debt long due." Rose was proud of the words she came up with; they sounded almost like something that might really be in a fairy tale.

"Ah," said the witch. "I know of only one dweller in this forest, and that's me. But I don't recall any debt from a young thing such as you."

"If you are the only one who lives here," said Rose, "then you must be – ." She hesitated. Her books didn't say if it was safe to call a witch "witch" to her face. But then she straightened her shoulders and plunged on. "You must be the Witch of the Wald, and it is you I seek." She looked at the fox, and it looked back at her. It seemed to smile.

The witch followed her gaze. "He was enchanted," she said. "A certain seamstress from a village not far from here wanted to impress her beloved and convince him to marry her. And as he was a toymaker, she decided to sew a toy, but because he made his toys of witch-wood they seemed almost alive, so she wished to make a stuffed creature just as lifelike. I gave her the fox skin and she made the toy and won her husband. The fox had been a naughty fellow and it seemed a fit punishment to make him a toy for a time. I think he will behave now, and he seems to like you." She paused to look closely at Rose-Perle again. "I wonder where you found him."

"I think," said Rose, "that the seamstress was my Grandmama and the toymaker my Grandpapa, and it's about them that I've come."

"Ah," said the witch. "I begin to understand."

"I have brought you all the silver that should have been yours," Rose said, and rummaged in her pack, pulled out the bag of coins, and held it out.

The witch took it, almost hesitantly, looking keenly at Rose all the while.

"That was not the terms for breaking the curse," she said.

"No," said Rose. "But it's your silver just the same."

"And the pearl?" said the witch. "You are a remarkable child."

"Well," said Rose. "In a story I read – Grandpapa and Grandmama wrote it in a journal – you wished for a girl child from your . . . from the first Holz in Schönstadt, but they always had boys."

"Indeed, clever girl," said the witch.

"You said a girl child would be a pearl beyond price."

"So I did. And there was a girl child. The seamstress of the fox married a Holz and I saw to it they had twins – a boy to keep and a girl…"

"For you?" Rose trembled, because she knew the witch could be dangerous, and because the quiet thoughtfulness of this lovely old woman was far more frightening than a raging hag would have been. But she looked the witch in the eyes and kept her chin up.

"Indeed," said the witch. "But I couldn't simply take her. That is not how bargains are kept."

An idea crept into Rose's mind. "Did you . . . Did you make the journeyman steal the silver?"

The witch looked startled, then thoughtful. "Did I? I suppose I might have given him a nudge. But I could never have swayed a truly honest man, no matter how many nudges or how hard."

"Why did you not simply ask for the girl child?"

The witch regarded her solemnly, not as an adult looks on a child, but as a person might look at someone of equal intelligence. "Were you her mama or papa, would you have given her over?"

"No," said Rose. "I suppose I wouldn't."

"I thought," said the witch, "that if I asked for her to break the curse – a pearl beyond price – that they might give her up to save their neighbor's children."

"But they didn't realize," said Rose, leaning forward urgently. "They never knew what you meant, even though they knew the story of the first Holz, even though they wrote it in their journal. They thought the pearl was a fabulous gemstone."

"I suppose I thought them more clever than that."

"Well," said Rose. "There is another pearl. One that's Holz on both sides. Another girl child."

"What is your name?" The witch sat very upright, and spoke sharply, like a stern teacher, but there was hope on her face.

"Rose-Perle Holz," said Rose.

The witch stared. "Who are your parents?"

"Jorinde Holz, called Rinde, and Joringel Holz."

"The twins?"

"Yes," said Rose.

"Incest," said the witch. She sounded horrified, and fascinated.

"I suppose so," said Rose, defiantly. She knew her parents should not be brother and sister, that it was wrong, and gross, but it was hardly her fault.

"Poor child," said the witch. She took Rose's chin between her fingers – they were warm and gentle and not at all witch-like – and turned her head this way and that. "Such a pretty thing," she said. She stroked Rose's hair, which had begun to come loose from its braid. "So fair." Then she sat back. "Why are you here?"

"To break the curse, of course," said Rose.

"Do you intend to throw me in my own fire? Drown me in the stream?'

"Of course not," said Rose. "Those weren't the terms. I am the pearl beyond price you asked for, and here I am."

"You would deliver yourself to me?" The witch looked bewildered.

"To save the children, to save Schönstadt, yes."

A tear trickled down the witch's face, but she did not seem to notice. "You are an extraordinary child," said the witch.

"I followed the terms," said Rose. "Will you break the curse?"

"Yes, yes, of course," said the witch, and she waved her hand in the direction of Schönstadt. "It is broken."

"What will you do with me?" said Rose.

The witch regarded her, and then smiled sheepishly – sheepishly! "I suppose I'll have to teach you magic," she said.

"Oh!" said Rose, delighted. She clapped her hands. The fox leapt from his stone to Rose's boulder and licked her cheek.

"And it seems you already have a familiar." The witch laughed. It was a lovely sound, merry as a flock of songbirds, but it sounded stiff, like she didn't use it often and wasn't sure how well it would work.

"Do you have one?" asked Rose. "A familiar?"

"I have many," said the witch. "All around us in the forest. Birds and beasts. Even a few insects, though they don't live long. A salamander or two."

"I see," said Rose. "I think one is enough for me. To start."

"Indeed," said the witch. "To start." She looked at Rose silently again, until Rose wanted to squirm. Then she said, "What else do you wish for, in your heart of hearts?"

"Normal parents would be nice," said Rose. "But I don't suppose that's possible."

"I'm sorry," said the witch. "I can't do anything about the twins."

"There is one thing, but it's silly."

"Nothing is ever silly, if you truly wish it," said the witch.

"When I was in the toy shop… Well, I wished I knew how to use Grandpapa's tools, and Grandmama's sewing things."

"You wish to be a toy maker?" The witch looked only a little surprised, and she sounded thoughtful.

"Can I be a toy maker and a witch, both?" said Rose.

"I don't see why not," said the witch. "But I can't teach you how to be a toy maker. I can only teach you to be a witch."

"Oh," said Rose. "I suppose I'll just be a witch, then."

The witch clapped her hands to her knees. "Nonsense! You are my pearl, daughter of my heart, and I will see that you get your wish." She looked very sternly at Rose and Rose met her eyes boldly. "You better be certain about this, though." There was a warning in her voice.

"I am sure," said Rose. "I want to learn to make toys that would make Grandpapa and Grandmama proud. And I'd like to be a witch, too."

"I believe you are sure," said the witch. "But it will be many long years of hard work."

"I can do hard work," said Rose. "I'm not afraid. And I won't give up."

"I don't believe you will," said the witch. "How remarkable." Then she picked up the bag of silver coins and weighed them in her hand. "Take this money," she said. "Give only as much of it to your parents as they must have to live. The rest you will use to buy your education when you are old enough. In the meantime, come here every third day and I will teach you magic."

"Oh, thank you!" said Rose.

"But be warned," said the witch, "this is a bargain you make with me, and you must keep to it and use the coins to learn to be a toy maker and for nothing else. Break this bargain, and there will be a new curse."

Rose nodded, all seriousness, and took the silver back from the witch. "I'm quite good at bargains," she said.

"So you are, my pearl. So you are."

When the witch stops speaking we all sit for a moment, looking at each other.

Finally, Alex says, "That's it?"

The witch turn a surprised look on her. "You want more?"

"Rose-Perle presents herself to the witch, and the story ends? I thought you said this was my story?"

"The story does not end," says the witch. "The *curse* ends. The rest is uninteresting."

"If you're Rose-Perle," I say, "And you became the Witch of the Wald, how did Alex …" I fish for the right words. "If you've been here ever since, but Alex is a Holz…"

"Where did I come from?" says Alex. "Where did my mother come from? My grandmother?"

"Where offspring always come from," says the witch. "Obviously."

"But…"

The witch holds up a hand. "The Witch of the Wald has a long life, if she stays in her forest. But she is not immortal. We choose someone to father a child. The girls we keep, the boys we send to their fathers."

"But your mother wasn't a witch," says Alex. "If you are Rose-Perle."

The witch laughs, not a creepy, witchy sort of laugh, but one genuinely amused. "The Holzes have always had witch-blood. We chose them often, to father our daughters."

"But –"

This time, it's a sharp glance from the witch that silences Alex.

"Your … hmm … your mother … or was it your grandmother?" The witch pauses and stares out the window into the afternoon light as if deep in thought. "Yes, I suppose she must have been my daughter. She left me. She didn't want to be a witch."

"I'm confused," I say, but the witch throws the same sharp look at me and I feel my mouth snap shut, almost against my will. I resist the urge to growl.

"I became the Witch of the Wald," says Rose-Perle. "Eventually. But there are seldom two Witches at once. So I also followed in grandpapa's footsteps. I became a toymaker. That is one of mine." She gestures at the box holding the carved fox head that sits where Alex put it out of the way of lunch, on a sideboard under the window.

"There was a local boy. I was pregnant when the Witch of the Wald … vanished." She looks briefly nervous, like there's something she's not saying. "So I became the Witch in her place. The child I carried would have been your grandmother. Or your mother. Or your great-grandmother. She lived with me in the summers in the wood, and the winters with her father in Schönstadt. Eventually, she chose to leave. She went to America, and one day had a daughter of her own."

"Sígrun," I say, the name suddenly coming into my head.

"No, that was not her name," says the witch. Her eyes have gone unfocussed.

"Sígrun was *my* ancestor," I say. "She was half *hexenfuchs*. She made you that garden," I say. "She loved you."

The witch looks at me, eyes still unfocussed. "Sígrun," she says. "My lover. My … my familiar."

"I thought…" I say, trying to remember all my dreams of my ancestors. The *hexenfuchs*, whose name I never learned. Her half-human daughter Sígrun. I don't know *my* story beyond the part where Sígrun and Rose-Perle became lovers. "I thought you chose *not* to make her your familiar."

The witch says, "I don't remember. I am old and tired." She stands suddenly, goes to a door across the room. "I will sleep. Tomorrow we will discuss your future." She waves her hand. "Help yourselves to food, drink, whatever you require. Sleep there." She points to a ladder, leading up into the rafters. I can just see the edge of a mattress.

Then the witch opens the door, steps through, and closes it behind her.

Chapter Nineteen

ALEX SITS HOLDING Li's hand, staring at the door the witch has vanished through.

"She's not what I expected," she says.

"She seems a bit … unhinged," I say.

Alex laughs, but it's short, sharp, bitten off. "Yeah," she says. "But I guess anyone would be, living all alone in the woods for … How old do you suppose she is?"

I shrug. "She's your great-grandmother, so, a hundred?"

"If she even *is* my great-grandmother. She didn't ask anything about me. She could be my great-great grandmother. Or just my grandmother, no great at all."

"Do you remember how many names were in your mom's album?" I try to remember what Alex has told me, but it won't stay clear in my mind. It's a struggle to focus. This whole trip has been a blur, and only by concentrating on the purpose of our visit have I felt like I've gotten anywhere. I shake my head.

Alex taps her fingers against the tabletop, like she's counting. "Me," she says. "Mom." She looks up at me. "There was only one name between Mom and Rose-Perle, I think. My gramma. I think I might remember her, a little. Or maybe I made her up because every child I knew had grandparents." She glances at Li, like she wants her opinion, but Li is facing straight ahead, her eyes closed like she's fallen asleep perfectly upright. Alex's shoulders slump.

"I don't know what to do," she says.

"We follow the plan," I say, with more confidence that I feel. "She's your great-grandmother. Or something. We ask her how to remove the binding." I think of meeting the witch in the woods and how she said the binding was incomplete. That should make it easier to remove, right?

"And Li?" Alex leans over to rest her head on Li's shoulder. Li doesn't move.

"Ask the witch to release her."

"And if she still wants something in return?"

"She's family. Maybe she won't."

"She's also the legendary Witch of the Wald."

"Who needs to train a successor. You have something she wants, too." I put my hand on Alex's and squeeze. "We'll think of something."

She sighs, but she straightens up and nods. "Okay," she says. "We're here, it can't hurt to ask."

Dealing with witches, I think, *it probably* can *hurt to ask*. But I don't say it out loud.

"Get some sleep," I say instead. "Or try to, anyway."

"And you?"

"I need to think," I say. "I'm just going to sit here a while. Maybe eat something."

I help Alex coax Li up from her seat. She's sluggish, and doesn't act like a sentient being, but at least she more or less moves where we tell her to, if pushed in the right direction. We get her up the ladder and lying on the mattress.

Back downstairs, I listen to Alex toss and turn, feel her anxiety through the familiar binding, and focus on ignoring her. Out the window, the light fades from the sky again and I wonder, vaguely, without really caring, what the old man at our hotel will think about his guests being gone for the second night in a row.

I shake my head and try to concentrate, try to care. But it's too hard to think of anything but the tightness around my throat. I wonder if this is what it will be like for the rest of my life if the witch won't help us. I don't know if I can live that way.

I slump across the table. It would be so easy to give up. If I take fox shape, I can just let my mind slip into fox-being and forget I was ever human. It would be better than being self-aware and unable to live my own life.

I slouch farther and my knuckles knock against the windowsill. I look up, see the dim shapes of trees. My eyes follow the flight of an owl – one of the witch's familiars, perhaps – as it passes by the window, and reappears in the next window, and then is gone from view. And there, on the sideboard beneath the second window is the box that holds the carved fox doll head.

I only have to lean over, half-rise from my chair, to reach the box. I look at it for a long time, remembering the odd experience the other times it was opened. Then I lift the lid.

There's no choking, no feeling of sorrow, nothing. No, not nothing. I feel a presence just brush the edge of my awareness. I make myself breathe deeply, kung fu breathing exercises, and let my awareness expand.

The witch's house is a bright spot inside which I sit. There is Alex, a brighter spark connected to me by a glowing line. Li flickers and wanes and flickers, like she's barely holding onto herself. A thin ray of light connects her to a void, a nothingness that hides and reveals the witch the same way her house was absent from the forest. I can almost see something in that void, but I dare not look too closely.

The familiars are all around, some near, some far, all connected to the witch's emptiness with a web of lines in different shades of bright. Few other animals venture into the sphere of the witch's house and yard. The fox doll head flickers like Li, but is far fainter, more a memory of light than a glow.

There is something – a membrane, a barrier – that surrounds the house. The same thing that kept it hidden from me when we were searching, I suppose. It is difficult to extend my senses past it, but something… there, just beyond the garden, reaching out to me from the forest beyond –

Abruptly, whatever it was is gone. I hear an owl screech and a rustling reaches my ears from beyond the witch's doorway. Alex turns over on the mattress in the loft.

Suddenly, I am overwhelmingly weary. I think about curling up in front of the fire. There is a blanket there, bunched up in an inviting way, perfect for a fox to curl up on to sleep. It would be warm. It would be lovely.

I realize, like a slap in the face, that it would be exactly what the witch wants. For me to lose myself in my fox nature, go willingly to be Alex's familiar, to accept the bond. Then Alex would be complete as a witch, but alone to face her ancestor.

We would all be lost. Li to the witch, me to Alex, and Alex to… her destiny? But I refuse to accept such a thing as destiny. We make our own fates, our own choices, our own lives. Accepting destiny means there is no point to anything. To freedom. I will not believe that.

So I get up, and I walk quietly to the door, and let myself out. I half expect the witch to appear, to forbid me to go outside, but she does not, and I climb down the ladder and walk around to the back of the house.

There's the garden, but it's overgrown. Weeds, brush, and flowers compete for space in the rare open area, even this early in the year. No one has tended this garden properly in years. I can still see where the different herbs and vegetables were carefully laid out in beds once, but soon even those traces of order will be gone.

It has a fierce beauty of its own, but I think about the dream I had of my half-human, half-*hexenfuchs* ancestor Sígrun who spent weeks climbing trees to cut branches to let in enough light for a garden this deep in the woods. She dug the earth, hauled topsoil from the banks of a not-so-nearby river, and laid drystone walls to create a place to grow edible things, beautiful things. She even made a beehive and got stung over and over trying to catch a wild bee colony so her witch lover could have honey.

I wonder if the witch stopped tending the garden in anger or in sorrow. I wonder how long Sígrun and Rose-Perle were together. Did Sígrun die or did she leave, like Rose-Perle's daughter left? Was that daughter born before or after Sígrun came into Rose-Perle's life? Did Sígrun know that Rose-Perle killed her father? Or *did* she kill him? My mind has gone fuzzy again, and I can't keep the details of my ancestor's story, of Alex's ancestor's story, straight.

Then I sense that presence again, just there beyond the far corner of the garden, in the woods a ways, past the edge of the witch's membrane. A spark in my wider senses.

A fox.

I want to run, to call out, but I don't. I might frighten him away. I walk towards him, thinking reassuring thoughts in case he can sense me the way I can sense him. His presence is a crackly spark, dim through the witch's barrier, but strong. He feels like joy.

I have almost reached him when I realize I can't go any farther. The edge of Rose-Perle's space won't let me out. No wonder she wasn't worried about me leaving the house.

I push against the barrier and Alex's binding tightens on my throat like a leash. I can't breathe, but I won't give up. I struggle, push, fight, and find myself on my knees, on my side, thrashing, silent because I couldn't draw breath to yell even if I wanted to.

And then it all goes black.

"Girl, wake up." The voice is masculine, deep, with a pleasant smoky burr. It should be a sexy voice, but there's something about it that isn't.

"Girl?" It sounds like my father's voice. The accent is almost the same, but there's a slight difference. I wonder if I have any uncles. I don't remember any uncles, but then I barely remember my father.

I open my eyes and the face peering into mine looks like Dad, too, but not. Like a close relative. I sit up and I'm not in the forest. I don't know where I am. I feel tightness in my neck and realize I can see Alex's leash, the familiar binding, like a white thread suspended in the air. So I'm not awake after all.

"Good," says the man. "You are awake. Or *not* awake, I suppose." He smiles and something in the set of his lips, the glint of his teeth, reminds me of myself, my own silly grin in the mirror. He has long canines like me, and amber eyes with vertical pupils.

"You're –"

"A cousin, I think," he says. "We are in your dreams. It is the only way

I can appear so." He gestures at himself.

"Appear how?" I say. He looks like a Schönstadt local. More farmer-ish, maybe, in work clothes of simple cut. His hair is short, but not recently trimmed, and his face is shaven, but stubbly.

He smiles his lopsided smile again. I always thought that expression looked silly on me, but Evgeny claims it's sweet. I think I can see what he sees now.

"As human," the man says.

"Oh," I say. I feel like I'm thinking through mud. Then I realize. He's the fox. "*Hexenfuchs*," I say.

"Only enough to communicate in this way," he says. "Outside of dreams, I might as well be a normal fox."

"Are we related?"

He shrugs. "*Hexenfuchs* are rare. I would not be surprised." He sits back on his heels and I realize he's been holding my arm the whole time. Now he backs off to give me some space.

"Your ancestor," he says. "She was a *hexenfuchs* who fled the hunters to shelter with the Witch of the Wald?"

I nod. "Not the current witch," I say. "The one before her, I think. Or … I'm not really sure."

He smiles again. "There is always a witch. Some are kinder than others at first, but in the end, they are all the same. In the end, they are cold, or crazy, or both."

I grope around in my memory, trying again to remember all the dreams of my ancestors, of the witches. They try to hide in my mind, but I still have so few memories to filter through I pull them out, like mice hiding behind the few books in my mental library. I am a fox, after all, bane of mice the world over.

"The *hexenfuchs* came across a house," I say. "There were two witches, an older one and a younger one with hair so fair it looked white. And there was a fox."

The man nods. "An ordinary fox," he says. "The witch's familiar."

"She was afraid of the witches, but more afraid of the hunters. And the fox made her feel the witches were the better choice."

"Maybe they were," the fox man says. "Maybe they weren't. She became a familiar, too."

"They had kits," I say.

He nods. "My ancestors came from that line."

"She fell in love with a human man, too."

"And your ancestors came from that union."

"The witch –"

"She killed the fox, stuffed him as a toy, and sent it with a curse, to the human man's family. He watched his baby sister sicken and die, and then his whole family.

"And then he died, and the fox spent many years as a stuffed toy until a child found him, brought him to life again, and made him her familiar."

I shake my head. "But we were just speaking of Rose-Perle. She was the younger witch, the white-haired witch. And her stuffed fox was made into a toy by a seamstress, to give to her beloved."

His smile grows sad. "This story has happened before, some variation of it. Twice, three times. More maybe. The witch, a fox familiar, a *hexenfuchs*. A younger witch seeking a teacher. Love and curses. Betrayal. And loyalty. Each time a little different, but each time much the same. She is caught in a circle of her own making, our Witch of the Wald. It traps her, but it also protects her."

"Protects her?"

"It is the same force she uses to keep this forest. But despite that, each year the Hexenwald grows smaller. She cannot keep the world at bay forever."

"Am I the *hexenfuchs* in this story? And you the fox?" He's cute enough, but he reminds me too much of my father for me to imagine having his babies, if I even wanted babies. The idea is absurd anyway, but I'm caught in a dream, so I might as well see where it leads.

He shrugs. "Do you believe in destiny?"

"No," I say, my voice so vehement it surprises me.

He grins, long teeth showing over his lips. "The perhaps you are not this *hexenfuchs*."

"How many times has it happened?" I ask. "The *hexenfuchs* being the witch's familiar and betraying her for a human lover?" If it's happened many times, it would explain why I'm so mixed up about when my ancestors lived and who with.

He spreads his hands. "Foxes are not so good at passing on stories. Even foxes with *hexenfuchs* blood."

"You can't guess?" I poke at my memories again. Of dreams and Alex's stories, and the witch's tale, and Li's writing.

"Twice, perhaps," he says. "The fox was a familiar, then a toy with a curse, then a familiar again. Twice he loved a *hexenfuchs*. Twice she had a human lover. But these things always come in threes." He looks closely at me. Am I the third?

"How many half-human children, then? Two?"

He looks thoughtful. "No," he says. "Or maybe." He shakes his head, cocks it to one side, shakes it again. "That part may be unique."

"My ancestor, Sígrun, she was half-human, half *hexenfuchs*. I think she was Rose-Perle's lover. The current Witch. Until she left."

The fox man smiles. "Yes. Sígrun. She was this witch's *hexenfuchs*. She met a young man, too, and left her witch for him."

"What happened to him?"

"He died, I suppose. Maybe he was cursed. But Sígrun never returned." He cocks his head the other way. "You did. Familiar-bound, with a young witch descended from *the* Witch. Are you sure you don't believe in destiny?"

"No," I say. "We came to learn how to break the familiar binding."

"Were you your witch's lover?"

"What does that matter?"

He shrugs. "It's part of the story."

"I was," I say, "Once. A year ago. More, now. Before I lost my memory, and … never mind. It's a long story. But now Alex is my friend, and she loves Li."

"The doll? Poor child."

"She's not a doll."

He sighs. "Not always, but the witch made her one."

"Why did you call me out here?"

"I wanted to meet you."

"What if the witch catches you? Binds you?"

"Then I become part of the story, too. So far this new tale lacks an ordinary fox."

"You're okay with that?"

He grins his sharp grin. "With you as a fellow slave, it wouldn't be so bad." Then his face grows more serious. "But she hasn't caught me yet."

"You should go far away."

"The witch may be dangerous, but her forest is the safest place for a fox with a touch of *hexenfuchs* blood."

I get up and pace. This dream space is grey and featureless. You'd think, since this is my dream, that I could have made it more interesting.

"Can you help me?" I say, stopping in front of him and looking down at him. His hair is reddish brown, like my dad's, like Kit's.

"Help you do what?" he asks.

"Get the witch to tell us how to reverse the familiar binding."

"How would I do that, short of offering myself as a prize in the bargain?"

"I wouldn't ask you to do that," I say.

"Good, because I might be tempted."

"Don't," I say, then, "Why?"

He gets up, too, and leans over to whisper in my ear. "To become a part of your story," he says. His breath on my neck sends a shiver down my back and I suddenly *can* imagine having his babies. Until I remember that outside the dream space, he's not human, but a fox. Ew.

"That's ridiculous," I say.

"I'm a creature from German folklore," he says. "Being part of a story is a sort of immortality."

"Well," I say. "One could say you're already a part of my story. Assuming mine is a story anyone would want to hear."

"I want to hear it," he says. "Other foxes will."

"I thought you said foxes aren't good with stories."

"Not to tell," he says. "But we make great listeners."

"Fine," I say. "Fine." I pace some more. "How can I bargain with the witch? Assuming she won't just help because Alex is her family."

"And assuming your Alex won't be persuaded to keep you and take her rightful place as the new Witch of the Wald."

"She won't."

"Not even it it's the only way to get her lover back?"

"She won't," I say. But I wonder, and feel ashamed for wondering. Would I betray Alex if it was the only way to keep Evgeny? It makes me feel small, human, almost evil, but hell yeah. I would. I would choose Ev if I had to choose. Fuck.

"I won't give up just because someone else decided I was meant to be a witch's familiar."

"Then maybe you will be the one to change this story. But first you must find a way out."

"You don't think the witch will help?"

"It's not in her nature. It is her custom to bargain, not to offer her services for free."

"So what do I do?" I say this mostly to myself, because I'm pretty sure the fox has no idea. But a thought occurs to me. "Did the witch bind Sígrun?"

"What?"

"Sígrun. Was she familiar-bound?"

"She left," says the fox. "So she must not have been. I think the witch loved her, in her way."

"Maybe she's not as bad as previous witches."

"Maybe not."

"When I first met her, the witch said my and Alex's binding was incomplete. Do you know what she meant?"

"Your witch is inexperienced, yes?"

"Yes."

"She must not have known how to perform the binding fully. She must have left something out."

"Like what?"

"I have never been bound. I don't know."

"If it's not complete, then it should be easier to reverse. Alex thinks she can undo it if she can figure out what she actually did to make it work."

"Perhaps."

"Perhaps? You're not much help." But of course he isn't. He may know more of my ancestors' story, but he doesn't know anything more than I do about witch magic, I don't think.

He looks at me carefully, though, like he's trying to see something in my face. Then I feel his presence brush against mine, sort of.

"You are the strongest *hexenfuchs* I have ever met," he says. "There's something in you that's fighting your binding already."

"How many *hexenfuchs* have you met?"

He looks confused. "I don't know. A moment ago, I'd have said you were the first." Then he shrugs. "But I don't think you are only *hexenfuchs*."

I think about the fox women who saved my life. A Chinese *huli jing*, a Japanese *kitsune*, and a Korean *kumiho*, who gave of their own blood, their own natures, to keep me alive, to heal me. It stole my memory, too, but it left me another kind of *otherness*, something older and more powerful. Something very different from any sort of *other* I'd ever encountered, before or since.

I tell him that, and he grins, teeth grown so long they project over his lower lip and touch his chin.

"She won't expect that," he says. "And I think these parts of you won't accept being enslaved, even if you agreed to it."

"So how do I use that?" I say.

Another shrug. "I think," he says, "that you can simply break the binding."

"I can?"

"Maybe," he says. "Maybe not. Maybe it will kill your friend. But at least you will be free."

Then he's gone and everything goes black again.

Chapter Twenty

I WAKE UP for real, on my side under a tree. I can breathe again, but each inhale is shallow, gasping. I push myself to a sitting position and think about how nice it would be to take fox shape, to set aside human worries.

Only knowing that if I do it I'll be lost keeps me from tearing off my clothes and changing shape right away. If I let myself lose my humanity, I'm pretty sure I'll lose everything.

I shift onto my knees, but I don't quite feel strong enough to stand. So I crawl back towards the witch's house, and each little bit I get closer, my breathing eases.

Inside, Alex sleeps restlessly next to Li, and Li is … who knows? Trapped in her own mind? Or trapped in the witch's mind? As for the witch, the void that both hides and reveals her seems quiescent. Maybe she sleeps, too.

When I get to the ladder, I stop, and sit back against it. I can almost breathe normally again, but my thinking is going fuzzy. It's worse since we arrived at the witch's house, when I most need my mind clear.

I realize I've zoned out completely when a stray beam of morning sunlight hits my face. I've been staring into the woods, not a thought in my head. Is that what it's like for Li?

I shift uncomfortably. How could I not have noticed I was sitting on a stick? But it isn't a stick. It's my tail, awkwardly manifested even though there's no room in the back of my jeans. It's sort of curled up next to my ass and numb from being sat on.

I've manifested my tail. Since I figured out how to change shape, to vanish and produce my tail and my fox eyes at will, to control my shifting, it's never happened without my knowledge or against my will. I prefer to have my tail, when it's safe, when no one will see, but I've been deliberately keeping it hidden this whole trip.

That it's appeared on its own must mean I really am losing it. I need to break this familiar binding and reclaim myself, and I need to do it now.

I vanish my tail, but it takes effort. I have to try twice before it goes and my clothes fit properly again. Then I drag myself to my feet and climb the ladder. I'm so tired, so weary, so sleepy, that each step takes concentration. It feels like it takes hours to reach the door of the witch's house, and I think I might even have blacked out part of the way up, because by the time I get there the sun is all the way up, filtering down through the branches and almost reaching the garden.

It's still dim in the woods, but definitely daytime again.

When I open the door Alex and the witch are at the table, sipping tea and nibbling at scones. Or, the witch is nibbling. Alex crushes hers between her fingers, but going by the pile of crumbs on her plate, none of it has actually gone into her mouth.

She looks up as I step through the door and something flickers across her face. I should be able to read that emotion, but I can't focus well enough.

"Not feeling well, little fox?" says the witch. "You should get some rest." She indicates the blanket by the stove and I actually take a step towards it before I stop myself. Instead, I sit in one of the chairs at the table.

Alex looks at the witch, then at me. She opens her mouth, closes it again, and looks like she'd like to cry. I can't remember if I've ever seen Alex cry before. I miss her Celtic goddess fierceness. Even her hair seems not so bright a red this morning. But then, everything looks duller.

No, not duller, just less colorful. I close my eyes, touch my eyelids. It's how things look when I'm in fox shape, except without the extra sharpness.

I pull in a deep breath, open my eyes, and look at the witch. "Will you help us?" I say.

She smiles. "I would like Alexandra to be my apprentice. My daughter, in a sense." Her eyes are too wide, her smile too big. She's crazy, I think. Completely mad.

Alex looks startled. "You do?"

"Of course. I may be the Witch of the Wald, but I won't live forever. Someone must come after me, and you are my blood."

"Oh," says Alex. I make myself focus on her face, stare until my eyes hurt, and I can see hope in her look, and uncertainty, and … pride, maybe?

The witch laughs. "You are the perfect choice. The only choice." She waves her hand at me. "And even though you have but one familiar, it is the best familiar a witch could hope for. You may even be a better Witch of the Wald than I."

"What about…" says Alex, but she trails off.

"Your China doll?" the witch asks. I remember another witch, in another place, calling *me* a China doll, and for a moment the confusion on Alex's face shows she must have remembered, too. But of course Rose-Perle isn't talking about me. She means Li.

"You can have your lover," the witch says. "Or she can have herself back, if that is what you wish. That will be my gift to you. But she can't stay here. You will get her a house in Schönstadt, divide your time between here and there, as I did."

"What about me?" I say, barely able to force the words past my fox teeth. I breathe through my nose, force my teeth back to human, and glare at the witch.

She looks at me like I'm an animal that thinks it can speak. And to her, I suppose I am.

"We came here to break the familiar binding," says Alex. Her voice is uncertain, and I know she's considering taking the witch's deal, getting Li back and becoming the new Witch of the Wald, eventually.

I can hardly blame her. I'd probably do the same.

But Alex has always been a better person than me, and when she speaks again, her voice is firm. "Show me how to unbind Su, and I'll be your apprentice."

The witch laughs. "You would give up your beloved for your friend? Touching, but is it what you really want?" She gets up. "I have things to attend to. Take the day to think. When I return tomorrow morning, you can let me know your decision." Then she strides to the door and is gone.

Alex and I look at each other.

"Alex…" I say. I don't finish the sentence, because what more can I say?

"I guess we got our answer," she says. Then she reaches over and touches my forehead and I can think clearly again, or almost. And I can stop fighting against taking fox shape.

"What are you going to do?"

She looks at the ladder to the loft. Li must still be up there, asleep. Or in suspended animation, or whatever.

"Alex?"

She turns back to me. "If you had the opportunity to find out all it means to be what you were born, would you take it?"

"If it meant enslaving a friend, no." My words come out harsher than I meant, but that *is* what she's asking. I think.

"If I can undo the binding before she returns, then you can go home."

"And you?"

"I'll stay. Learn to be a real witch."

"And Li?"

"If I stay, I think Rose-Perle will release her. Then she can make her own decision about… about me. Us."

I reach over and snag one of the scones the witch left on her plate and bite into it. No matter how anxious I get, how scared or tired or sick, I can always eat.

When I've swallowed, I say, "Just now, when you touched my forehead, it cleared up my thinking. Thanks."

She shrugs. "It's only what Evgeny used to do for you, before you learned how to block out witches."

"I never really learned that," I say. "It just happened when I figured out how to change shape. It's like that unlocked everything else."

"Anyway," says Alex. "I've been thinking, and I might have an idea about how to release you."

"You couldn't have thought of it before we came all the way here?" I try to joke, but it falls flat.

She fishes in her pocket and pulls out a clear quartz crystal on a leather thong.

"Is that…?"

She nods.

When we helped Evgeny by creating the familiar binding in the first place, we used a quartz crystal. Alex did some kind of spell or something on it – "manipulating the strands of probability" she said at the time – so if I thought I needed to combine our strength by submitting to the binding, all I had to do was put the crystal around my neck and then Alex could activate it and we'd be bound. I thought the crystal was in a box in my loft, but I guess Alex took it, and brought it along.

She sets it on the table between us.

"What do we do?" I say.

"I'll try to … to undo the binding through the crystal. To focus through it."

"In my dreams," I say, "the binding is like a white cord. Can't you just cut it?"

"I tried that, a bunch of times. Nothing happened except I got a sort of electrical shock."

"I should have known it wouldn't be that easy."

She smiles, almost. "You just sit there while I try this."

I munch on another scone, and sip the witch's tea – one thing about my fox nature: I'm not so particular about who has touched the things I eat or where they've been anymore.

Alex frowns and stares at the crystal. For a moment, the tension at my throat eases and Alex smiles, then it suddenly snaps back tighter, and I'm choking on scone and falling sideways.

And again – how many times is that now? – I fall out of waking and into my own head.

I'm suspended in nothingness and I wonder if I've lost my

imagination along with my focus. Last time I was inside my own head, it was grey and featureless, but at least there was a ground, an up and down, a surface to sit or stand on. This time there isn't even grey. Just nothing.

Then something comes into focus in front of me. It's the carved fox doll head, only huge, and it looks at me from golden glass eyes. No, not glass eyes, *real* eyes. I can see the narrow pupils expand until they're round to try to let in light where there is none.

"Daughter," it says, or *thinks*, I suppose, since its mouth doesn't move and no actual sound hits my ears.

"What?" I say. My voice sounds harsh and out of place. I think the fox winces, if a disembodied head *can* wince.

"There is no need for noise here," it says.

"Aren't we inside my mind?"

"In a manner of speaking." I want to ask what that means, when it goes on. "How did you come to be here?" it says – or *she* says, because she feels female to me.

I try thinking to her instead of speaking. "I came with my friend, to look for a way to…" I hesitate to tell her, this fox, that I let myself be familiar-bound, which is stupid, because she's a toy fox head inside my own mind. But I think about how this carved object has had a spark of consciousness since the first time I encountered it. Her. In my expanded awareness, she feels like a living creature, and more than that, a *thinking* creature.

"I know you are leashed," she says. "I can feel it. But it is weak and you are not."

"So everyone keeps saying, but I don't know what that means. I don't know how to use it."

"We always discover our strengths too late, our kind," she says.

"I don't understand. Who are you? *What* are you?"

"Sígrun," she says.

I shake my head. "Sígrun was a real person," I say. "My ancestor. Not a toy fox."

"I was," she says. "I was real, and naive, and now I am a facsimile, and wise." The carved wood shifts and she is smiling, the giant toy fox head floating in front of me. "Or maybe not so wise, since I remain trapped here."

I know I should ask her questions, try to find a way to break the binding and get myself out of here, away from the witch. And Alex and Li, too, if I can manage it. But there are too *many* questions, too many thoughts, and I can't concentrate. I can't pluck one thought out from the others as more important. So I ask the first words I can form.

"How did you end up as a toy?"

"I made a mistake," she says.

"You fell in love with a human man."

"No," she says. Her eyes are sad. "That was never a mistake. My mistake was thinking I could return to Rose-Perle when my husband died."

"Why?" I say.

"Why did I return? Rose-Perle was cold, and clever, and already a bit insane when I left her, but she was my first love. I never stopped loving her. I thought I could return, healed by my time away from her so I could be strong for her again."

"What happened? The fox in the forest said you never came back once you left here."

"Rose-Perle vowed revenge on my husband and our children, down through the generations. And she did the one thing she had promised never to do when we were first together."

"She bound you."

The fox is silent, but I know I'm right. Her presence radiates sorrow, and strangely, love for Rose-Perle.

When she speaks again, even though her words are not really sound, she's so quiet I can hardly hear. I know that doesn't make any sense, but I can't explain it any better.

"I was born of a *hexenfuchs*, but I had always worn human shape. Rose-Perle taught me to use all my fox magic save the ability to take fox form. I believed it was not a skill I possessed, and I never missed it. I think now that she did not want me to change so she would not be tempted to bind me, to make me her familiar."

"She already had a fox familiar," I say, remembering part of the story we pieced together.

"Yes, and for a time, he was her favorite of all her familiars. But he was old when she bound him, when she learned how to break the curse that had made him a toy."

"He died?"

"He died and after that she began to joke about making me his replacement. I reminded her of her promise, and didn't worry about it because I believed I was not really a fox anyway.

"Then she took a lover, a man from Schönstadt – she still divided her time between here and there in those days – and she lost interest in me. I don't think she loved him, but she wanted a daughter to succeed her someday as Witch of the Wald.

"So I spent more and more time alone. Until I met Hans. He was not a local man, and knew nothing of witches or foxes or magic. He was a scientist, and smart, and though it took a year to happen, I fell in love.

"And the next time Rose-Perle joked about binding me, I ran away with him. We were married and had a child, and I believed Rose-Perle forgot about me."

She falls silent and I try to figure out when she was alive. Is she my grandmother? My great-grandmother? Does it matter how many generations there are between us?

"Hans grew old and died, and I hardly aged at all. My son left for England, then Canada, and I went back to Rose-Perle, to see if she had got the daughter she wanted, if she remembered me."

"Because you still loved her."

"Yes. And she did remember, but she had grown colder, and cleverer, and even more insane. Her own daughter had fled from her to live with her father's family. And Rose-Perle could not have revenge on my husband, who had died, or my child, who was out of reach."

"So she… turned you into a toy?"

"No."

"I –"

"At first, she seemed to return my love and we went back to our old ways. I was happy. She told me about her daughter, who became a toymaker in Schönstadt. And she finally taught me how to take fox shape.

"One day I ventured into Schönstadt to sneak a look at Rose-Perle's daughter and learned that the young woman had left the Oktober

Mountains many years before. That was the day Rose-Perle forced me into fox shape and bound me as her familiar.

"She never let me take human shape again, so the forest foxes would probably only remember me as *hexenfuchs* – I was not human long enough after I returned to make much of an impression. Eventually my fox body aged and died because life as a familiar adds years to a common animal's life but steals years from a magical being."

"But how did you end up as a toy?"

"As my spirit slipped free of my body and I leapt joyfully away to the freedom that the nothingness of death bestows, Rose-Perle tightened her grip on my leash and bound me instead to a fox doll. The last toy her daughter made before fleeing the country."

We had thought Rose-Perle had made the fox doll; even the witch had claimed so herself. I wondered what other half-truths and outright lies she had told us.

"But how?" I ask.

"I don't know, but I learned then the true tragedy of the *hexenfuchs*. Once bound, the *hexen* who holds the leash can keep us enslaved even after death. And that was Rose-Perle's revenge on me for loving another."

"But she had a lover, too."

"She would say she was fulfilling her destiny as Witch of the Wald by producing an heir."

I can feel a tugging at my throat now, where before I sensed barely a hint of Alex's binding.

"Your witch is calling you back into awareness," says Sígrun. "Be careful, my daughter. Even those who love us will chain us, if the circumstances are right."

Then she grows bigger, the huge fox head swelling so one eye becomes a door I could almost step through.

"How can I free you?" I say.

"Only by destroying me. But it is yourself you should worry about. Your *hexen* holds your leash tightly." She blinks and peers at me again, and I feel that if I stare into her pupil, I'll fall right in. "But she has tied the end of your leash to a stone and not to her own soul. There is hope for you."

Then the binding pulls tight, jerks, and I'm on the floor, staring up into the rafters of the witch's house.

"Ow," I say, and my voice comes out as a croak.

"Sorry," says Alex. "I wasn't expecting that to happen. Are you okay?"

"Yeah, but I could use a drink." I'm thinking Scotch. Just two fingers, neat, and no more, but Alex pours me tea, which is probably a better idea, anyway.

I half expect it to be dark already, but the angle of the sun, what little I can tell of it through the trees, seems about the same as before I blacked out. Not that I'm that good at telling time outside of dawn and dusk. Or at all, in this forest.

We sit at the table again and Alex plays with the quartz crystal while I stare at the carved fox in its box. I know I should tell Alex about Sígrun, and about the fox man I met earlier, but I can't quite get the words out of my mouth.

I feel horrible, like the worst friend in the universe, but I'm hesitant to trust her now. She's always tried to do the right thing, as far as I know, but what the right thing is for her, or for Li, might not be the same as what the right thing is for me. I know I can trust her with my life. Absolutely. But my freedom…

But no. She's done nothing but try to unbind me since she first cast the spell. And the binding was my choice in the first place. I did it to save Evgeny.

And I suddenly realize I haven't called or texted or emailed him since we got to Germany. I bought a stupid cell phone so I could keep in touch. And even more disturbing is the fact that *he* hasn't tried to contact me.

And all sorts of thoughts start surging through my head then. Fear that something's happened to him and I'm not there to help – hell, I did save his ass twice, after all.

What if the demon in his head gets loose again, or worse, what if it manages to take him over from inside?

But if something happened to Evgeny, Magne would have let me know. At least I think he would have. He *has* been kind of distracted by his new love.

My head is in such chaos I'm totally unprepared when the shockwave of whatever Alex has just done with the quartz crystal hits me.

Electricity tingles down all my limbs to converge on my crotch and suddenly I'm feeling wave after wave of almost violent orgasm. Then Li starts screaming from up in the loft.

Chapter Twenty-One

THE ELECTRICAL TINGLING cuts off abruptly as Alex jumps to her feet and scrambles up into the loft.

I'm left clutching at the edge of the table, shaking, trying to stop the pulsing aftermath of climax so I can think again.

"Li, sweetheart, are you all right?" I hear Alex say. Li's screams trail off into a keening moan and then soften into whispers before finally stopping. I hear the mattress shift, blankets moving, as Alex settles next to Li. She says, "Fuck," so softly I would never have heard it without my fox-enhanced hearing.

But it's like that's happening very far away. What's foremost for me is trying to stay conscious. I'm so tired of blacking out, of dreaming other people's dreams, of talking to things inside my head. I grip the table so hard my nails make dents in its hardwood surface. Oak, quartersawn, and polished gleaming. The quartz crystal is an even brighter spot on its surface.

For long moments I stare at the crystal. "She has tied the end of your leash to a stone," Sígrun said. Did she mean *that* stone, the quartz? It would make sense.

Then I looked at the carved fox. Its glass eyes are more yellow than the giant fox in my … my dream I guess you'd call it. In that nothing place in my mind.

When I asked how to free her, she said, "Only by destroying me." If I burn this fox head, will she be free? I suppose it means death, nothingness, but if she's anything like me, she'd prefer that to servitude.

But at least I always have the hope of future freedom. Sígrun has nothing else.

I lift the fox free of its nest of wood and linen and it feels warm. I expand my awareness and feel the crackle of her presence. I can't communicate with her, I don't think, but I think she can feel my presence, too. I bring the toy to my face, press it against my cheek and maybe it's only my imagination, but I think I feel love, welcome.

I could keep her with me, a reminder of what I am and where I came from. But she would still be tied to Rose-Perle, trapped in a wooden prison. I look over at the stove. It's radiating heat, so it must be lit. Fire destroys wood. I wonder if it will hurt. Will Sígrun feel the flames consume her?

I have the door to the stove open when I'm startled back to full awareness by Alex's voice.

"What are you doing?"

She's standing at the bottom of the ladder and her eyes are red from crying. I didn't hear her weeping, and I didn't hear her come back down.

I show her the fox. "I'm setting her free," I say. I forgot I didn't tell her about Sígrun, trapped in the toy.

"That belongs to me," she says. "The old man gave it to me, and it's all I have of my ancestors." She reaches for it and I step back. The heat against the back of my legs tells me I'm too close to the stove.

"You have all this," I say, nodding my chin at the house around us.

"Not if I choose not to stay."

That stops me. I hadn't considered she might not stay. I thought her choices were to free me and stay to become a real witch and try to free Li, or to stay and bind me in order to free Li. If she doesn't stay, what becomes of Li? Of me?

"Sígrun is trapped in this carving," I say. And then I have to explain how I know. But I don't tell Alex everything. Not yet. Not until I know which path she'll choose.

A flame leaps up in the stove behind me, heating my legs painfully and sending a glint of light off the quartz crystal on the table. I make myself *not* look at it. I think I may know how to free myself, too, but I need to know what Alex intends to do, first. And I need that crystal.

Alex's shoulders drop and she sighs. "Su, I don't know what to do anymore."

"What do you *want* to do?"

She shakes her head. "I want to find out how to free you. I want Li back. And I want…"

"You want to learn from Rose-Perle," I say. "It's okay. I would, in your position."

"No," she says. "I don't think you would. You would never trade your freedom for knowledge. That's where we're different. Anyway, you have those fox women, back home, and you don't go see them much."

"I don't think they're interested in having me around. I'm too human still for their taste."

"And maybe I'm too human to be a real witch."

"Can't you be both?"

"Remember what you said to Mathilde?"

The oldest witch in the city, back home, had been at the heart of trying to destroy Evgeny. I accused her of trading her humanity for her *hexen* abilities.

"You're not like Mathilde, or like Rose-Perle," I say. "You might trade your own freedom for what she can teach you, but you'd never trade mine. Or Li's."

Her eyes slide away from mine and I know she's been considering exactly that.

"Mathilde thought I needed to bind you in order to make progress as a hexen," says Alex. "What if she was right?"

"She wasn't," I say.

"But what if?"

"Then you need to decide what you want more. What actions you can live with."

"And if I choose to keep you bound?"

I shrug. "I can't blame you if you do. You get to learn magic, and save

Li."

"That's it?"

"No." I look at the fox head in my hands, then back at Alex. "You're my friend. I love you and I want you to be happy, but I won't be your slave. I'll fight the binding with everything I have. Everything I am."

She nods. "Okay." Then she goes back up the ladder to Li and I can finally step away from the heat of the stove.

Okay. Does that mean she's decided, or is she just acknowledging what I think?

Again, I look at the fox toy, then I turn, toss it into the stove, and slam the door shut in one motion.

I'm expecting something to happen, but nothing does. The stove still keeps giving out heat, and the world goes on. But then I hear the crackle and pop as the flame catches on the dry old wood, the oil-based paint, and I feel something swell in my head, my heart. For an instant, I feel flames, taste smoke in my throat, and then there's coolness and I feel like I'm surrounded by stars.

"Thank you," I hear Sígrun say, and then she's gone, and when I extend my awareness, I sense nothing at all from her.

But I do sense the witch. She's far off, well beyond the membrane that shields her house, but the void of her is briefly full of raging green fire. Then it slams shut, vanishes from my awareness altogether, and I can't stop the violent shiver that runs through me.

The Witch of the Wald knows what I've done, and she's not happy.

"Is she free?" says Alex. Hours have gone by and the forest has grown dark and the witch has not come back.

She said she would give us until morning – give *Alex* until morning – to decide what to do, but after I burned the fox head, I thought for sure she would return. I've spent the whole time sitting at the table, waiting for her, while Alex murmured to Li in the loft.

I look up at her now, as she steps around and pulls out a chair. I've never see her looking so tired.

"Yeah," I say. "And the witch, Rose-Perle, I'm pretty sure she knows."

"You're waiting for her to come back," says Alex. "What are you going to do?"

"I don't know. I guess that depends on what you decide."

She sits down, accepts the lukewarm cup of tea I give her, and sips.

Li makes a noise from the loft, and Alex glances up. "I love her," she says. "More than anything. But she's not in there anymore. She's not in that body. Or if she is, Rose-Perle has her locked up so tight inside her own mind I can't reach her."

I put my hand over hers. "So take Rose-Perle's offer. Become her student. You get Li free, and you learn to fulfill your potential."

"I want to," she says. "I can't tell you how much I want to. But I could never forgive myself if I have to… to bind you to do it. I can't trade your freedom for Li's."

"I wouldn't blame you." Maybe I would, but I won't tell her that.

"I would. Li was… was Rose-Perle's creature before I met you. Maybe her loving me… maybe that was all part of the witch's scheme. All along, she's been trying to bring me here. Or if not me, then one of her descendants."

I shake my head, squeeze her hand. "I don't believe that. Maybe the witch sent Li to find you, but Li loves you all on her own."

"You can't know that."

"Well, she'd be crazy not to."

She smiles wanly at that. "I guess we should go then, before Rose-Perle gets back."

I glance back out the window, where I can just see the shape of an owl, watching from a tree. The witch may be away, but her familiars are all around us.

"No," I say. "Stay. You take the bargain. Be the best witch you can be, and get Li free of Rose-Perle."

"I can't keep you bound." Her voice is nearly a sob.

"You won't have to," I say. I hold up the quartz crystal. "I'll be free, too. And long gone before Rose-Perle gets back."

"But how?"

"Sígrun was trapped inside that wooden fox. She said I had to destroy her to set her free. So I burned her prison and she escaped into death.

Nothingness."

"I won't let you kill yourself so you can be free." Her voice is fierce and she sits up very straight. I can't help grin because the Alex I've always known, strong Alex, is suddenly back.

"I'm not going to kill myself," I say. "Sígrun also said the reason our familiar binding is incomplete is because you bound me to you via this crystal, and not directly to yourself."

"She said that?"

"Well, not in those words, but I'm pretty sure that's what she meant."

"So you destroy the crystal."

"Right. I'm just worried that there might be some backlash. That it might hurt you."

"I can handle it."

"What if it kills you?"

She looks at the crystal, and a line appears between her eyebrows as she considers.

"No," she says. "If the connection is incomplete, I don't think it will kill me. Remember when you defeated the *hexen*?"

The witches back home had used a bottle of ashes as a focus to attack Evgeny. When I struck back at them through it, I gave the lot of them nasty headaches, but didn't really hurt them.

"This is different."

Alex shrugs. "Maybe not so different."

"No," says another voice. "Not so different at all." Rose-Perle steps through the door, takes two long steps across the room, and plucks the quartz from my hand before I can react.

"Do you see, my child, how a beast that thinks can be a dangerous thing? Much better if you do her thinking for her."

I lunge for the witch, for the crystal, but I'm too slow. Too clumsy. She only laughs.

Alex gets up too, steps towards Rose-Perle, but I grab her shoulder. "No," I say. "Stay out of this. You still have till morning to decide what to do. In the meantime, don't take a side."

"But –" The witch may be her family, but Alex has always stood up for me.

"Trust me."

She nods, reluctantly.

"Stay with Li," I say, gently.

She nods again, and makes her way to the loft. I think – I hope – she understands that the only way all of us can get what we want is for me to win my own freedom.

Now I just have to get the crystal back from Rose-Perle and figure out how to destroy it.

I face her across the room. Her pale hair seems buoyed by static electricity and it floats around her. She is terrifying, and quite beautiful, and I think I can see why Sígrun loved her, and why Alex wants to learn from her.

Then she laughs and insanity creeps into her eyes and I shiver.

"I'm not *your* familiar," I say. "You can't control me."

"Oh, silly animal," she says. "I may not be your mistress, but I hold your leash." She holds up the quartz and I leap for it without thinking, but she's fast and I miss. Instead I hit the wall, hard, and it knocks the breath out of me.

I turn and she looks like she might simply have vanished from where she was standing to reappear across the room. The smell of spices, of vanilla and anise and mint, is almost overwhelming.

"Here, in my house, you are weak, *hexenfuchs*. You cannot hope to catch me, to take back this trinket and free yourself."

"I can sure as fuck try."

She scowls. "Young people and their filthy language. Learn your place, fox." She points at the floor and suddenly I find myself on hands and knees.

"You should see this, daughter," the witch calls out. "You should be learning how to discipline your familiar."

"Alex, don't," I say. "I'm fine." I can hear Alex shifting on the mattress, but she doesn't look down the ladder.

"Now take your proper place, and your proper shape." The witch points to the blanket by the stove, and I crawl towards it. Oh hell, I try not to, but I can't resist her command. I'm not her familiar, and even with her holding the crystal I don't think she should be able to command me, but she does, and she can. Maybe if Alex told her not to… But no, I asked Alex to stay out of this.

I curl myself into the smallest ball I can on the blanket, and then I feel my tail appear, squeezed too tight in my snug-fitting jeans. The colors bleach out of the room, but I can see with surreal clarity, and my teeth push against my lips until I taste blood.

I resist, and for a moment I think I can reverse the change, hold my human shape, and win free of the witch. Then something gives and I'm small and furry and tangled in my human clothes. I don't move when the witch pulls away my jeans and t-shirt, plucks my underwear and bra out of the way with a sniff of disdain.

"Now doesn't that feel better?" she says.

It does.

I was afraid that if I was forced to take fox shape here I would lose myself. Out in the forest, it was so inviting, so rich with magic and… and *age* that I could imagine living there forever in fox shape and being perfectly content never to be human again.

I like being a fox, but it's only part of what I am and in this witch house up on stilts that make no sense, full of witch magic, I believed I would surrender to my fox nature and forget the rest.

It is Rose-Perle's house, and Rose-Perle's rules. And being in fox shape feels so good. So *safe*.

But I am not just *hexenfuchs*. And I am not just human, either. Something like a year and a half ago, I nearly died. To save me – and I still don't know why they chose to, because they believed at the time I was just human – the *kitsune*, the *huli jing*, and the *kumiho*, the three fox women who live in the Japanese garden outside of town, each gave me something of themselves, to make me what they are.

If I *had* been human, the blood they gave me would have made me like them. A fox woman with powers out of Japanese, Chinese, and Korean mythology.

But I'm not human, I'm *other*. I'm descended from *hexenfuchs*. By everything I know about *others* – witches, werewolves, vampires, and the like – you can be born *other*, or you can be made *other*, but you can't be both. To attempt it is death.

Except that's not true. Not always.

What the fox women did for me should have killed me just as surely as what my attacker, my rapist, had done. But it didn't.

Maybe it's because my *other* nature was fox, and what they gave me was fox, too. But somehow, I didn't die.

If I was only *hexenfuchs* and human, Rose-Perle's trick of forcing me to take fox shape would probably have worked, as it worked on Sígrun. I would have subsided into my fox nature to only take human form or have human thoughts when allowed to.

But I'm also fox woman, and fox women don't take well to being forced to do anything. The *kumiho* once told me that her kind – our kind – are creatures of vengeance. Hurt us and you make us stronger. I think she's always been disappointed that I'm not violent by nature. But I don't take shit from anyone.

And while a *hexenfuchs* is in some ways stronger in human form, a fox woman is in some ways stronger in fox form. And the strength I need now is fox woman strength.

So when the witch is tossing my clothes into a heap in a corner and standing over me gloating, quartz crystal dangling carelessly from one long elegant finger, I'm recovering my presence of mind.

In fox shape, I don't think quite like a human does, but it's not true fox-thought, either. I lay still, catching my breath, waiting.

Rose-Perle smiles. "Poor beast," she says. "Like most animals, you'll find you'll be happier without the confusion of thoughts." She bends down to stroke my head and I force myself to hold still, to relax, even. Then as she straightens, confident that she has subdued me, I strike.

I don't attack her – after all, Alex needs her to free Li – but I leap for the crystal, grab it in my teeth, and am across the room in a flash of red fur.

"No!" says Rose-Perle. "Bad fox. Return to your place." She points to the blanket, and I feel a vague pressure, a weak desire to go and lie down, but it's easy to push aside.

I snarl, and she comes after me.

She's fast, Rose-Perle. She moves nearly as quickly as Evgeny, and he's just about the fastest creature I've ever met.

But the thing about my abilities is, I can't always call on them at will, but put me in mortal danger and they kick in. That peculiar circumstance kept me alive before I knew what I was. Now, it makes me faster than the witch.

She flashes like lightning, pale hair flying around her, black dress billowing, and her speed is terrifying. But I'm a shadow, slipping away from her crackle of searing light, always moving away from her. I dance around her, flow like the forest breeze past her, and slip into that state of mind I always aim for when I practice kung fu. I don't think, only act.

Again and again I move away from her, until finally she stops dead.

"I cannot catch you," she says, surprise in her voice. She laughs and she actually sounds delighted instead of angry.

She's crazy, sure, but if defeat pleases her instead of angering her, maybe she'll be a good teacher for Alex after all.

Then she goes utterly still and I feel something gathering in the air. I don't know what Rose-Perle is doing, but it doesn't feel good.

The air seems to squeeze me from all sides and when I try to move I find it like wading through mud. The air has become thick, and it holds me.

As I stare across the room at the witch, I know I need to destroy the crystal now, because even if she wasn't turning the air against me, I can't run around the room forever, and in fox shape I can't open the door.

But how? I guess I was thinking a big hammer and a hard surface to pound it on. But quartz is a very hard rock, not easy to break, let alone pulverize.

I watch, helpless, as Rose-Perle crosses the room, smiles, and pats my head.

"I do *like* you," she says. "In other circumstances, we might have been good friends." She considers me. "Or perhaps not friends," she says. "But allies, at least."

And as she reaches for the leather thong hanging out of my mouth, I do the only thing I can think of. I bite down on the quartz, as hard as I can.

And everything goes stark, painful, white.

Chapter Twenty-Two

CHOMPING DOWN ON a quartz crystal should shatter my teeth. Instead, my teeth shatter the crystal. The shards stab into my lips and gums, filling my mouth with blood.

Light fills my head, searing me, burning me from inside. For an instant I can feel Alex as clearly as I feel myself. All her thoughts and memories are laid out before me. Then the connection between us is severed and I discover how utterly alone I am.

The light fades and I shift forms without really thinking about it. I just don't want to be smaller than the witch. I stand facing her, unbothered by my nakedness. My hair flows down my back and over my shoulders like a cloak. Was it quite so long when I braided it in the hotel room before we left Schönstadt? It's almost to my ankles. I keep cutting it and it keeps growing, but surely it was only to my waist a few days ago.

I look at the witch, turn my head to spit out crystal shards and blood, meet her eyes defiantly. She blinks rapidly at me, and I realize something in my vision has changed. I have the extra clarity of my fox eyes, but in full human color.

I flick my tail and something feels different there, too, but I'm not sure what it is. I want to turn and peer back over my shoulder to see what has changed, but I'm not ready to turn my back on Rose-Perle just yet.

We face each other across the room again, two tall women with crazy long hair, mine black, hers white, like negatives of each other, almost. Then she smiles.

"You are magnificent," she says. She places a hand over her heart. "You would have been such a fine familiar, but I see now that my granddaughter was right."

I stare at her, feel my head tilt like a dog's or a bird's. "Okay," I say. She seems to expect me to say something.

"You do need to be free," she says. "Bound, you would have been only a *hexenfuchs*. Useful, powerful… but nothing like you are now. Remarkable."

She pulls out a chair from the table, and sits, still staring at me, smiling. "Come down, Alexandra. You *must* see this."

Alex shifts on the mattress. "Su?" she says.

"It's okay," I say. "I'm fine. Unbound. I think everything's fine."

Alex comes down the ladder, turns to look at me, and *stares*.

"What?" I say. Being naked is finally starting to bother me.

"Wow," she says.

"What?" Louder.

"You're…"

"I'm what?"

"Your hair is all super long and… floaty."

"Floaty?" I look down at where the black strands lay across my skin. Some of it does seem to have lifted free of gravity. "Weird."

"And… um…"

"And what?" I look back at her, and she's grinning.

"Your tail," she says.

I *knew* something was different.

"It's…" she says, "Well, bigger."

"What?!" Now I do turn, strain to see my own backside. What I notice first is that the fur on my ridiculous appendage is no longer a bright russet red. Instead it's a shade paler, more orange, like the embers of a fire. And when I flick it from side to side I think I'm seeing double, but no, it's just twice as fluffy. Twice as long.

"I need to sit down," I say. Alex slides over a chair and I sink into it.

"Just when I'm used to my tail, it gets bigger," I mutter.

I suppose I shouldn't be surprised, though. After I first met the fox women – not counting the time they saved me, which I only recently remembered – I read everything I could find on Asian fox lore. According to Japanese myth, the *kitsune*, as it ages and gains wisdom, becomes paler-furred and every so often grows a new tail. When it reaches its full power, it is pure white, and has nine tails. I guess I should be glad I didn't sprout a whole other tail.

What happens after that, the stories don't say.

"Well," says Rose-Perle, clapping her hands. "What fun!"

Alex and I just look at her.

Perhaps we could all use some rest," she says, finally. "Then, Alexandra, you have a decision." She looks at me. "Though I expect it will be an easier choice to make, now."

"What about Li?" says Alex.

"In the morning," says Rose-Perle. Then she gets up and strides to the inner door, steps through, and closes it behind her. Outside the window it's still dark. I wonder how much of the night is left.

"Do you think you can sleep?" I say.

"I don't know if I'll ever sleep again," Alex answers.

"Earlier," I say, unsure if I should even ask. "Why was Li screaming?"

Alex shakes her head. "Bad dreams, I think. If she can dream, in her state."

"She quieted, when you went to her. Maybe she is aware, on some level."

Alex looks towards the loft. "Maybe." There is a lot of doubt in her voice.

"Well, I could use some rest," I say.

"And some clothes," says Alex, a grin creeping onto her face. "And incidentally, thanks for the headache."

"Oh," I say, dismayed that I haven't even thought about how the destruction of the crystal must have affected her. "It is bad?"

"Bearable. Especially knowing you're free. How did you do it, anyway?"

"I bit it," I say, knowing how dumb that sounds.

"You *bit* it? Geez."

"I didn't think it would work, but I didn't know what else to do."

"But it did work."

"Apparently."

We sit for a while, not talking. Then I get my clothes from the corner, shake them out, and put them on. I have to vanish my tail to get my jeans on, but that means I don't have to try to get used to my new state just yet, which is fine by me.

Then we go up the ladder and stretch out on the mattress, Alex on one side and me on the other, with Li – still and quiet – between us. I wait until Alex's breathing softens with sleep before I let myself relax.

I think about trying to fight off sleep, so I won't dream, but I know I need the rest. I don't think I've really *slept* since we left our hotel in Schönstadt. So I finally let go of my tension and let the dark take over.

The smell of bacon cooking wakes me. It's full day – as bright as it gets in this forest – and Alex is gone. I must have been really tired if I didn't wake when she got up.

I feel strangely good, and happy, and I realize I didn't dream at all. Or not that I remember, anyway.

Li lies still next to me, breathing softly. I let my awareness expand a little and sense her as a crackle and flickering spark, just like before. Like she's there, but not there. Alex is a bright beacon, and today even Rose-Perle is a glow instead of a void.

I breathe easier.

When I climb down the ladder, Alex is busy propping bread to toast on top of the stove, and the witch is turning bacon over in a cast iron pan with a fork.

Eating breakfast like a normal group of people may be the most surreal thing that has happened on this very strange vacation. Rose-Perle is cheerful and Alex seems cautiously optimistic. I can't wait to get the hell out of here.

When we've eaten and cleaned up, Rose-Perle vanishes back into her room.

"So," I say. "I thought I'd head back today."

"So soon?" says Alex, and laughs sheepishly when I raise my eyebrows at her.

"You're staying, then," I say.

She glances at the ladder to the loft, then at Rose-Perle's door. "She actually offered to return Li to her old self, and let us all leave together."

"But you want to stay." I don't need to make it a question.

She looks at her hands, the stove, out the window. Anywhere but at me.

"It's okay," I say. "I expected you would."

"I can learn so much," she says.

"I know."

"I'll be home eventually."

I think about how Rose-Perle probably expects Alex be the next Witch of the Wald; Sígrun said Rose-Perle took a lover so she could have a daughter to take over for her some day. And once Alex has learned all she can, will she really want to go back to the dingy city we came from?

"Sure," I say. She walks with me outside, all the way to the edge of the membrane that hides the witch house from the outside world. There she stops, digs in her pocket, and pulls out a piece of green linen that I recognize from the carved fox's box. When she hands it to me, I can feel small hard things shift inside.

"What's left of the crystal," she says. "I thought you should keep it." I wonder if she means it as a simple keepsake, or if it's because witches are supposed to be able to do magic on people using things they've owned. That quartz *was* awfully closely tied to me, and got doused in my blood, too.

"Thanks," I say. I fish in my own pocket and hand her the silver coin I found in the old clearing. "Something to bargain with," I say, joking.

Then I turn and look at the witch's membrane, or at the empty air where I know it to be, anyway. I wonder if I can get through this time, or if I will struggle against the barrier in vain, like before.

But I step through and suddenly Alex and the house and the witch's garden vanish. I sense only nothingness. For a moment, I almost step back through. I didn't get to say goodbye. Not properly. But maybe this is better.

Quick and painless.

Or quick, anyway.

All the way back to Schönstadt I sense the fox following me. Finally, when I reach the clearing where we sat to open the box with the fox toy, I stop, turn towards him, and say, "I know you're there."

I sit on a stump and twine a stem of new grass around my finger, and wait. After a few minutes, he steps into the sunlight, hesitates a moment close to the safety of the trees, then he hops up onto a stump near mine and sits down.

He's bigger than I expected, bigger than I am in fox form, and his fur is black-tipped, giving him the look of a banked fire, the bright red embers half-hidden by charcoal. The black on his legs extends to his elbows, and the white tip of his tail almost glows in contrast.

Foxes use their tails to communicate, waving them like flags above the grass to keep in contact when they hunt together. He waves his at me now.

"Hi," I say.

He opens his mouth and lolls his tongue out, almost like he's making a silly face. It's faint, but I sense a return greeting in my head.

Can you hear me? I try thinking at him. He grins wider, and again, I feel an affirmative, a bit stronger this time.

Thank you, I say. *What you told me about the witch… it helped.*

He nods, human-like, then stands and turns to go. I feel regret from him, like maybe he was hoping I would stay. But I also sense joy. He's happy I'm free, I think.

Then he turns back, leaps so quickly I don't think to react, and lands in my lap. He swipes his tongue across my face and I feel an impression of laughter as he leaps away again, and disappears into the forest.

Even being a fox myself, it still amazes me how they can so quickly vanish into the neutral background, when they're so brightly colored.

In Schönstadt, the people look at me oddly, but even the little old man at the hotel doesn't comment on my absence, or the fact that of three guests, only one has returned. He only smiles and greets me, as asks if I wish to stay another night or catch the afternoon train back the way I came.

I could stay a while. My ancestry is here, too, as much as Alex's is. Or half of it, anyway. But now that I've left Alex and Li to follow their own paths, all I want to do is go home.

Evgeny is waiting for me, and there are things I left undone. There's the mystery of John Pradip and his connection to my murdered father, and there's the possibility, however unlikely, that my younger sister could still be out there somewhere, alive.

Someday I'll come back here, learn what there is to know about foxes and *hexenfuchs*. I'll visit Alex, and Li and Rose-Perle. Someday, too, I'll go to China and Korea and learn about the other side of my family.

But now that I'm thinking straight again, I'm full of the urgency of those unfinished investigations I left behind to come here. So I buy a train ticket at the tiny station and go to the hotel room to gather my things.

I look around the room. I never actually unpacked, so I pull out clean clothes, shower, and stuff my dirty things into my suitcase. Then I go to Alex's room and Li's in turn, and pack up their things. I ask the old man to send Alex and Li's luggage to the little history museum in the old toy shop. I figure the curator there is the person Alex is most likely to see, when she comes to town to find a place for Li to stay, since Rose-Perle doesn't want her in the forest.

Then all that's left is to wait for the train. On the long ride back into the city I finally remember to look at my cellphone, and discover the battery is dead. No wonder I haven't heard from Evgeny. I hope he's not too worried that I haven't contacted him.

Fortunately, the train is modern and sleekly European, and supplied with plenty of outlets for electrical devices, so I plug my phone in and stare out the window while I wait for it to charge. And I guess all the tension of the past few days catches up to me and I fall asleep.

I open my eyes and Sígrun is watching me from the opposite seat. In my dreams, I've almost always seen her story from her perspective, like I'm acting out her role, so I've ever actually seen what she looks like, yet I know for sure it's her.

She's got that same reddish brown hair my dad had, but darker. Her eyes are green, too, but every now and then they shift color when she turns her head and they catch the light. Then they're brighter, yellow-amber, and her pupils contract to vertical slits.

Her face is narrow, foxy, and she has faint freckles. There's a definite look of *otherness* about her, the sort of thing no one can quite point to, but that makes people stop and stare. She keeps her eyes down, and her shoulders slightly hunched, as if trying to be invisible.

But when she sees I'm awake – if I really am awake – she straightens, and smiles, and I can see her long foxy teeth. I think she's amazing, and beautiful, and I grin back.

"Thank you," she says. Her voice is quiet, like a forest breeze stirring the leaves in passing.

"I killed you," I say, and the reality of that sinks in.

She smiles again. "You *freed* me."

"Was it so bad?"

"Many years, I was shut inside a box, as well as prisoned in a toy. Not even an entire toy, but a part of one." She leans forward and touches my hand. "Yes, it was that bad."

"I'm glad, then."

She sits back. "Good. I am, too."

"But you… I thought you vanished into nothing. How are you here now?"

"Perhaps I am not," she says, and I hear laughter in her voice. "Or perhaps I lingered long enough to see my granddaughter free herself."

"Did you help me? When I was fleeing the witch, when I bit the crystal, I was stronger. Was that you?"

She shakes her head. "I was free of my prison, but had no agency. I could do nothing."

"Then who? The fox in the forest?"

She laughs. "People these days. Why are you so reluctant to believe you can do things on your own?"

"I've never been that strong. That fast."

"And were you always able to take fox shape? To block others from your thoughts?"

"No. Those things just sort of… happened. When I really needed…" I have to stop and consider. Every big jump in my abilities has happened when I was in peril, when I would have died otherwise, or lost something – or someone – important to me.

"That was all me?" I can't keep a little wonder from creeping into my voice.

"It was."

"Wow."

"You are stronger than I ever was. Stronger than any *hexenfuchs* I've ever heard of."

"I'm… I have other… something else…" I don't even know how to describe what I am. I'm not really sure I understand myself. Just when I think I have it figured out, I learn something new that changes everything.

But she nods. "The daughter of *hexenfuchs* is only half of what you are," she says. "I can smell other things in you. Other fox magic." Then her face goes serious. "But you must be cautious. You can't know how those things will combine. It's never happened before, that I know of."

"It's not supposed to be possible," I say. "But I'm not the only one both born and made *other*."

"It is very unlikely," she says. "Unlikely it would happen once, impossible that it would happen again."

"But it has," I say. "Evgeny was born a witch, and made a vampire. He…"

I stop because a look of horror has crept over her face. "You love this… Evgeny?"

"Yes. The witches call him an abomination, and the vamps want to use him, but he's sweet. He's…"

She's shaking her head. "You are smarter than I was," she says. "But I beg you to be careful, daughter of my heart."

"Okay," I say. Then I notice she's kind of going transparent.

"You should wake up," she says. "I think your phone is ringing."

My phone? Did Sígrun even know what a cellphone was?

"Farewell, daughter. You will not see me again."

Then a persistent buzzing penetrates my awareness and I open my eyes.

I wake for real this time, and discover my phone, battery now charged, has been vibrating out a whole slew of notifications.

I look at the texts first. Evgeny, all of them. The oldest ones are sweet notes, with a few naughty comments. Then they get concerned, then a bit frantic-sounding. Then, two days ago, they stop.

My stomach is clenching as I dial voicemail. Several "I love you"s and "where are you"s, then one that leaves me cold.

"I don't know if I'll be… if I'll be *me* when you get back. Fuck, Su, I hope you're all right. I know you're probably busy tracking down witches, but…" It trails off in a choking sound. Then it starts again and Ev's voice is clipped. "Don't come home. Don't look for me when you get back. Something's happening. I don't want it to get you after it takes… No, never mind. Don't worry about me. I'll be fine."

I can't listen to the last message. I hang up and just stare at my phone. What's been happening while I've been gone? Why the hell couldn't I have remembered to check my messages?

I'm back in the city, curled up on a bunk in the hostel, waiting for it to be time to get up and go to the airport, before I finally muster the courage to listen to the final voicemail.

It's not Ev, but Magne. "I hope you're on your way home," he says. "And if not, please come back soon. Ev's… he hasn't been well. Long story, and I'll fill you in when you get back. He's… he's going to be okay, but he's not the same. He might not want to see you."

There's no way I can sleep after that, so I just stare at the dark until I can leave for my flight home. And just as I'm about to shut my phone off for takeoff, another text comes through. It's Magne again, texting in almost full sentences. Maybe it's an *other* thing, because that's how Ev texts, too.

O'Malley dug up some info on your sister. Don't get your hopes up. He still thinks she's probably… not alive. But he thinks he may have a lead.

I shut the phone off and stare out the little window. I was terrified of going home yesterday. Terrified of whatever I'd find when I saw Evgeny again, assuming he'd even want to see me – and why the hell wouldn't he?

But now I have a good reason to get back no matter how fucked up my boyfriend might be. Yeah, Magne said not to get my hopes up, but hell, I'm an optimist.

And Kit might still be alive.

BROTHER of DEMONS

read on for a preview of book four of the *Fictive Kin* series

Chapter One

It starts when I kiss her goodbye. I could say it started before that, with the mood swings and irrational anger I keep telling myself are stress. Work stress. But my job is not stressful.

I could say it started with the nightmares, each ghost in my head replaying its memory of fear and brutality and death. They are not simple bad dreams you awake from and they fade away leaving only a lingering bad feeling. They are *memories*; not mine, but they might as well be. Each beating, each violation, each torture I live through in a dream, and can't wake up until the ghost dies in my dream and when I do it takes time to remember those things did *not* happen to me, and each time it takes longer to remember.

When Su is with me, I do not have those dreams. Instead I dream of the forest, a lake, the stars. Wild dreams. I dream of slow lovemaking, her skin against mine. I dream of fucking, of burying my face between her thighs, of her voice crying out in pleasure. And then I wake up and I can kiss her for real, hold her, smell her, taste her.

But something makes me retreat from her from time to time, as if I need to see those terrible ghost dreams. Like I can only be rid of them once I see them all over and over until they *are* my memories. Or until they drive me mad.

But I don't hear the voice until I'm kissing her goodbye.

She's leaving, my Su, on a trip to Germany with her friends Alex and Li. It's a long story, and complicated, but there's magic involved – Alex is a witch, a *hexen*, and Su... To save my life, Su combined her own magic with Alex's, and ended up bound to her friend as a familiar and they can't undo it. And Su needs to be free.

Su is... I don't know what Su is. She is a thing that shouldn't be possible, just as I am. But she was born a *hexenfuchs*, inherited from her German father. And later she was made something else. A fox woman. Three old fox ladies were trying to save her life, and ended up *changing* her. What she is now is simply glorious.

And she needs to be free, so she's leaving me to find a way.

"I'll text you," she says, and I smile, remembering my attempts to teach her how to use her new smartphone.

"I know," I say. "I'll miss you."

"I know," she says. "Me too."

"My heart," I say.

She smiles, her eyes taking on an amber glow. If she lets them, they can become fox eyes, slit pupils and all. A strand of black hair escapes its pins and elastics, and I twine it around my finger.

She grins, takes hold of the strand, and severs it with a quick snap of her fox-sharp teeth. "To remember me," she says, as I stare at the lock of hair she twists around my wrist as a bracelet.

"As if I could forget you," I say. Then I kiss her, soft, tender. She parts her lips, deepens the kiss, and I wish we had more time, even though we spent most of last night making love.

Throw her against the wall and fuck her, says a voice in my head, and I know that voice. I almost choke on our kiss.

"Are you all right?" she says. "Ev?"

I nod. "Yes," I say. "I just tried to breathe at the wrong moment." I don't like to lie, and I abhor lying to Su. But she needs to go to Germany, to get free of the magic that binds her to Alex, and if I told her the demon had re-formed itself again, enough to make words in my head, she would insist on staying to help me.

She puts her hand on my cheek, warm and vital. I can feel her pulse on my skin. My own pulse is slow, so slow compared to hers, even after a sexy kiss to speed it up.

"I love you, crazy Russian vampire witch boy," she says.

"I am your very own abomination."

She frowns. She doesn't like to hear me called abomination, even when I try to make it a joke. I forgot that. How could I forget that?

"I love you, my glorious foxy German-Chinese woman," I say.

"You forgot Korean," she says. "One of my grandmothers was Korean."

"German Chinese Korean," I say. "North American woman."

Outside, the taxi driver leans on the horn.

"Gotta go," Su says.

I nod.

On the floor, says the voice. *I bet you've never fucked her up the ass.* I pretend not to hear it.

I have to step back away from the spear of sunlight as Su opens the door. If not for the sun, I would see her to the airport, drive her there myself; Magne would lend me his truck.

She turns and waves one more time as she gets into the taxi, and then it pulls away and she is gone.

And I am alone, except for the demon in my head.

My name is Evgeny, and as Su said, I am a crazy Russian vampire witch boy. I was born in Russia, and lived there long enough before my parents brought me to the New World to always sound like I'm not from around here.

I don't have a Russian accent anymore, not unless I want to, but I've never quite shaken the slightly-too-formal English my parents taught me before we left the motherland.

I didn't know I was a witch until after I had been made a vampire. Being "reborn" as the other vampires like to say – they prefer to be called that, as well. Not vampires but Reborn. I don't associated much with my kind. They haven't treated me well.

But there are two kinds of non-human sentient creatures lurking in the shadows. Some, like witches and *hexenfuchs*, are born what they are. Some, like vampires and werewolves, are made what they are. No *other*, it is said, can be both born and made. Either one dies in the process, or one's inborn nature defeats the invader, or the invader defeats the genetics.

Mostly, it means death.

But it can happen. Su was born *hexenfuchs*, and made a fox woman. She lived, and now she's both. Or something greater than either. She thinks it's because *hexenfuchs*--that means "witch-fox" – and fox woman are both foxes, so they didn't fight, so to speak.

But that doesn't explain me. Though I didn't know it, I was born a witch. Witches, for reasons unknown, are all female, except in a few rare families. The royal family of Imperial Russia was one such family. They all died, but young Prince Alexei lived longer than anyone supposed. Long enough to have a son, and to be used by a mad sorcerer trying to create a powerful puppet.

The sorcerer was defeated and my great-grandfather had to be burned alive and his ashes imprisoned in a jar to defeat the demon he was becoming.

History repeats. I was a vampire before I knew I was a witch. I should have died, but instead my witch powers grew. And the other witches saw me as an abomination. Not for being a male witch, but for being both witch and vampire. An impossible thing.

They tried to use Great Grandpapa's ashes as a focus to combine their power and take over my mind, to force me into the sun and kill me. It almost worked, but instead they unleashed a demon, a consciousness born of the senseless death of hundreds of innocent people in pain and fear.

And Su defeated the demon and the witches, but it bound her to Alex, and that's why she's gone, and I am here alone with the demon we thought was dissolved into memories.

You should have tied her up, the voice in my head says, as I retreat to my dark bedroom. It is rich with the smell of Su, of our sex. I ignore the voice and burrow into the blankets and breathe in what's left behind of my lover.

"Su," I whisper, as if her name alone can keep away the voice. *It's only a voice,* I tell myself.

Only a voice.

In my dream, she's there, behind me somewhere. I can't see her in the shadows when I turn to look. Contrary to popular superstition, vampires don't have good night vision. We use other senses to hunt. Not that we're stupid enough to hunt much these days. It is too risky, and bagged blood is no different from fresh once you heat it up. As long as it's not *too* old.

I can see vague tree shapes, but once I've turned back the way I'm headed, I can't turn to look for her again. I can only stare ahead as a tall, lean form steps out of the dark.

My stomach clenches. *Demon*, I think. But the demon never took such form.

Instead, it's a man with Asian features. Japanese, I think, as he steps near enough I can almost see him clearly. His eyes look flat black and I think I have seen him before.

"Evgeny," he says. His voice is cold. Not devoid of emotion, only filled with something I can't name. The faint moonlight finds a gap in the tree cover and glints for a moment off his teeth and I can see the slight gaps where his canines would fit if he extended them, unfolded like the fangs of a venomous snake. Vampire.

I shiver, and from behind me, I can smell Su's fear. I didn't think Su was so afraid of anything. Something nags at my memory, like I should remember more about this man, this vampire who feels older than time, but who has nothing of the shrivelled look very old vampires usually get.

I don't answer him. I'm not sure I can make my vocal apparatus work.

He looks at me closely, shakes his head. "How disappointing," he says. "I thought you would become something interesting. Perhaps you are not as strong as I believed." He steps away again, disappearing back into the trees and darkness.

"You're just like all my other degenerate offspring. No better than your father."

The "father" he refers to is not my human father, but my vampire sire. Su calls him "Papa Vamp." He was cruel and clever and it may be because he fed me on witch blood – which is supposed to be toxic to vampires –

that I didn't die in the process of being reborn.

"Su killed him," I say. I don't know why I say it, though it is true.

The other vampire pauses, a blacker shadow under the trees. "I believe she did," he says. "A pity you didn't do it yourself."

"He was evil," I say.

His shape moves and I think he may have glanced back. "Some would say we are all evil."

"I refuse to be," I say, and I think I can feel Su draw closer behind me, feel the heat of her skin.

The old vampire laughs. "That may be your undoing," he says. Then he's gone, between one eyeblink and the next, but as I wake, groggy and disoriented, I think I also hear him say, "Or it may be your salvation."

I suppose for some, being made a vampire would be an exciting change, an adventure full of new possibilities. For me, it is mostly an inconvenience.

My existence is no more exciting now than it was before. In many ways, it is more mundane, save only that I would never have met Su if I hadn't been reborn.

I still need a job so I can pay rent and buy food, only now I have to work after dark and my groceries are in liquid form. Mostly. I refuse to give up all human things. As a vampire, I need not eat solid food, but I still *can*. Not a lot, mind. It doesn't digest well in large quantities. But I can still taste flavours, even if some are stronger than they once were. And I have always loved to cook.

So I go to work each night, walk my night security rounds at the local mall, evict drunk teenagers from the roof. I collect my pay, pay my rent, buy groceries.

I am trying to return to the creative pursuits I once had. Before I was made what I am now. Right now, the only thing that makes my life mean anything is Su, and Magne keeps telling me I shouldn't invest everything I am in another person. It's not healthy, he says. Like he should talk. He's so besotted with his witchy new girlfriend. Nosy werewolf.

Except he's probably right.

So it's Magne's fault, I suppose, that on my first night off after Su leaves, I gather up my camera and a portable flash unit and go looking for something to photograph.

Before I was made a vampire, I liked to shoot street scenes: people doing strange things, juxtapositions of signs and objects, little oddities and quirks people don't notice until they're pointed out.

At night, there is nearly as much going on in some parts of the city as during the day. In some places, there is even more happening. The light is more difficult to work with, more contrasty with bright hot spots and shadows devoid of detail, but the challenge should be fun. Exciting.

Instead, I see nothing at all I want to capture in my lens. The camera hangs from my shoulder like a stone, banging against my ribs, and I'm really regretting bringing the extra burden of the flash. I wander the streets, wishing Su was next to me. She always noticed the little details, pointed out things to make me laugh. She was always so happy to simply exist, even with all the terrible things she's seen, the terrible things she's had to do, and to endure. I used to be like that. I remember how the shape of a leaf or a smile from a stranger could make me feel good to be alive.

When did that change? When I died and was brought back as something different from what I used to be?

Magne would tease me if he knew I was pining for Su like a lovesick boy. *Su* would tease me. Though she would be nicer about it. Here I am, trying to find a way to exist without her, and she is all I can think about.

I find my steps have turned away from populated areas, have carried me to the park. Here, Su and I had to defend ourselves from a whole pack of vampires who had been sent to capture me. It wasn't the first time I discovered how easy it was for me to kill, but it was the most obvious example. Su managed to disable two of them, and in that time, I took out the rest. I don't know how many there were, and I try not to think too hard about it. I don't want to know.

Instead, I steer my thoughts to happier memories. Last time we were here, we sat on a bench and shared a dairy-free milkshake. Chocolate tofulati with a hint of peanut butter. Su had most of it, but she made sure I had plenty of sips.

This bench, here, is where we sat, drawing glances for drinking a cold summer treat after dark, when the air was rapidly cooling to night chill.

And we just grinned back at those people and they smiled and shook their heads at two people stupid in love.

I sit on the bench and lean back, watching the moths flit in the light of an electric lamp nearby. A pale blur, too large for a moth, I think, captures my eye and I have to get up, walk over to it, fluttering at the lamp's base.

It *is* a moth, pale green with reddish edging on its upper wing, and transparent spots. It is the size of my hand, almost, and so fuzzy I want to stroke it like a kitten. I reach out a finger tentatively, and touch it lightly in the centre of its back. It flips its wings fully open, but it doesn't seem bothered.

Its hind wings taper into long, gently twisted tails and I think I have seen a picture of one of its kind before. A lunar moth? No a *luna* moth. No "r". I stroke it again and it is a soft as the delicate fur behind a cat's ears. It fans its wings.

Then I reach for my camera, check the aperture and shutter speed against its built-in light meter. I still shoot film, not because I'm a Luddite, but because I like the hand-work involved in developing my own film and printing my own images.

I wish I had brought a tripod instead of the flash, but I brace the camera on my knee and am for once thankful for my vampire nature, that lets me go more still than is natural for any other creature. I hope that and the lamplight will be enough for a sharp image.

The click of the shutter cheers me. Magne was right, I do better with something outside of Su to focus on. Though of course the whole time I'm thinking how I can show her the image when she gets back, or scan it and email it to her, maybe bring her here to see if another luna moth will come so she can see it for herself.

I bracket my shots, one f-stop on each side of what I think is the correct setting. Then I bracket the shutter speeds, too, just because. One the five should be useable, I hope. I almost wish had loaded colour film, to capture the delicate green of the animal's wings, but black and white will exaggerate its ghostliness, and it suits my mood.

As I put my eye to the viewfinder for one final shot, I notice a detail I didn't see before, something Su would have noticed right away. Something

I would have noticed if I'd been paying attention to my sense of smell instead of concentrating only on what I could see.

Where the pale moth rests on the grey concrete, there are splatters of dried liquid. It looks black in the contrasty lamplight, but I know in daylight it would be dark red.

There is blood on the ground here and, unless my vampire olfactory acuteness has suddenly failed me, it's not entirely human blood.

About the Author

NICO SILVER LIVES like a hermit on the edge of the woods, but haunts used bookstores like a wraith. They fully expected to be found someday as a mummified old corpse crushed under a toppled to-be-read pile, but the rise of e-books has made that somewhat less likely, though the books will always outnumber even the dustbunnies. Nico will read just about anything, including the instructions on the back of medicine bottles, but has a particular fondness for good stories with a hint of magic. They write dark, sexy urban fantasy, and sometimes dream in black and white.